HAMSIKKER

RUSS WATTS

Writing is not a solitary journey, no matter the hours spent alone.

For unwavering support and help, this book is for Karen.

"When you can't make them see the light, make them feel the heat."

Ronald Reagan

PROLOGUE

"Thanks for coming, thanks a lot. Please, go on in." The words came out of his mouth, but he'd said them so many times over the last thirty minutes they had lost all meaning. It was like he was regurgitating a prayer, over and over, like some deranged priest.

"Mrs Danick, thank you for the flowers. Please, head on in. Thanks a lot for coming." She had aged a lot since he'd last seen her, but she still had a wicked glint in her eye, and he remembered all the trouble he'd caused his neighbour over the years when he was growing up with Janey. He watched Mrs Danick accompany a frail, elderly woman into the church, their arms linked and their feet shuffling slowly.

As he shook another hand, kissed another cheek, and handed out another tissue to wipe the tears away, he wondered if he had slipped into a parallel universe. Wasn't *he* the one who was supposed to be in mourning? How come everywhere he looked people were crying, holding each other, supporting each other with words of kindness and recalling memories of happier times? Why was *he* the one standing by the church gate, handing out condolences and hymn sheets like some kind of admin assistant?

There was a brief respite at the entrance as Mrs Danick entered the church, and he realised he was probably getting sunburnt. The back of his neck was hot and itchy, the thinning hair on top providing no cover for his head. Using a wad of hymn sheets, he fanned himself, knowing only his father would've died in the middle of a heatwave. It was as if the old bastard was having one last laugh at his son's expense. Jonas reached into his pocket and pulled out a crumpled navy blue kerchief. He dabbed his moist forehead before shoving it away, as a family approached the church gates. Putting on his best smile, he prepared himself for another clammy handshake from yet another distant relation he hadn't seen in twenty years, and prepared to repeat the speech he had given everyone else.

"Thanks for coming. Please…"

"Jonas Hamsikker, how're you doing?"

Jonas looked at the large man facing him, and was momentarily thrown. This was not a friend of his father's, just another acquaintance, or an old uncle; this was a face he knew well. It had been a long time since he had looked into those piercing blue eyes, and the red hair was unmistakeable. Thick sideburns grew down the man's cheeks like a lava flow, filling in the burly man's creased skin and crow's feet. Jonas gripped the firm hand he was offered, and shook it enthusiastically.

"Erik? Jesus, man, how long's it been?"

The two men embraced quickly and then Erik introduced his family.

"Hamsikker, this is my wife, Pippa. These two role-model citizens are Peter, my son, and my daughter, Freya."

"Pleased to meet you," said Jonas as he shook their hands in turn. Freya giggled as she shook Jonas's hand and then slid shyly behind her brother.

"I heard you were back in town, and of course I heard about your father. Sorry, man. I hope it's okay we came. I wanted to pay my respects. Seemed only right, given how your old man looked after me back then."

"Of course, of course," said Jonas, pleased he was finally able to talk to someone he knew. He still couldn't believe Erik Lansky was standing in front of him. He might have aged twenty something years, and added twenty pounds, but otherwise, he still looked like the same Erik he used to goof around with at school.

As more people filed into the church, Jonas shoved hymn sheets at them as they passed. It was almost time for the service to begin, but he didn't want to miss out on catching up with Erik.

"Pippa, go on in with Peter and Freya, I want a quick word with Hamsikker," said Erik standing to the side so the others could take the path into the church.

"Sure is a hot one," said Jonas.

"And it's only spring. You forgotten that glorious Kentucky sun already?" asked Erik. "I hope going out west didn't turn you into a pussy."

Despite his awkwardness, Jonas sniggered. It felt good to see his old friend again. Erik looked tough and given his larger-than-life stature, he could scare off people before they'd even spoken to him. But he was a kind man, always ready with a joke or a line. That was what made him such a good cop.

"Say, I wanted to ask how long you're back for. This a permanent move, or what?" Erik dabbed at his sweating forehead with a hand and then wiped it on the back of his suit jacket.

Jonas frowned. "To be honest, I'm not sure. I've a lot to sort out now. There's a whole heap of things I need to do, and Dad's place is a mess. He was a hoarder. You want a stack of newspapers from the nineties?"

Erik slapped a hand on Jonas's back. "No thanks. Look, old collections of newspapers aside, I'm here for you, man. Where are you staying? At your father's? You'd better not tell me you've shacked up in some downtown motel. You know we can find a room for you, no problem. Pippa would be glad to have you over. I'm serious."

An ambulance suddenly sped past, and it turned its sirens on just as it rushed by the church. It was swiftly followed by another, and Jonas wondered where they were off to in such a hurry. Jeffersontown was a quiet place, and without the sounds of the speeding ambulances, the only audible sounds had been the faint tweeting of a cardinal, and his own thoughts. The ambulances disappeared taking their warped sirens with them. Jonas looked up into the blue sky. There was not a cloud anywhere. He saw the trace wisp of a plane's vapour trail, a fleeting line of white arching across the sky.

"Thanks, Erik, but I'm staying at Dad's place. I really need to get on top of things there, so it's handy for me to stay in the house. I'll be around for a while, so we can catch up. You coming to the crematorium after?"

"No can do. Sorry, but Freya's got netball, and Peter's in the middle of exams. Why don't I swing by tomorrow? You free for lunch?"

"Sure. If we don't catch up later, you can meet Dakota then. You'll love her." Jonas heard the priest calling to him, and waved a hand to let the priest know he was on his way. The service was about to start, and it would not be cool to be late for your own father's funeral.

"Dakota? You finally get a woman? How long did that take you?" Erik removed his hand as the two men began walking up to the church together.

"Been married almost eight years now. Met her in Phoenix. Couldn't imagine life without her, you know?" Jonas wanted to get inside now. He wanted it over with. He wanted to fast forward time, and skip the next three hours at least. He wanted to go straight to drinking, to remember his father, and then to forget him. Dakota was waiting for him, probably sobbing her heart out even though she had never met his old man. That was just the way she was. She cried at the news, she cried at movies, and she cried at the funerals of people she didn't even know.

"Say, is Janey inside already?" asked Erik. "It'd be good to say hi after all these years."

Jonas knew Erik had always had a thing for his sister, going way back to when all three of them hung out as teenagers, but there would be no reconciliation today. He shook his head. "She couldn't make it."

Erik looked surprised. "For her own father's funeral?"

"She's busy, truly." Jonas didn't know why he felt guilty explaining Janey's absence. His father had never made excuses for her, and he shouldn't have to justify why she wasn't here. Then again, Erik believed the Hamsikkers were a happy family. He didn't know what happened when the doors were closed, and the lights went out.

"Janey's a dancer now. She moved up to Canada years ago. Married, three kids, the whole works."

Erik's bushy red eyebrows turned down as he processed the information. "A dancer? Janey?"

Jonas could see the surprise on Erik's face. "Not *that* kind of dancer, Erik. She's with a theatre company up there. Does all sorts of musical theatre, shows, film adaptations, everything. Keeps her busy, and I know she loves it. She's got an important production on at the moment, so she couldn't get the time off. Honestly, she's a workaholic. I talk to her on the phone a lot, but don't get the chance to get up there much." Jonas felt bad lying about why Janey wasn't at the funeral, but the truth would've been much worse. He changed the subject, eager to steer the conversation away from his sister. "So how about you? You're quite the hot shit cop around here. Lovely wife, a house in the 'burbs, and to top it off, a boy and a girl. How's that working out for you?"

"Living the dream, brother, living the dream. My kids are smart, cute, and costing me a fortune. How about you? Any kids?" asked Erik.

Jonas shook his head again, and they reached the priest who was impatiently waiting at the church doors. "Happy as we are, thanks. Look, I have to…"

"Absolutely. Sorry, man. I'll see you later." Erik disappeared through the massive oak doors of the church, and Jonas turned to the priest.

"Ready when you are," Jonas said feeling a bead of sweat roll down his back.

There was a fluttering of nervousness as Jonas entered the church, and he felt like he was ten years old again, walking up to the stage at school to take assembly. He had always hated being the centre of attention, and didn't doubt that he always would. As he walked, he made a point of not looking at anyone in the pews. The mumbling and sobbing told him enough. He didn't need to see their eyes, their grief, their accusations and shame, because he felt enough of that himself without anyone else's help.

He sank down into the pew at the front next to Dakota and she slipped her hand into his. It was reassuring, yet cool, and he became aware again of how hot he was. He loosened his tie, pulling it down just a fraction so he could breathe. The sweltering heat from outside had been replaced by cool air and icy stares. His suit could protect him from only so much, and the moment he was dreading was upon him. The priest had taken up residence by the lectern, and motioned for Jonas to step up as he said a few words.

Dakota leaned over to her husband. "I'm here, honey. I'll go up with you if you want?"

Jonas looked at her. They could have been climbing the Rockies, flying over a volcano, or crawling through mud; it didn't matter. He knew she would be there for him, just as he would be there for her. It had been a conscious decision not to have children, much to the chagrin of Dakota's parents. They loved each other so much that they just didn't want anything to come between them. Neither had any urges to raise children, and so they decided not to. Of course, now and again, doubts crept into their minds, and it wasn't an easy decision. Right now though, he knew it was the correct decision.

Dakota looked beautiful. Normally, she wore bright colours, but today was a black day. Her shoulder length hair was tied in a bun, and a few grey hairs were exposed. They normally hid behind her ears, showing themselves only when she was nervous, or when she tied her hair up. Jonas knew she could go bald, or dye her hair purple, and he would still love her.

"No, it's all right. I'll go."

He gripped her hand and then let it go. Walking slowly, he approached the open casket. It was nothing fancy, just what they could afford, but without children, they had managed to save well. He didn't really care if his father was buried in a cheap suit and a garbage bag, but then Dakota would've started asking questions: questions he didn't want to answer. He and his father had grown apart over the years. He knew he should've come back sooner, when he'd found out about the illness, but there was always something stopping him. Well, he was back now. He had seen his father just once in the last ten years, and that had been last week. He had left Dakota behind, not knowing it was as urgent as it had turned out to be. His father had barely known him. He was so frail that he couldn't even get out of bed, and Jonas was shocked at his appearance. Why hadn't the old man told him sooner? Why had he not asked him to come home? Jonas preferred to remember his father as a young man, when he could still play ball and get around on his own, instead of lying in a hospital bed with a bag to piss into.

And there he was. His father, or at least his father's body, laid out for all to see like a prize at a local show. Religion had not played much of a part in Jonas's upbringing. His mother had died when he was ten, and with it, so had his father's faith. As Jonas looked down into the casket, he decided he should've paid extra for the velvet lining. The varnished wood looked fine, but now he felt cheap. All those watching eyes, all those people at his back who were undoubtedly thinking the same thing, were pressing down on his head. Poor old Mr Hamsikker, let down by his failure of a son again, stuffed into a cheap wooden box, ready to be sent to the bonfire-house just so his son wouldn't have to visit the grave.

His father's eyes were closed, and the skin slightly discoloured. They had done a good job, he had to admit. His father looked better now than last week. Death suited him. The soiled bedclothes had been replaced by a navy suit Jonas had found. It was the same suit that his father was married in. After all these years, it still fit, and it seemed only right to send him to rest in it. After his mother had died, Jonas's relationship with his father had soured. It hadn't happened overnight, or even been based on one single event. Becoming a teenager as his father wrestled with grief had been difficult. Jonas had his own grief to handle too, and eventually, they had gone their own ways. His mother's untimely passing hadn't brought them together, but had driven a wedge between them so deep that nothing was going to free it. What had followed, what had passed between his father and Janey could never be forgiven, or forgotten, and it seemed fitting that the old man had suffered before his death, just as he had made others suffer. Jonas rested a hand on the casket.

"I hope you're with mom," he whispered, "say hi from me."

Was he supposed to cry now? Is that what they expected? He felt bad. He felt guilt, misery, shame and sorrow, but he didn't feel like crying. As he stared at his father's dead body, he remembered his mother more and more. He always pictured her with him, never alone. Vacations at Myrtle Beach, shopping at Jeffersontown Mall, buying his first school uniform; wherever his mother was, his father was too. He guessed they were in love, as much as him and Dakota maybe. He rarely thought of them like that, but why not? They were happy back then. They were happy until the illness and the one-way trip to hospital for his mother.

Sighing, he took a step back from the casket as another siren went past outside, the high-pitched wailing breaking his thoughts. He looked up at the priest and gave him a courteous nod. The eulogy would come soon, but right now, he wanted to be back at Dakota's side, pretending none of this was happening. He indicated to the priest that he needed a minute to compose himself, and returned to the front pew. Dakota squeezed his hand as he slipped down quietly beside her.

"We meet here today to honour, and pay tribute to the life of Francis Jonas Hamsikker," began the priest.

As the priest went on, Jonas stared at the casket. There was a hush around the church now, and the sunlight made the windows seem alive with life, whilst the rest of the church suffered in darkness. There was a groaning sound, and Jonas thought that perhaps the priest had made it. But the priest kept talking and made no sign that he was ill. Jonas heard the groan again, and was certain it was coming from the front of the church somewhere. Other than the casket and the priest though, there was nobody else up there. He looked at Dakota to see if she had heard it, but her face was buried in her hands and a pile of tissues. It was surely nothing, just someone behind him crying and the sound reverberating around the church. His ears were playing tricks on him, and he gently felt the inside pocket of his suit jacket. He had been up late last night rewriting the eulogy, and he was going to have to get up to the lectern soon to face everyone. He couldn't claim to know everyone, but he had recognised old family friends, uncles and aunts, even people from the hospital who had come to pay their respects. They would all want to know what glorious things Francis Hamsikker's only son had to say, and what happy memories he would share with them.

Jonas heard the groaning again, and then a collective intake of breath. He looked up and saw his father slowly climbing out of the coffin. His face was deathly pale, and the navy blue suit hung off his thin frame, but there was no mistaking that it was his father that now stood by the lectern. The eyes opened slowly and looked about the church.

"What the hell is this?" shouted a voice from the back of the church. "Is this some kind of sick joke?"

Jonas couldn't believe what he was seeing. His father was standing upright, just in front of the altar, bony hands hanging loosely at his side. It crossed his mind that it was a sick joke, and that his father had conned him into coming home just so he could prove a point. Quite what the point was, he didn't know, but he had to find out what was going on. Dakota was squeezing his hand so tightly that he had to prise her fingers off one by one.

Jonas stood up and looked from his father to the priest and back again. All around him people were standing in shock, asking what was going on; was Francis alive, what should they do, who was in charge? The priest appeared to be in shock, and was gripping a bible in both hands, staring at the standing body a few feet away that had just climbed out of the casket. Jonas had heard of people mistakenly being pronounced dead, but such cases were extremely rare, and he'd thought things like that only happened in gossip mag's and bad B-movies.

"Jonas, honey, what...what is this?" Dakota stood next to her husband. She had screwed up a hymn sheet into a ball and held it ready to throw. Jonas wondered what she hoped to achieve, but it was an instinct in her to protect herself.

"Sit down, I'll sort this out," said Jonas having no idea how he was going to sort anything out. His father had died two days ago, of that he was quite sure. He had seen the body, felt the cold lifeless hands as he held him one final time. He had to do something though.

"Hamsikker, what's going on?" asked Erik as he approached Jonas, hitching up his belt as he did so. His face was stern, his tone serious. Erik had slipped into cop-mode instantly, and Jonas was relieved he wasn't on his own.

Jonas answered him with a shrug and stepped out into the aisle. He heard his father groan again, this time louder, and the dead man's eyes widened. Francis coughed, and then seemed to take in a long breath. Jonas and Erik looked at each other nervously. Some of the people at the back of the church were leaving, and now that the church doors were open, they could hear more noise from outside: shouting, screaming, and lots more sirens.

"Dad?" asked Jonas timidly, ignoring the growing rush for the exit behind him. "Dad, are you...are you..." Jonas didn't even know how to finish the question. How do you ask a dead man how he's feeling?

"Our father, who art in heaven, hallowed be thy…" As the priest began reciting the Lord's Prayer, he held the bible aloft, a large, thick book bound in red leather.

Jonas watched as his father swung around and without warning, without uttering a word, ran full steam at the priest. Francis knocked the priest down, and Jonas heard him crying for help.

As if in slow motion, Jonas saw Erik charge up to the altar, and he wanted to follow, he really did, but his feet were stuck to the floor. Fear had replaced sorrow, and logic had been replaced by terror. His father was dead. Francis Jonas Hamsikker was cold and dead, so how had he climbed out of the casket? Why was he attacking the priest? Erik brushed aside Jonas's father, and the three men rolled about on the church floor as if they were playing a game. Jonas heard Dakota scream, and suddenly time sped up again.

"Jonas! Help him!" Dakota practically pushed Jonas forward, and he rushed to Erik's aid. The man had Francis pinned down on the floor, but this was no ordinary dead body. Francis was thrashing and writhing, trying to push Erik off. His head lunged forward and his teeth snapped inches away from Erik's arms and hands.

"Jesus, Dad, what the hell?" Jonas grabbed his father's head, and held it down as Erik shouted for more help. With his father under control, it was then that Jonas looked across at the priest. The man's smock was covered in blood, and the bible lay at his feet. The priest's eyes rolled back in his head as his pale hands tried to stem the bleeding from his neck. There was blood not just on the priest, but also on the carpet, the bible and Erik. It was too much, far too much for one person to lose, and the priest's hands fell away as he relinquished his life.

"Erik, what the fuck? The priest, he's…he's dead."

"I know, man. Your Dad was biting him when I dragged him off. Looks like he tore out his jugular. Hell, Hamsikker, what is this?"

Hell sounded about right, thought Jonas. His father was still struggling to get free, and showing no sign of tiring. Dakota approached Jonas cautiously, and he asked her to call the police.

"I already did, but the line's busy." She looked at Francis in amazement. He had been quite dead only a few minutes ago. His eyes were wide, and when he saw her, it only served to reinvigorate him.

"Francis? I'm Dakota, Jonas's wife. Do you…"

The dead body continued wriggling, and Jonas's father didn't answer Dakota.

"You're telling me 911 is busy?" asked Erik. His face was burning red, showing the effort it was taking to keep Francis pinned down.

"Try them again," said Jonas. "We can't hold him down much longer."

A scream sounded from outside the church, and they heard tyres coming to a halt on the road outside. More screams followed it, and the sound of breaking glass reached them.

"I gotta check on my family. I gotta go, man," said Erik.

"Wait, please," said Jonas, "I can't do this on my own. I can't…"

Dakota held the phone out in front of her. "It's still engaged. I can't reach…"

As the priest slowly sat up, he reached a hand out and grabbed Dakota's ankle. She yelled out and frantically tried to kick him off, but the hand holding onto her was strong.

Jonas looked at Erik. "I'm sorry." He let go of his father's head, and rushed to help his wife, leaving Erik to fight his father.

The priest lost his grip on Dakota as Jonas aimed a kick at the priest's head, and Dakota tumbled backwards. The priest sprang to his feet, eyes wide, and blood dripping from his jaw.

"Get back!" shouted Jonas to Dakota.

The priest barrelled into Jonas before he had time to move, and he felt his legs give way as the man crashed into him, knocking them both to the floor. He threw a punch at the priest's head, but only succeeded in hitting him in the shoulder as they rolled around. He vaguely heard Dakota screaming something, but he was too occupied in keeping the priest's snapping teeth away from him to hear what she was saying. The priest was an old man, almost as old as his father was, but he had such strength. Jonas hadn't been in a fight since he was fifteen. Tommy Parker had called his mother a dead bitch and that fight had not ended up well for either of them; Tommy lost two teeth, and Jonas got a month's detention. Now he was fighting a priest. A *dead* priest at that. As Jonas pushed his arms up off the floor, he felt the weight of the priest rise up off him. He saw Dakota with her hands around the man's waist, helping him up, and then he heard the shot. The priest's head exploded into a mist of blood and brain. Jonas was showered with fragments of skull and warm blood. As he rolled out from under the priest, Dakota dropped the lifeless body.

Jonas wiped the blood from his eyes as Dakota helped him up. "Did you get through to the cops? Who is that? Who's shooting?"

There was another two gunshots, and Jonas saw Erik coming back from the altar. He was panting heavily, and wiping blood from his face. Jonas asked him who was shooting, if the police had finally arrived, but he was met with a blank stare.

"I don't know. Later, Hamsikker. I've got to find my family."

Erik barged past, and Jonas saw the body of his father lying beneath the casket. He was truly dead this time. There was a bullet hole in his forehead, and another shot had taken off his jaw. Francis' eyes were closed now, and Jonas was certain they were going to stay that way. A figure stepped down from the altar, and paused by Jonas, looking him up and down.

"You'd do well to get yourself armed, son. You're in Kentucky now. It looks like we're in for trouble. You seen what's going on outside?"

Jonas wiped his hands through his hair, and saw a pair of tidy flat shoes standing in a slick pool of blood. The green dress the woman wore seemed familiar, and then he remembered who it was.

"Mrs Danick? Is that you?"

The elderly woman tucked the revolver back into her handbag, and began shuffling off to the church doors. "Get out of town, Hamsikker. Your father don't need you no more. And get that lovely wife of yours someplace safe."

Jonas took one more look at his father. He was truly dead. Jonas wasn't sure if his father was at peace, or what had just happened was real, but he was sure of one thing, Mrs Danick was right; they had to find someplace safe. He took Dakota's hand and they ran after Mrs Danick. The church had emptied, and everything seemed unreal, as if it was a dream. Jonas looked back at his father, and the dead priest, and wiped warm blood from his face. This was no dream. The three of them stood in the church doorway looking outside. The sky was still blue, and the cardinals were still flying amongst the trees, but everywhere else he looked, Jonas saw death. Countless cars had crashed into each other, and plumes of smoke were rising from the direction of Louisville. The church pathway was littered with bodies, and in the distance, he heard sirens drifting over the breeze.

"What's happening?" asked Dakota as she linked her arm with Jonas's.

A man came from around the corner of the church, dressed in a black suit, and Jonas recognised the figure as someone from the funeral. Uncle Nevin? Uncle Newton? The name escaped him, as it was hard to identify the man with half his face missing. Something, or someone, had ripped off the left half of the man's face, and one eye dangled from its socket. Blood dripped from the man's mouth, and when he saw Jonas, he growled.

A sedan suddenly came to a screeching halt at the roadside, and the driver's window automatically wound down. Jonas could see the car had four occupants, but only the driver was clearly visible through the blacked out windows.

"Get in," shouted Erik. "Get the hell in, *now!*"

The path between the road and the church was blocked by the dead man, who was now staggering toward them. Another figure was rising from the ground beside a poorly maintained grave. The earth was fresh, and there was no headstone, just a simple white cross that was crushed beneath the dead man's feet.

Mrs Danick calmly took the revolver from her handbag, and cocked it. "You go," she said to Jonas and Dakota as she raised the gun and took aim at the approaching figures. "I've got this."

CHAPTER ONE
A FEW MONTHS LATER

She was dead, no doubt about it. The discoloured skin, lifeless eyes, and slack jaw made it pretty obvious. The next clue was in the way she walked, so slowly and aimlessly, drawn to any noise like a dumb animal. Dead feet scraped the ground as the zombie shuffled forward, meandering across the grass verge towards them.

Javier put his hand across the gun that was aimed at the zombie's head, and lowered it. "Don't waste your time. She's too far away to worry about."

He could see the disappointment in Rose's eyes, but he wasn't about to waste a bullet.

"Oh come on, it's not like there are any others around. We can drop her and move on. I need the practise," said Rose as she raised the gun and squinted down the length of the barrel.

Javier rocked back on his feet, sucking in a mouthful of warm morning air. "No. We're low on ammo and…"

The zombie's head exploded as Rose fired, hitting it squarely between the eyes. The body fell slowly to the ground, and then silence resumed. A lone bird flew from a tree in the distance, startled by the gunshot, but otherwise, they were completely alone.

"Bagged me a zombie." Rose jumped to her feet looking elated. "Down in one."

Javier looked at her coolly. His blue eyes sparkled in the morning sunlight, and he took a step toward Rose. "What did I *just* say?" He could see her happiness fading, the light in Rose's face diminishing with each second, as pride was replaced by uncertainty.

"Oh, come on, cupcake, it's just a zombie," she said. "We've killed a thousand already, so who gives a shit? It's not like..."

The sting of his hand knocked her backward, and Javier grabbed the gun from her hands as Rose stumbled away from him. He holstered it, and then held out an open hand to her. She was more shocked than anything, and he knew he hadn't hit her that hard. She'd taken worse. It was really just a warning, a reminder of who was in charge.

"Come on." He felt her slip her thin fingers into his, and he pulled her up. Facing him, the light illuminated her long blonde hair, and his lips curled into a thin smile. She always looked beautiful to him, though even more when she was submissive. He didn't like it when she got cocky. He wasn't the only man to find her beautiful, but he sure as hell wasn't about to let anyone else get a piece of his Rose.

She looked up at him, and he saw the faint red glow blossoming on her cheek where he had slapped her. She leant in and kissed him, then drew her arms around his neck.

"I'm sorry, baby."

Her kisses tickled his neck and he pushed her away. "No harm done."

Javier turned to the low brick wall where they had stopped and he sat down. He faced the park they had just passed through, and stared at the treeline, trying to guess what lay beyond it. Tall elm trees littered the fringes of the park, and further still, lay thick scrub over hilly terrain. It was going to be another long hot day, and he wanted to push on. Jeffersontown left him cold. It was so bland, so suburban, so very apple-pie, college football, God-damn *American*. He hated it. He wanted to keep riding, just to keep going until he found someplace he could call home. He had come with his parents over the border years ago into Texas, and they had moved around a lot, sometimes several times in just a few months. Very quickly, his father had shot through, and from then on it had been different schools, different friends - different fathers, depending on the mood his mother was in. Eventually, he gave up on trying to settle down, and simply went with the flow. His mother had left him as soon as she could. One day, he came home to find a scribbled note stuck to the fridge. She had taken off with her latest boyfriend, a truck driver from Ohio, leaving him a cold slice of ham, her discoloured wedding ring, and twenty dollars to get by. The bitch had probably whored herself all the way to Canada by now, and he let out a small laugh.

"What's up?" asked Rose as she sat down beside him. It was warm, but early, and she zipped up the black leather jacket they had found discarded in the back of an SUV the previous night. You had to take what you could now. There were no more stores, no more hand-outs, and the law of the jungle ruled the streets now.

"I was just thinking. Where do we go from here? I mean, Jeffersontown did us fine, but I'm ready to move on, you know? Why stay here?" asked Javier.

"Can't we stay, just for a few more days? That place we crashed in last night was comfy. It's nice to sleep in a bed instead of the back of a truck for a change, and I know you enjoyed it too, right?"

Javier felt her run a hand over his thigh to his groin and she started squeezing him. He arched his eyebrows and looked at her. "You're a good fuck, Rose, but there's more to life than your tight ass."

She brought her hand back to her lap and smiled, but he could see he had annoyed her. Her eyes were distant, her smile forced. Inwardly, he wanted to smile too, but right then, there were more pressing matters than playing games with her.

"So what then, we keep going?" Rose asked. "Just going and going and going, right?"

Javier nodded. "Stick to the plan. Keep heading north. It's still our best shot."

Rose mumbled something, but he didn't hear her. It didn't really matter what she said, so he stopped listening. He knew full well that she would go along with him, no matter how much she complained. She could be a bad-ass when she needed to be, and they got on well most of the time, but he wasn't beholden to anyone, and he wasn't about to let Rose tell him what to do. Last night *had* been good, that was true. They had found a deserted house, and taken full opportunity to use the luxury at their disposal. The occupants were long gone, probably joining the ranks of the undead months back. The house was locked up tight, but he had easily broken in via a back window. There was no alarm, and they had swiftly checked all the rooms. Evidently, a fairly well off couple had lived there given the size of the place and the expensive looking décor. There were no children's toys, or clothes, and the pantry still had a few tins of food which they'd guzzled down greedily in the darkness. The boxes of oats, cereals and pasta had either gone off, or been eaten by rats and mice. The fresh food in the fridge had turned into small piles of mould, and the fetid smell was revolting. Nothing worked anymore: fridges, streetlights, televisions, computers, phones, nothing. Along with the power that had gone off months back, all those gadgets and devices supposed to make everyone's life easier had been turned off. They were as useful now as yesterday's newspaper.

"You've not given up on me, have you?" he asked Rose.

She shook her head. "Javier, you're my hero, you know that. I'm never leaving you."

He rolled his hand across her back, and brought it up to the nape of her neck. The sun behind them was slowly warming their backs, but still, he felt her shiver when he touched her.

"And Canada? You remember the plan?"

Javier gripped her neck tighter, just increasing the pressure of his fingers a fraction. She flinched, but not once did she take her eyes off his.

"Of course I do. Your brother is there, I get it. I'm with you, Javier, I promise. Straight up."

Javier brought his arm back around, and cupped her face. He leant in and kissed her. Those kisses made him feel alive, more alive than he had since before the shit had started. Back then he had been nothing; a nobody doing nothing of value, not understanding how he fitted in with the world, or where he was going. He had drifted, and he knew he couldn't blame his mother for that entirely. The bitch certainly hadn't helped, but he had been too chicken-shit to do anything about his life. Since the outbreak though, he had grown up. He realised what he had to do to get through life. He was head honcho now, and he was proud of what he had become. Rose had come along at just the right time, just after the uprising. It was a chance for a fresh start. Those big blue eyes had drawn him to her, and they hadn't looked back. Sure, sometimes he had to keep her in check, but on the whole, he could trust her. She was his forever, and that was as long as he wanted it to be.

"You're my eagle," she whispered to him as he held her. "Forever and ever."

Javier had told her early on in their relationship how the bald eagle mated for life. He'd spent a lot of time sitting in front of a TV picking up lots of useless information. He admired the eagle, so powerful and majestic: The King of the Skies. They were loyal too, a quality he admired, but had yet to experience. Rose was like a faithful dog, always at his side, but not always obeying him. She just needed a little more training.

"Forever," he whispered back, and he brushed his fingers through her long hair. He wasn't sure if he loved her, but he knew she loved him.

"Let's move." Javier stood up and walked over the rough yard to the bike. It was nothing special, just something they had picked up a month back outside of Owensboro. He had ridden Yamahas before, so he found it easy to handle. Annoyingly, the bike was ten years old, and as smooth as riding a donkey down a dirt track. He was on the look out for a Harley, or maybe even a Ducati, but so far, they had been out of luck. The only garage they had come across recently had been ransacked. There were nothing left but spare parts and a dead man with a bullet in his skull.

Javier mounted the bike and felt Rose climb on behind him. Her arms wrapped around his waist as he stirred the machine into life. More zombies were coming through the park now, probably drawn by the noise of the gunshot. There was nobody else around, certainly nobody alive to pique the zombies' curiosity. Turning around, Javier pulled them out onto the road, and let the engine idle as he looked around at Jeffersontown one last time. It had been a brief, but necessary rest stop. Having been on the road for several days, and running low on supplies, they needed the break. He knew it was too dangerous to go into the cities, and Louisville was no exception. It had succumbed quickly to the disease, and was now full of rabid zombies who for the most part, stayed there picking off the final survivors. Javier had no intention of becoming just another victim, and had only gone in as far as he had to. The back of the bike was packed full of food and water, a couple of guns, but not much else. They travelled light, and he liked it that way. The houses they had come across in town had been stocked, so they could have taken a hell of a lot more, but the more crap you carried, the more difficult it was to run. Moreover, they had done plenty of running of late, far more than he would've liked. The dead could still sneak up on you if you weren't careful, and in the early days, he had spent a lot of time running from one place to another, not really knowing where he was going, or what he was doing. There were runners too, really fast motherfuckers who could just run and run and run. Avoiding them wasn't easy.

Then he'd met Rose. She was holed up in a small Korean grocery store, and by chance, he had run in there to escape the attention of a herd of dead school kids. She hadn't even locked the front door, just pushed a few crates in front of it, which he had easily brushed aside. They stayed quietly inside for a full day waiting for the dead to leave, to go and find someone else to eat. In the meantime they talked, ate, drank, and finally fucked. Ever since then, since those days spent cooped up together, she had been by his side like a loyal hound. He hadn't quite known what to make of her at first, but she was interesting. He asked her about her past, but she kept it brief and glossed over a lot of it. It was all irrelevant now anyway. It helped pass the time, but where you came from had little relevance to where you were going in a world full of the dead.

Javier sped up and drove down the deserted streets, past burnt out buildings. Cars littered the road and the sidewalks, but there were few bodies around. At first, the dead had been left to rot in the streets, but eventually, they had either reanimated, or been eaten by the others. Only skeletal carcasses were visible now, and it was possible Javier and Rose were the only people still alive in Jeffersontown. It had been a couple of days since they had seen anyone alive, and even then, it was only from a distance. They'd passed a gated school just off I-65 and kept well away. A crowd of at least fifty zombies had it circled and were battering at the doors and walls. Up on the roof there was a figure, too far off to see clearly, but most likely one of the teachers who worked there.

The figure waved their hands above their head and shouted, but there was nothing they could do for them. Javier kept driving and watched the school recede into the distance as he drove them on, away from danger. They had a limited supply of ammo, and he wasn't about to waste it on some old fart who would only be a drain on their resources. Javier knew asking for help was a sign of weakness; he didn't expect any, and didn't give any.

As they reached the edge of town, Javier turned a corner and hit the brakes. Right in the middle of the road stood a boy, no older than fourteen or fifteen, staring right at them. He wasn't moving, speaking, or doing anything, just standing there as plain as day right on the centre line. Javier stopped the bike ten feet short of the boy, and looked him over. The boy had probably been scavenging for months. He was skinny and dirty, with pale skin that was covered in spots. His dishevelled hair was long and greasy, and his clothes torn and filthy. The boy raised a shaking hand.

"Please," he whispered. "Please, I need…"

The boy swayed before collapsing to his knees. Javier dismounted and looked around. It could be a trap. The boy might be playing a trick, or his friends could be lying in wait nearby, ready to pounce and take the bike and supplies. They'd most likely kill Javier, and take Rose too. That was *not* going to happen. Javier carefully looked at the houses on both sides of the street, scanning the gardens and fences for watching eyes, but he found none.

"What's happening?" asked Rose.

Javier watched her withdraw a blade from her boot. "Just keep your eyes open. Yell if you see anything. I'm going to check it out." Rose remained seated, as Javier hopped off the bike. He walked slowly up to the boy.

"What's your name?" Javier asked. There was no friendliness in his tone, and he wanted it that way. If he showed the slightest hint of weakness, the boy was likely to use it. In this world, strength was the new currency. Weakness meant you were a victim, and victims died quickly these days.

"Please, help me," the boy whispered. He looked up and wiped wiry hair away from his eyes with grubby fingers.

Javier pinched his nose. It smelt like the boy had soiled himself, and on closer inspection, it seemed his clothes were drenched in blood. Javier pulled his gun out, but kept it low by his thigh.

"Name. Now."

The boy's breathing was shallow and he shuffled forward on his knees. "Noah. I'm Noah. Please sir, I heard you coming and I..." The boy hesitated when he saw the gun, before continuing. "Please, I haven't eaten in days. Take me with you. It's hell here. They're spread thin, but they're everywhere. I don't know how to drive. My parents are dead. Well, you know, they were before they came back and... I can't live like this. Please, sir, please, you have to help me."

Javier could see the pain in the boy's eyes; he was telling the truth. He had done well to survive this long if he was on his own. Without weapons, without help, going from house to house looking for food and clean water was no way to live. Javier could testify to that. He heard Rose come up behind him.

"He's just a kid," she said. She sheathed the blade and folded her arms. "Is he bit?"

"You hurt?" asked Javier. There was a lot of blood drying on the boy's clothes.

Noah shook his head. "No, I'm okay. I'm just hungry. Do you have any food?"

The boy's eyes betrayed his desperation, and they looked from Javier to Rose before settling on the bike, and then the pack of supplies tied to the rear. Javier took a step to the side to block the boy's view. Young Noah was getting ahead of himself.

"I need to know you're not bit. Pull up your shirt and turn around, slowly."

Noah got to his feet and did as he was told. He unbuttoned his shirt, and lifted it showing them his pale, grimy body. His slender frame was filthy, but there were no bite marks.

"I told you, I'm clean," said Noah as he buttoned his shirt back up.

"You're hardly clean," muttered Rose, "stay there."

She took Javier's arm and drew him back to the bike so she could talk without being overheard. "Javier, what are we going to do with him? If I shuffled forward, we could just about squeeze him on the back of the bike. Or, I suppose we could find somewhere safe to stay? Maybe feed him up a bit before we send him on his way? We can't just leave him."

Javier looked back at Noah, who was waiting patiently. The boy was harmless. God knows how he had made it this long. His parents had probably saved him from much of it, but evidently, they hadn't quite stuck around long enough to see it through. The boy was starving, and unlikely to make it much longer without help. "You remember me telling you about the native American Eagles. The way they soared through the sky was amazing, so effortless and powerful and free. I saw a programme once where the male returned to the nest, only to find his mate was dead. She'd been poisoned. You know they only mate once in their lives. A dumb animal like that showed more loyalty than any person I've ever met."

Rose looked up at Javier with puppy-dog eyes. "*Hey*, I'm right here."

"Present company excluded." Javier knew that was what she wanted to hear. He tapped the gun on his thigh as he thought. "I'm not so convinced we can take him with us. We travel light, remember? We only have enough water for two, and it's gonna be *real* snug on that bike with three. We've got a lot of riding before we even get close to the Canadian border. You want to ride all the way there with Noah holding onto your ass?"

"No, but, oh I don't know. It's up to you, honey. You're my eagle." Rose got onto the back of the bike. "Better hurry up though. I think we've got company."

Javier looked to where Rose was pointing. An assortment of people, all dead, was slowly making their way down the street in the direction of the bike. Drawn by the noise of the engine, the zombies had emerged from hiding, from the shops and houses, the park, and the abandoned vehicles. All were now heading directly for Javier and Rose.

"Get her started." Javier watched Rose lean forward and turn over the engine. She winked at her lover, and then he returned to Noah.

Noah smiled, showing Javier a set of brown teeth. "Thank you. I promise I won't be any trouble. I haven't got any stuff so we should get going. Should I sit behind your girlfriend?"

Javier sighed. "I'm sorry, kid, but you're not coming with us."

"What? But I'm clean! I mean, I'm not bit. I showed you. Come on, man, just take me as far as you can and..." Noah could tell his pleading was falling on deaf ears.

Javier slowly raised the gun, and pointed it at Noah's chest. From this range, he could not miss. Hell, he wouldn't miss if he was fifty yards away and it was raining frogs. He probably had a minute before the dead reached them, and he felt for the boy, he really did. At least when his own mother had abandoned him, he had been half prepared for it. He had grown up on the streets, moving from place to place. This kid had almost certainly gone to a good school, been looked after, been well fed by his loving parents, and was in no way prepared for the life he faced now.

"What happened to your parents, Noah?" Javier asked.

"They're dead, I told you. Look, what's that got to do with..."

Javier cocked the trigger. "What happened?"

Noah looked frantically from side to side, but the empty streets offered no salvation. "They got caught a few days ago. We were out looking for food and... It was an accident. I managed to get away, but they..."

Noah was trembling. His eyes were filling up, and Javier could guess the rest of the story. Still, he wanted to know.

"Go on."

Noah wiped his eyes and smeared fresh dirt across his face. "They came back. Yesterday. I didn't know what to do so I ran. I just left them, and I ran and I ran and... They followed me, along with some others. I tripped and ended up in a creek, just behind the warehouse over there. It was full of dead bodies. They'd all been shot through the head, and they were rotting. The smell was horrific. It was *so* disgusting that I would've puked if I had anything inside me to bring up. It must've worked as they eventually gave up and left me be. I stayed there all night and day. Then I heard you coming and..."

Noah began sobbing and Javier lowered his weapon. He put it back in his belt as he approached the boy. He slipped an arm around Noah's shoulders, and the boy instantly clung to him, soaking Javier's shirt with his tears.

"Hush, Noah, hush." Javier looked over to see the zombies approaching. He had about thirty seconds to spare. Rose was looking anxious, and signalling for him to hurry up.

"You know what?" Noah kept crying and Javier stroked the boy's tangled hair. "I had a rough time of it too," said Javier. "I know how hard it can be on your own, on the streets. I took a shine to a dog once, just a stray, but he seemed to like me. I guess we had something in common so we hung out for a bit. Tucker. Don't ask me where that name came from, but it stuck. I was young and stupid. Anyway, he started walking with a limp one day, and it just got worse. I was living rough, and didn't have the money for a vet, so I just let him drift. The day after, he could barely walk at all, and the day after that, he wouldn't move at all. Tucker was dying, I knew it, but I didn't know what to do. I just stayed with him until he finally passed. He was in pain, I knew that too, but still I let him live as *long* as I possibly could. He was *my* dog, and I wanted him with me as long as possible. That mangy dog hung on for four days, whimpering in pain at all times of the night. I learned my lesson though, and I vowed never to let a wounded creature suffer again. I was selfish. Best to put 'em out of their misery right away. You know what I'm saying, son?"

Noah didn't answer. The crying had stopped, but the boy was holding onto Javier; he had nothing else to hold on to. He was shaking and Javier could almost feel the boy relax. Silently, he drew a knife out from a hidden pocket.

"It's for the best. I'll stay with you," said Javier as he flicked the knife open.

As the blade pierced Noah's neck, the boy began to struggle, but Javier held him tight. He plunged the knife further, severing the boy's major artery, and warm blood spewed out. Javier was careful to keep most of it away from him. He didn't relish being covered in blood. Human bodies could break so easily. Most of the undead died cleanly: no blood, no mess.

Noah kicked, and gripped Javier's waist, but the life was quickly slipping away from him. The boy hadn't the energy to fight, and in just a few seconds, it was over. Javier carefully laid Noah on the ground, and wiped his knife clean before sheathing it.

"Sleep well, boy."

Javier strode back to the bike and got on. He gripped the handlebars, and said nothing. Rose wrapped her arms around him, and let her head fall on his strong back. The bike started moving, and the zombies groaned almost as one as their prey left them. Rose watched them recede with the rest of the town, and began to wonder where they would end up next.

As they passed Noah's body, Javier looked into the boy's lifeless eyes. He couldn't afford to waste a bullet, and had tried to make it as painless as possible. The poor kid would've been dead before the week was out. Being eaten alive was no way to go. He had tried to prepare the boy too, as best he could. Javier was not a religious man, and prayers meant nothing to him. He had tried calling on God for help many times when he was younger, but there was never an answer. He hoped the story about Tucker had given the boy some sort of peace. Javier had never had a dog in truth. Who had the time to look after one when you barely had food for yourself? It seemed like the right thing to say at the time. Devoid of any knowledge of the Bible, it seemed like it was appropriate.

Rose looked at Noah longingly. It had been so long since she had felt the life drain out of someone that she wished Noah had come along on the bike. She could've slit his throat while he slept, or seduced him and had some fun before she let him bleed out. Javier never let her have fun anymore. The blade in her boot was aching with the need to kill, and she didn't know how much longer she could hold out. Taking down a zombie just wasn't the same. It was already dead. Where was the fun in killing something already dead? She needed to feel the warm breath of a man on her face as she cut out his heart. She forced herself to forget about it, and held onto Javier's waist. One day, Rose thought, Javier won't be around, and then the time will come.

The bike sped up and Jeffersontown was left behind. The sun rose higher illuminating the barren streets, and the zombies fell upon Noah's body, devouring it quickly, leaving only scraps of clothing and his shoes behind. They sucked on his bones, wiping them clean, licking off every last inch of blood and tissue. When they were done there was nothing left, so they continued their meandering deadly sojourn down the streets of Jeffersontown, following the trail of the bike.

CHAPTER TWO

"Kill the dead! Kill them all!" screamed Jonas. Saliva and rage flew from his mouth as he launched himself at the nearest zombie, the axe in his hand jarring sickeningly with bone. The zombie's head neatly fell to the side leaving the decapitated corpse blundering about aimlessly before sinking to the floor. Jonas swung again, heaving the bloody axe from side to side, and sinking its delicious blade into arms and heads. There was no time to think about what he was doing. Within seconds, it had turned to chaos, and he had no idea who was safe and who wasn't. All he could do was fight.

"Help!"

Jonas turned to see who had cried out. It was Anna. She was locked in the embrace of a dead woman with the creature's arms wrapped around her body. As Jonas turned to rush to Anna's aid, the zombie sunk its teeth into the side of her face, tearing off a massive chunk of flesh. Anna howled in pain and Jonas could see the top row of teeth through the hole in her cheek. The zombie sunk its teeth into Anna again, and was quickly joined by another who bit Anna's neck. In seconds, she was engulfed by them, and Jonas no longer heard any cries for help. His friend was gone, submerged beneath a pile of moving corpses.

A hand grabbed his shoulder, and he whirled around to find the fragile, bony fingers of a zombie gripping him. Grunting with the effort, he managed to lift his axe with his free hand, and slice off the creature's arm, leaving its bony hand still wrapped around his forearm. He swung again and the axe embedded itself in the dead man's cranium. Jonas lost his grip on the axe as the zombie fell to the ground, the weapon still firmly lodged in its skull.

Two gunshots rang out, swiftly followed by more, and Jonas looked about him. Cordite and blood filled his nostrils and he pushed another zombie away. Someone was shooting. He prayed they could tell the difference between those who were alive, and those who were dead. The axe was out of reach, and another zombie charged him. Jonas side-stepped the attack at the last second. Grabbing the zombie's shoulders, he threw it as far away as he could. Its head collided with a concrete wall, and its body slumped to the ground as its skull cracked open. The room began to spin, and all he could hear was shouting and gunshots. The voices were loud, but he didn't hear a word. The dead moaned and sighed, their soulless whispers fading in and out amongst the tortured screams of his friends. Something pulled at his leg, and he looked down to see the decayed corpse of a young man trying to pull him toward his mouth. He freed himself easily from its grip, and hefted a large boot into the zombie's gaping jaws, cracking its head back against the cold, hard floor.

As he reached down to retrieve his axe, he realised the attack had stopped. The sounds, the cries, the gunshots, the fighting and breathing and dying; they all ended as abruptly as they'd begun. Jonas left the axe where it was, still stuck in a dead man's skull, when he saw Tyler with his back against the door. The young man was leaning forward, doubled over as if he was about to vomit. When Tyler looked up their eyes met. Jonas saw such a lack of hope and utter desperation in the young man's innocent eyes that he wished he could trade places with him. Cliff stood in the middle of the room unloading a clip into some poor dead idiot's skull, and Jonas knew then who had been doing all the shooting.

"That's it," said Cliff as he fired one last time. "That'll do, pig, that'll do."

As the room fell silent, the three men looked at each other in horror. All about the room lay dead bodies. They had walked right into it. The garage was supposed to be safe, supposed to be somewhere they could take solace for a while, and rest. Instead, it had turned into a slaughter. Jonas silently thanked God the others had stayed outside waiting for the all clear. They must have heard the gunshots, yet they had stayed outside. It didn't matter why, it just mattered that there was still someone alive. After all this, someone still had to be alive.

There was a banging on the door at Tyler's back, and he turned around. Jonas could see the gun trembling in the young man's hand, and went over to him.

"I locked it as soon as I saw them coming. They couldn't have helped us; they would've just got in the way. I'm not sure what happened to Anna though. She ran in and... I didn't think they..."

Tyler fell to his knees and Jonas caught him, lowering him slowly to the bloody ground.

"I'm sorry, I... I need a minute," said Tyler. His eyes were wild, and Jonas could feel the man's whole body shaking. The kid had probably never been through anything like that. Hell, none of them had, at least not for a good while. Jonas couldn't speak for everyone, but it had been a long time since he had been forced to put one of the dead down. The banging on the door increased, and Jonas heard voices from the other side.

"What the hell is going on?" shouted one. Was that Peter or Erik?

"Let us in, let us in," shouted another.

"God damn it, let us in!" The second voice sounded like Pippa's.

Jonas could hear sobbing too, and put his hand on the door. The vibrations as it shook in its frame were reassuring, a reminder of gravity, of reality; it was something simple and yet his mind was close to breaking. The shaking door was pulling him back to Earth.

"Hold up. We're okay. Just hold on and stop shouting, or you'll draw more of them."

The banging stopped. Jonas heard faint sobs from the other side. The adrenalin still coursing through his veins wanted to tell him to run, to get away from here, and keep running; just keep running and running and not look back. He put a hand over his mouth as if it would stop the nausea, but the slickness of the blood on his fingers only made him feel worse. A woman's voice whispered to him through the closed door, becoming muffled as it tried to work its way through the oak.

"Jonas? Are you okay? Jonas?"

There was a lone gunshot from behind him in the room, and the hairs on his neck stood up. The woman's voice was familiar, yet strange. His senses were highly attuned, yet his memory momentarily left him. What was going on? Who were these people? Why was he standing in a room full of dead people?

"Jonas, please, I need to know you're okay." The woman's voice was faint and broke up into sobs. "Who's shooting? Please?"

"Hold up," Jonas said as he tried to recall whose voice it was. Dakota. The woman was Dakota. Random thoughts came to his mind as he pushed the images of the zombie attack to the back of his fizzing brain. She had long brown hair, laughed at bad sit-coms, hated ironing, played tennis on Thursday evenings, liked pizza, hated politicians, and yet, and yet... Something important forced its way to the front. She loved him. She loved *him*. Dakota loved him. God he loved his wife.

"Dakota? Honey, I'm fine. We'll be out in a minute."

His stomach churned, and he fought down the still rising urge to vomit. He turned to face Cliff. The man was holstering his gun and scanning the room casually, sizing it up as if deciding on what wallpaper to pick out.

Jonas couldn't wait any longer. The others wanted answers, and so did he. They had come here on the basis it was safe. Jonas had even said they should all get inside off the street immediately. It was only Erik who had suggested some of them wait, just in case. He always made the right decision. It was something Jonas was trying to do, but he wasn't convinced he was achieving it yet. Today was a classic example, and now people were dead.

Jonas approached Cliff, looking him up and down. The mechanic's greasy overalls were covered in bloodstains, the dark grey cotton now a muddy brown.

"You hurt?" Jonas asked him.

Cliff wiped the sweat from his eyes, grinning. "They never laid a finger on me. Easy as pie, brother. Reckon I took at least a dozen down. How about you? I saw you take a few down. You are one mean motherfucker when you're cornered, Hamsikker." Cliff removed his cap and slapped it on his thigh. "Hoo-hah!"

Jonas punched Cliff square in the jaw. The mechanic reeled backward, too shocked to react, and he rubbed his jaw. As he slid to a halt, Cliff's feet found traction on the slain body of a zombie, and he braced himself. He raised his fists, and snarled at Jonas.

"What the hell is *your* problem?" Cliff's dark eyes were set on Jonas, and he was all too eager for a fight.

"My problem?" Jonas was astounded that Cliff even had to ask. "Do you think this is a game? That was a fucking massacre. Look around you, Cliff. How many of us are left?"

Jonas could see confusion in Cliff's eyes. They shifted around the room lazily, taking in those who were left standing, and those who had fallen.

"So what?" he shrugged. "It's not my fault they haven't learnt how to defend themselves by now." Cliff softened his stance. He knew Jonas didn't want to fight; he was just making a point. They had argued bitterly over the last few weeks, and today was just another fight.

Jonas clenched his teeth together, and walked over to the body of a woman wearing slim jeans and a grey cardigan, now drenched in blood. He pointed at the body. "Anna Redburn. Been with us four months." Jonas pointed out another body in the corner of the room. "James Bracken. Three months. The woman next to him, his wife, Gloria, cooked us supper last night. You may remember telling her the soup needed more salt?"

Jonas bent down putting his arms around the neck of a smaller body. It was just a girl. He carefully lifted the child's head so it was facing Cliff. Her wide lifeless eyes stared out, her pale cheeks splattered with blood and a ragged, gaping hole in her neck proof of how she had been killed. Jonas's voice softened. "Mary Redburn. Six years old. Think she should've defended herself better? Huh, Cliff? I guess it's her fault she's dead."

The mechanic looked away. Jonas couldn't tell if it was through embarrassment, or boredom.

"How was I to know? I thought it was safe here. I thought…" Cliff trailed off and looked down at the gun in his hand. His thick sausage fingers were red and sore.

"Sorry, what was that?" asked Jonas. "Was that an apology?" Jonas gently laid Mary down on the sticky floor of the garage.

There was so much blood he could almost swim in it. It soaked into his shoes, and squelched every time he took a step.

Cliff looked up, his jaw locked in a stiff expression of anger. "Fuck you, Hamsikker. You can't make me feel guilty for this. Look there's likely to be someone still upstairs. I'm sure I saw them moving. We need to move on quickly and..."

"Move on?" scoffed Jonas. "Cliff, do you even hear how you sound? I very much doubt there is anyone alive up there given the state of things down here. Most likely, you just saw a zombie, and took us on a wild goose chase. This place is nothing but a death-trap."

"I told you, I thought it was safe. How was *I* to know?" Cliff visibly bristled.

"How were *you* supposed to know?" Jonas couldn't stand any more of Cliff's defensive attitude. For months, Cliff had been irritating everyone, and his bad attitude was bringing the group down; now he had cost some of them their lives. "Maybe because *you* were the one who told us this was safe. Maybe because *you* were the one who scouted the garage out, and brought us in here. If it isn't your fault, then whose is it? You're a first class moron, Cliff, and I'm done with you. You need to leave us. Make your own way from here on in. I can't do this anymore. I can't bury any more of my friends. With you around, there won't be many of us left soon."

Cliff raised his gun at Jonas. "You know what, Hamsikker? If I have to listen to one more of your sanctimonious bullshit speeches, I'm going to throw up. You've been on my case since day one. I came to you, remember? I gave your group everything I had: my guns, food, matches, everything. Do I ever hear a 'thank you, Cliff,' or 'you're welcome, Cliff'? No. All I hear is you bleating on about eating too many rations, or that damn bitch of yours, Dakota, telling me to pray to Jesus. *Cliff do this. Cliff do that.* Well fuck you. I'm sick of this pathetic group you have. I'm sick of the lot of you. I *will* make my own way. I'll be better off on my own without you lot dragging me down. I'm taking my shit with me. *My* guns and *my* food. It's all going with *me*."

Jonas couldn't contain himself any longer, and he hurled himself at Cliff. He saw the surprise in Cliff's eyes, but he didn't care anymore. The man was a liability. If he was leaving the group, then it was going to be on Jonas's terms.

Cliff didn't expect Jonas to attack, and without even thinking pulled the trigger. The gun was aimed straight at Jonas's head, and Jonas wondered why he was still standing. He flinched as Cliff pulled the trigger again when Jonas was only a foot away. They both realised at the same time that the clicking noise they could hear was the gun's empty chamber. Cliff had used all the bullets taking down the zombies, and finishing off the wounded survivors making sure they didn't come back.

Jonas barged into Cliff and they went down in a heap. A large powerful fist crunched into Jonas's jaw, and he was sure he felt a tooth dislodge itself. He had the advantage of being on top though and head-butted Cliff, breaking the man's bulbous nose. Jonas pushed himself up off the floor, and punched Cliff square on the chin, causing the man to squeal in pain. Now the man's nose and jaw were broken, and Jonas couldn't stop himself. He didn't care what happened. He couldn't see, feel, or hear anything, except the pathetic creature beneath him howling in pain. He launched a tirade of punches at Cliff, repeatedly striking him in the head, raining down blows on the man's face until Cliff's arms began to sag. Jonas screamed as he pummelled Cliff into the ground. A tornado couldn't have stopped Jonas then, such was his rage. The mechanic's eyes had swollen shut, and his face was a bloody, broken mess. The man was not just a liability, but a murderer.

"Jonas, stop, you're going to kill him." Tyler put an arm around Jonas. "Leave him."

Jonas sank back, his chest heaving as he drew in breath. He spat out bloody saliva, and turned to face Tyler. "That's the least he deserves."

Tyler nodded. "Maybe so, maybe so. Here, let me help you." Tyler lifted Jonas to his feet, and the men looked at each other. Nothing needed to be said about what had just happened. They both understood the gravity of the situation.

"We need to get out of here," said Tyler. "There'll be more. There always is."

"Just a second," wheezed Jonas. From where he stood, he could still see Mary's body, and his rage hadn't dissipated yet. He didn't want to go back out there to Dakota, to the others, and still be worked up like this. He needed to let it out. Beating Cliff had seemed so just, and so right; so why did he feel so bitter? Why did he want to cry? He hadn't hit a man for a long time, much as he had been tempted to during the past few weeks. He had to clear his head. Once they were back outside, they had to be alert, careful, and quiet. If he wasn't on the level, he was a liability, and there was more than just Dakota to worry about. The whole group looked up to him and Erik for leadership. If he couldn't get them out of this mess, then it was all up to Erik. The man had a family though, and neither of them wanted to put more responsibility on the other. It wasn't fair. Cliff had royally fucked them over.

"What do we do about him?" asked Jonas. He couldn't bring himself to look at Cliff. He could hear the rasping breaths behind him, and knew that if they took Cliff with them, they would have to carry him. If they didn't take him, they were essentially condemning him to death.

Tyler looked at Jonas. "You want to bring him with us? Even after this, after what he did? Where do we even go? I mean, Jesus, we've lost our safe house, we've nowhere else to go, and it'll be sundown soon. There are zombies out there who will have heard this, you know? If we leave him, he'll die, no doubt about it. Perhaps between two or three of us, we could carry him, but…"

Jonas grabbed Tyler's gun, turned around, and pointed it at Cliff. He wanted to fire a bullet straight into the man's temple. He wanted to forget this nightmare, to get rid of the bad egg, but he couldn't do it. He lowered the gun and handed it back to a startled Tyler. Rage had turned to defeat, and Jonas's shoulders slumped.

"We'll say he was bitten. He wouldn't have made it. He'd have just slowed us down until he turned. Understand?"

Tyler nodded, and looked at Jonas as he took the gun back. "I got it. There were too many of them and…"

"I don't want you to lie for me," Jonas whispered. "Your conscience is clean. This is on me." Jonas looked at Cliff, and he knew he couldn't leave him like that.

Jonas plucked his axe from a zombie's head, feeling his bones ache as he bent down to retrieve it. He had to do it quickly. His hands shook, and sweat stung his eyes, but he had to do it; just not think about it, and do it. Before Tyler cottoned on to what Jonas was doing, he brought the axe down on Cliff's head, the blade splitting Cliff's skull open, killing him instantly.

"Jesus Christ," said Tyler turning away as Cliff's brains oozed out over the floor.

Jonas put a hand on Tyler's sweaty back. "Remember, Tyler, this is on me. Forget about it. This whole fucking thing has been a nightmare."

They walked over to the door as the pounding on it increased. Jonas unlocked it, and Erik nearly knocked him over as he charged into the garage, an aluminium baseball bat held high above his head.

"Relax, Erik, they're dead, they're all messed up," said Jonas, pushing him back. He knew Erik could see the mountain of dead bodies behind him, but he didn't want him to explore it. Once Tyler had followed Jonas out of the garage, back into the forecourt, he closed the door. "There's nothing you can do now. They're all dead."

"What was that, Hamsikker? What the hell happened in there? Why'd you lock us out?" asked Erik. He only saw a fleeting image of the bloody room, but it was enough to know things had gone bad. His mouth dropped open as he realised only Jonas and Tyler had come out. "Where's James? Anna? Oh Jesus, not Mary too?"

Dakota rushed to hug her husband. "Jonas, I thought…" Her words became muffled sobs as she buried her head in his shoulder.

More of the group filed closer to hear the conversation, demanding to know what had happened. Mrs Danick and Pippa were already crying, and all too aware that their friends were dead.

"What happened?" asked Erik. He rested his baseball bat by his side, unable to believe so many zombies had found them so quickly.

"Cliff sold us down the river," said Jonas. "He said the garage was secure, but when we got in there, two doors on the far side opened and they just poured in. I don't know what he was thinking. He probably never scouted it out at all. Tyler and I managed to take a lot of them down, and Cliff did most of the shooting, but…"

"Anna and Mary didn't make it," said Tyler. "James too. I saw him go down fighting. He was a tough son of a bitch."

"Cliff too?" asked Erik remembering the larger-than-life mechanic. "They got him?"

Tyler and Jonas looked at each other.

"Yeah, they got him," said Tyler. "They overpowered him, and he got bit. I made sure he couldn't come back."

Erik murmured something about it being the right thing to do, and then turned to Jonas. "Any sign of the person upstairs Cliff thought he saw?"

Jonas shook his head. "Nothing. It was just a zombie. There's no one alive in there."

"So, what now? We're going to have to make tracks. Who knows how many more are hiding around here." Erik looked around the forecourt nervously. Standing out in the open in this world was never a good idea.

"Where are we going to go?" asked Pippa.

"Yeah, Dad," said Peter. "This was supposed to be safe. We can't just wander the streets looking for somewhere to go." Peter was holding his sister Freya by his side, wishing she didn't have to hear this stuff. He wished for a lot of things that didn't come true anymore.

"We should go back," stated Terry plainly. He was an unassuming man, and rarely spoke up. He had been hiding with them for a few months, having been travelling with Anna and Mary. Jonas thought of him as something of a rarity amongst them. He was usually calm, and claimed to have despatched a lot of zombies into hell in protecting Anna and Mary. He was like a kindly uncle, always there in the background, never complaining, just waiting for his moment.

"We should just go back," Terry repeated. "I know there's no food left, but we do know that it's safe. If we can retrace our steps, then…"

"Then what?" asked Erik. "It's a big ask to retrace our steps to start with. The gunshots will draw more out, and getting back to where we started just seems like a backward step to me."

"I agree," said Peter. "We should go forward. Find somewhere new."

"I agree with Terry." Quinn was the same age as Peter, but she had twice the confidence, and had recently joined the group. She was assertive and bold, and would most likely lead the group herself once Erik and Jonas stepped down. Her youthfulness was only betrayed by a lack of vision. She could be headstrong, and that was why Jonas kept her on a leash. He was surprised to hear that she wanted to go back too.

"I have to say I think I side with Erik. We might be able to get back, but if we did, then what? We need to find food. If anything followed us back, we'd be stuck in that house with no food. We're better to carry on, find somewhere else."

"Anywhere that isn't here," said Dakota quietly. She tucked her hair behind her ears and stood by her husband's side.

"Quinn, please, trust us, going back is never a good idea," said Jonas.

"One thing we can't afford to do is stand around debating it." Erik slung his bat over his shoulder, walked to the closed door, and rested a hand on it.

Jonas was worried he was going to open the door. The chance of Erik noticing Cliff was slim given the amount of bodies piled up inside, but there would be some awkward questions if he did. There were a million reasons they had to get moving, most of them blood-thirsty zombies, but Cliff was one, and a very important one.

"I'm sorry for them, truly I am," said Erik. "I don't want to leave them like this, but there's nothing we can do now. Anna, Mary, James, and yes even that asshole, Cliff, deserve a decent burial. If we get a chance to come back then we'll do right by them. But Jesus himself would haul ass if he was in our position."

"Amen to that," said Randall. He was another in the group that rarely spoke up. Jonas found him a little tempestuous, but he didn't make waves, and he often helped to look after Freya. He was almost as old as Mrs Danick was, didn't eat much, or make much noise, but could be relied upon. He was always looking out for others, and never complained.

"May our brothers and sisters rest in peace," Randall said quietly.

Erik took a length of licorice roll out, and began chewing on it. Jonas was relieved to see that Erik hadn't opened the door and he whispered an 'Amen' with the rest of the group to the brief prayer for the fallen.

"Best to leave then," said Quinn. "After you, Hamsikker."

Jonas appreciated that she wasn't arguing with him, or Erik. There had been others, Cliff particularly, who always seemed to find fault, who always wanted to pick and pick until the discussion turned into a debate, and the debate turned into an argument. Quinn voiced her opinion, but knew what battles to fight.

"Erik can take the lead," said Jonas wearily.

"Come on, Pippa," said Erik. She followed him, still crying, and their children Peter and Freya followed. Quinn, Terry, Randall and Mrs Danick followed them, leaving Jonas with Dakota.

"The noise will attract more, you know," said Dakota. "Where do we go from here? What's waiting for us on the road ahead?"

"We were stupid to trust him. *I* was stupid. We should've gone in alone. It's not all on Cliff. I promised Anna I would look out for Mary, and now…"

"We work as a group remember? This is on all of us. Besides, you have your own family to look after. Don't you ever do that to me again, Jonas Hamsikker. You're all I've got. When I heard the shooting, I thought… Well anyway, you're okay, I'm okay, and the others are waiting for us. Let's go."

Jonas could see Dakota was on the verge of breaking down. Her lips trembled as she spoke, and her eyes were clear. He could understand what she was thinking. If it had been the other way around, if she had been trapped in there with him on the other side of that door, he would've killed anything in his path, and moved Heaven and Earth to get to her. Losing her was not an option he could think about.

Jonas was pleased when the garage was behind them. He still couldn't relax, but as it fell further behind so did the dark thoughts and anger. They were replaced with fear and uncertainty. They hadn't ventured out into these streets before, at least not since the funeral. An hour ago, there had been fourteen in the group, and now they were ten. He felt responsible for all of them, and he intended to find a bed for every single one of them. The problem was he didn't know where they were going. The part of town they were in now was the business district, and the shops and warehouses offered no protection at all. Large glass frontages could be broken easily, and the few warehouses they tried were locked up with no way in. They needed food too, and pushed on in search of houses. The streets were awkward to navigate, and progress was slow.

At one junction, telegraph poles and street lights barricaded the way. They'd fallen over each other and been left in a criss-cross formation, like an obscene obstacle course made of collapsed crucifixes. Jonas was reminded of the battlefields from the First World War. He couldn't imagine being in that situation; even the amount of death he had faced lately paled into comparison to what those soldiers had gone through. A length of wire hung across the street. Dismembered limbs hung from it, rags and torn pieces of clothing in tatters flapping gently in the breeze. The wire had been put there on purpose, specifically to stop the advance of the dead. More lengths of wire lay on the ground where it had been pulled down, and they stepped over it carefully. Some of it was barbed, and chunks of rotten meat covered in flies were trapped in its sharp barbs. Jonas tried to ignore the stench, but it was impossible to avoid altogether, and he heard Dakota gag as they ventured through the junction.

"Come on, honey, let's get past this." He felt for her hand and she took it gratefully. The sun was fading, and they could do with a break. He could sense the frustration and disappointment within the group that the garage hadn't worked out. He needed to get a result, to get them focused again, to get them somewhere safe, and he pushed on.

"You think we can find somewhere to stay?" asked Dakota. "Somewhere safe?"

"I'll bet we can," he replied. Dakota was no fool, and she wasn't easily convinced. He smiled at her, trying to reassure her. "We'll be fine, I can feel it." Jonas hoped the tremor in his voice didn't give away his true thoughts. He felt far from fine, and was beginning to doubt they would fine anywhere safe in Kentucky, let alone Jeffersontown. It was going to be a long day.

CHAPTER THREE

Creeping through the streets was unnerving, and Jonas could feel a million eyes staring at them, but they took it slow. Along with Erik and Quinn, they made their way down deserted roads. It was essential to keep quiet, so as not to draw the zombies, and so that they could hear any approach. Some of the dead were more agile than others, and whilst the slower ones could be dispatched swiftly, some of them could run, fast. Those were the ones you heard coming. They didn't care what they banged into or over as they ran. The slower ones were like silent assassins, and could catch anyone out who wasn't paying attention.

Erik directed them onto a larger road, and Jonas realised they had hit the Bluegrass Parkway. It was clear, lined with grass verges that hadn't been mowed in months, and trees thick with leaves. The sun was achingly hot, but he made them continue. They had to put as much space between themselves and the garage as possible. Jonas hadn't travelled on the Bluegrass since he was a teenager. It was a road he had used so many times that it was like second nature now. So much of his past he remembered, and yet so much was forgotten.

Travelling through Jeffersontown, Jonas was struck by how different it was from when he had last ventured out. Before the outbreak, the town had been bustling with activity; people and shoppers everywhere, lots of traffic, noise and vibrant colours. The town's edifice had slipped, and the colour had been replaced by grey. Smoke still drifted through the air, and soot had stained many of the downtown shops and buildings. Surfaces not tarnished by the fires were dirty, or caked in blood. The roads were starting to crack with weeds pushing through after months of neglect. Many road signs had been knocked over by cars full of people desperate to escape. The streets of this once vibrant town were more like a war-zone.

A lonely canvas 'For Sale' sign fluttered by, its stark red and white lettering with painted, smiling faces at contrast with the deathly atmosphere of the town. They walked carefully amongst the debris, as if picking their way through the aftermath of an explosion. Jonas tried to imagine what it was like in Fallujah where his cousin has been stationed during the last conflict. So many civilians had died in the last round of fighting, so many homes destroyed, that there were rumours the US were pulling out, abandoning the town to its own fate. He couldn't imagine having to try and find loved ones amongst so much rubble and death. Jonas passed a burnt corpse, and there was almost nothing left of the person. All that was left behind was a faint imprint of their soul, a charred shadow etched onto the tarmac.

The façade of the local cinema where years ago he had snuck in with Janey, and an underage Erik, to watch Army of Darkness had crumbled, exposing the seats inside. A truck had obviously smashed into the front of the building, weakening the already old structure. The huge empty screen was just visible through the bricks, towering over rows of dusty, vacant seats. The red velvet seats, lightly coated by dust, were now a shade of pink, and a huge vending machine had spilled its contents all over the pavement. Unfortunately, all that was left were empty cans and sweet wrappers.

Jonas was struck by a memory of Dakota laughing uncontrollably in similar seats at some dumb romantic comedy. The film's name escaped him, but his wife's face was perfectly clear, a perfect image frozen in his mind. He could sit through a thousand dumb films if it meant Dakota was happy, and he would give anything to see her smile again. Looking at her now, her eyes were full of sadness. The world was a shitty place, and he was at a loss how to turn things around. All he could do was lead them forward as best he could, find somewhere safe, and wait for things to calm down. People like Cliff came along once in a while, and he was going to have to be more careful from here on in. Cliff had been a bully, throwing his weight around, and demanding more concessions from the group; more food, more water, and continually raising expectations that could never be met. When they'd run out of food, and Cliff had told them of the garage, it seemed like a good idea. Jonas was glad Cliff was gone. The group would be better off without him.

Up ahead, Erik gripped his daughter's hand tighter. Jonas had never heard the girl speak in all the time they had been forced to live together. Back at his father's funeral, she had screamed as they'd driven away from the church. She had screamed for the whole time she was in the car. There were so many explosions and crashing cars around them, so many people running, shouting, and crying, and so much blood spitting across the windscreen, that it was amazing she hadn't gone completely insane. When Jonas thought back to that first day, it all became a blur. It happened so fast. Mostly, he just remembered Freya screaming.

She shouldn't have to be seeing this, she was too young. What kind of world did they live in now? How many had died? How many had lived? At the start, a lot of people had stopped by Erik's house, whether looking for someone, or just looking for help to get out of town. The undead had passed by too, unaware that Jonas and others were hiding inside. It was Erik's place, and Jonas was all too aware back then who had been in charge, but over time, Erik had backed away from leading the group, wanting to put more time into looking after his family. At first, it was just Jonas and Dakota, sharing the house with Erik, Pippa, Peter and Freya, and of course, Mrs Danick. Jonas couldn't help but smile when he thought of the old woman. She had proven to be tougher than any of them and practical too. The only downside was her requirement for medication. It had run out a week back, and since then, she had become more withdrawn. She never let anyone help her, and even now stubbornly refused any assistance. She walked tall, always with a shawl around her shoulders despite the heat, and expected to do her part in protecting the group. It didn't matter what he or Erik said, she steadfastly refused to accept her age, and told them she would pull her weight come what may.

Randall, Quinn, Anna, Mary, and James, had joined them over time. Finally, Cliff had arrived. There had been others knock on the door, but they had been moved on. Jonas and Erik had agreed to refuse entry to anyone who refused to give up their guns. Society had broken down quickly, and Erik knew many of the scum in the neighbourhood from his patrols. Usually, a warning shot was enough to scare them off, and they had luckily escaped intrusion. One man had threatened to kick the door down, demanding to be let in, but when confronted with Erik's police issued Glock 22, and Jonas with an axe, he had soon backed down and run off. Jonas couldn't remember where he had picked up the axe. Somewhere between the church and getting into Erik's place, he must have picked it up. They had been forced to abandon the car a couple of blocks from the house, and it had been a nightmare just getting those few blocks. By that time, the dead were everywhere, and people were openly brawling on the streets. Jonas shuddered when he recalled that day. As if burying his father wasn't bad enough, he had discovered the world was coming to an end too, and he'd witnessed things he thought were only true in Hollywood movies.

The end of summer couldn't come quick enough. The days were hot and long, and seemed to drag into one another like one hot, horrible, tedious day. He longed for fall genuinely to kick in. The Dog Days of summer had gone, taking the thunderstorms with them, but he would give anything to feel that west coast wind again. The storms had flattened out, stirring up nothing but nervousness, but the temperature stubbornly refused to drop. Jonas was always on edge that another big storm might hit, and they would have no notice. Early on, they had all been worried a tornado could hit them without warning without a working television or radio. Erik's house had no storm shelter, and if one did strike, it would've flattened them in seconds. Thankfully, they had gone through tornado season and not seen a single one. No doubt, there had been some, but whenever a storm had blown up, they just sheltered together in the basement and prayed. Dakota had far more faith than Jonas, and usually took them all through the Lord's Prayer. Remembering those dark days in the basement, all holding hands while the winds whipped around outside and hail pelted the roof, he was thankful for his wife. She was a calming influence on everyone, and he knew Erik was especially pleased. Freya was barely ten, and having someone to help Pippa look after her was invaluable. When the winds had died down, and the storm had passed, he would kiss his wife and promise her they would make it through this. Quite what 'this' was, he wasn't sure anymore. Zombies were something out of comic books and films, not real life. They were apparently here to stay though, and he would make sure Dakota was safe from harm, no matter what. She was all that he had right now. He still planned to get to Janey, to make sure she was safe, but Canada might as well be a million miles away. He had to trust that she would look after herself and the kids. He felt responsible for her, not just out of a natural sibling's love, but he felt a duty to protect her. He had failed so miserably at it after their mother had passed, and now he wanted to make up for it. Once they had found somewhere safe to rest, and eat, he would venture the plan again to Dakota. Not knowing where Janey was, or if she was still okay, was gnawing away at him like a leech, and slowly sucking the life out of him. He hadn't spoken to Janey for some time, and the last time they had spoken, she promised him she would stay home and wait for him, where the kids felt safe. He couldn't be sure she would stay indefinitely though. How long would she be able to wait?

Jonas knew fall would make things colder, but at least it would take the edge off. Everyone was irritable, and he wasn't sure how much longer the group would stay together. He and Dakota did not intend to leave Erik and his family, and he still hoped he could convince Erik to join him and Dakota in heading to Canada, to Janey's. But the others had occasionally mentioned finding somewhere else to go, somewhere by the coast, and it was tempting. With no firm plans in mind, or anywhere specific to go, they had kept the coast as just an option, rather than a real choice. Randall and Quinn wanted to try for the eastern seaboard, head to South Carolina, to try to find somewhere quiet. Terry had convinced them at one point that Pensacola was the answer, and they had contemplated heading south, but eventually the idea had floated away like dust. So many ideas did that. With nothing concrete to hold onto, with no real idea of how they would get anywhere, they had stayed put, and their hope had died. It was clear that rescue was not coming, and they had no idea what was going on in the world. The dead had risen up so fast that it had taken everyone by surprise. Jonas remembered the last time he spoke to Janey, of the worry in her voice when she told him about the dead marching through the streets of Montreal. He'd made her promise not to go outside, to stay in with the kids, until he could reach her. That had been months ago, and now the world had been turned upside down.

The power had failed so quickly there had been little chance of finding anything more out. Television studios were abandoned, and satellites tracked off course so the internet rapidly disintegrated as well. For all they knew, the zombies had only emerged in the US and Canada. Perhaps the rest of the world was still fine; perhaps people were still going to work, still making love and watching sitcoms and drinking beer and playing games, and they had watched on, wringing their hands as the US had fallen. The thought they had been abandoned made him shiver. Then again, the whole world could be covered in walking corpses.

Every day was like a dream, a kind of survival groundhog day, just avoiding zombies and finding something to eat. Conversations in Erik's house had grown stale like the air, and every day Jonas went to sleep wondering if he would wake up. Sometimes the thought of zombies attacking in the night, killing them all swiftly as they slept, held a certain appeal. This was no kind of life, and not going insane was an achievement in itself. Jonas couldn't imagine ever seeing the sea again. He was thankful they hadn't been in central Louisville when the dead had risen. So many people had died that day that there were surely no survivors from the city now.

Louisville's infrastructure had disintegrated as quickly as everywhere else, hanging on a little longer than St. Louis, yet imploding far faster than Cincinnati or Nashville. Local industry had been ticking along nicely, keeping thousands employed right up until that fateful day when everything had imploded. Once the zombie outbreak began the city crumbled, taking the suburbs with it before the National Guard even had a solitary finger on the trigger. The mayor had put a bullet in his brain, the emergency services had been overrun, and within twenty four hours, everything they had built up over the last two hundred years was gone.

Looking around Jeffersontown, Jonas was pleased he had been somewhere he knew. LA had never really been home, just a stop on the way to somewhere unknown. He, Janey, and Erik had grown up in Jeffersontown, and whilst he had moved away and things had changed, many of the streets were still familiar to him. Jeffersontown was unexceptional really, just another satellite town feeding a big city. It was certainly no Babylon, and didn't deserve what had happened to it. Jonas had moved out as soon as he could, hopeful of finding success in LA. His parents had put a lot of pressure on him to be a success, and at best, he had been nothing more than mediocre at school. There had been little interest in sports, and all the other subjects had passed him by without grabbing any real attention. They had been happy, a real family, and it was only when his mother was knocked down by cancer that things turned sour. Once she was diagnosed, she'd made it another three months, and then she was gone. In a flash, their father turned from a happy family man into a drunk, quick with his temper, and quicker still with his fists. Janey had suffered worst, and Jonas had tried to stand up for her, but it was useless. He had been too young, and his father too strong. He was clever too, only taking it out on them where the bruises wouldn't show.

Once Jonas had graduated, he moved to LA, hoping to find work, and maybe fame and fortune, and leave small-town suburbia behind. He and Erik had drifted apart, despite a promise not to let the distance divide them. Growing up they had been as close as brothers, and with Janey in tow, they had been close. His sister was only a year younger than he was, and he always wondered if she and Erik might have progressed beyond friends once they were older, but his father put a stop to that. Erik had been focused for some time on joining the force, but all Jonas ever dreamt of was leaving. When the time came, he hadn't looked back. He had abandoned Janey to her fate, and it was to her credit that she still talked to him. She said she didn't blame him for what happened, but he blamed himself. He had almost not turned up to the funeral either, but someone had to sort out the estate, and Janey wasn't about to waste her time on her father anymore.

When he'd reached LA, Jonas started working in a bar in the daytime, and working out in the evenings. A succession of women had passed through his room over the couple of years he'd lived there, but fame and fortune never found its way to his door. He'd become a drifter, not knowing what to do with his life, nor really caring. He had coasted for a few years until he'd met Dakota, and then things had changed. Everything he had been running away from suddenly became exactly what he craved, and she was his world. Looking at her now, he saw the dirt streaked down her cheeks, her once beautiful hair tangled and greasy, and her shoulders slumped as she walked wearily beside him without talking. There once was a time when she would just talk and talk and talk, until he had to kiss her to get her to stop. She was half the person she used to be, and he hated that he couldn't fix things. All he was to her now was a shoulder to cry on at night. Sex was virtually impossible when you were living with a dozen people in a house built for four. It wasn't that they were falling out of love, just that they were less of a couple, unable to share any intimacy or privacy. One day, this will all be over, Jonas thought. One day, things will go back to normal. He kept repeating it over and over in his mind, but he couldn't force himself to believe it. Things would never go back to the way they were.

Following a curve in the road, Jonas saw Erik and Pippa had stopped opposite a large sign advertising plots for sale amidst a new redevelopment of luxurious townhouses.

"Out of your price range," said Jonas as he approached Erik.

"Just wondering if we could try one of them to rest up a bit," replied Erik.

Mrs Danick loosened the shawl around her shoulders. "Sure is hot out here today. Even my blisters have blisters," she said hopping from foot to foot as she rubbed her ankles.

Jonas looked at Dakota. "What do you think?"

Dakota shrugged. When she was noncommittal, it didn't mean she didn't care; just that she hadn't made her mind up yet. She liked to think things through before making a decision.

"Um, guys, I think we need to check it out," said Tyler. "I thought I'd heard something, but I didn't think anything of it as it sounded so far away. Look down the hill."

Jonas stared back at where they had come from. Like a steadily boiling pot, the noise had only been increasing incrementally as they'd left town, and he hadn't noticed anything. Now he was looking though, he could see what Tyler meant. A tsunami of zombies was advancing upon them, and the rushing sound of dead groans filled the air. Wave after wave, they kept coming, crushing the slowest walkers, and filling the streets entirely. There were no gaps in their ranks, and the miserable sight filled Jonas with despair. He thought they had left them behind, leaving the garage successfully without attracting any attention. It appeared all they had done was draw more, and now there was an army of the dead, only minutes behind them.

"Right, let's get somewhere to hide, and fast. If we're sharp, we can be out of sight, and they'll pass us by."

The housing complex up ahead was little more than a building site full of half-completed roads, and abandoned trucks. The complex hadn't been finished, and many of the houses were just shells, but he took it as a good sign. If it hadn't opened yet, then nobody lived there, and if nobody lived there, then it was likely to be empty: no people meant no zombies.

Jonas jogged into the development. With the rest of the group following him, he knew he had to find somewhere fast. The first row of houses looked to be the most complete. Various tools, pieces of wood and pots of paint decorated the dirt yards, but the homes had four straight walls and solid roofs. He tried the door handle of the first house, and it opened immediately. Whilst it was dark inside, it was obviously empty, and that was good enough for him. "Hurry up," he said as he ushered everyone in. "Get in, get in."

Jonas closed the door and told everyone to go upstairs. As he followed them, he brushed his hands along the walls. They hadn't been finished, and were rough to the touch. The floors were bare, uncarpeted, and he winced with each step. As he climbed the stairs, every step creaked, and he prayed they were far enough away not to be heard. Enough light came through the windows for them to see by, and he anxiously followed Erik into a large room. The group had taken residence on what appeared to be a large bedroom, and they were sitting on unvarnished floorboards. The hollow houses had no furniture or dressings, and judging by the amount of paint slopped across the walls, they had been abandoned in a hurry.

"Get down," said Erik as Jonas approached him.

Sinking to his knees, he realised everyone was crouching or sitting, keeping well away from the solitary window in the west facing wall. He rubbed Dakota's back as he crawled over to Erik beneath the window.

"You think they saw us?" Jonas asked Erik in a whisper.

Erik turned up his nose. "I hope not. We don't have the firepower, or energy, to fight that lot off."

"Shush." Quinn poked her head up to get a look outside. "We need to know for certain."

Jonas watched as Quinn tentatively hauled herself up to the windowsill, and peered outside. She kept her movements to a minimum, and he felt sure the zombies wouldn't see her. But what if they had seen them go into the house? Erik was right. Between the Glock 22 and the pistol in Mrs Danick's handbag, they had enough bullets to take down no more than a dozen zombies. After that, they would be reduced to axes, knives, and bare fists. He looked at Quinn, wishing she would hurry up and tell them what was happening. It seemed to take an eternity for her to assess the situation, and his heart was pounding. What if he'd led them into a dead-end, nothing but a prison where the dead would pick them off one by one?

Quinn lowered her head slowly, and then crouched back down. "I think we're in the clear," she whispered. "It looks like they're heading up the hill, past the turn off to this place. If we keep quiet, we may just catch a break."

Even though nobody spoke, it seemed like the room fell even quieter. Jonas could practically hear everyone draw in a breath, and a silence fell over them like a warm blanket. Seconds turned into minutes, as they kept quiet. The drone of the dead continued unabated outside as the horde passed. They were so close, and yet so far. One sneeze, one cough and it would all be over. Jonas nervously fingered the bloody axe, wrapping his fingers tightly around the shaft in case he had to use it. He had visions of the dead suddenly running up the stairs and crashing into the room where they all hid. He could see it now, hundreds and hundreds of them pouring in, overwhelming him, biting Dakota, biting Erik and Quinn and Pippa, and eating them all alive. The moaning chorus grew louder as the thick crowd of zombies reached the top of the hill. Where the dead turned next was crucial. If they stopped, or turned around, they were in serious trouble. He needed the zombies to continue, to carry on over the hill in their quest for meat. If they became lost, or attracted by anything, the group could be stuck in the house for days. Randall carried a knapsack full of food, and Peter had a bag of bottled water, but it would not last long. It was only intended to keep them going for around twenty four hours. Jonas assumed when they'd left Erik's place that they would find somewhere else. He had assumed the garage was safe, but trusting Cliff had turned out to be a bad mistake.

The groaning that came in through the window, and bounced around the room like the whispers of ghosts, eventually faded. Minutes trickled by slowly, but Jonas knew they were leaving. Whatever impulse was keeping them on their feet was carrying them further away. Once the noise had faded to almost nothing, he asked Quinn to take another look. When she came back down from the window, she was smiling.

"They're gone. I can't see any. They must've carried on over the hill," she said in a low voice. Even though the dead had apparently gone, they spoke quietly, fearful of bringing them back.

"Okay," said Jonas, "let's go downstairs quietly. We'll double back to the city, find another road out of town, and maybe head up north. Just watch out for stragglers. Yell if you need help."

Jonas took point, and once downstairs, he asked Erik to keep hold of the Glock. "You're a better shot than me. We can't afford to waste any ammo. I've got my axe, and that's all I need."

Erik stuffed it carefully into his belt. "You know, we could check this housing development out. What if the contractors had a show home ready, and they fixed up the kitchen? Would be an awful shame if we missed out. There could be a heap of stuff we could take with us."

"Do we really have time?" asked Quinn. "I mean, if we're not intending to stay here the night, I think we're better off moving on."

"Agreed. It doesn't feel right up here. It's too quiet," said Jonas. "Let's round everyone up and get out of here. Even if they had any food stored, it would likely be off by now. It's not worth us rooting around for something that may not exist."

"Hey, guys, there's someone in here." Randall was standing by a small shack looking excitedly at a green door. It looked like an office, with one square window, and a pile of tools stacked up outside. Set back from the road, the shack probably served as the foreman's office, and Randall was pulling at the handle. "I can hear them. We have to help."

"Shit," said Jonas. Randall was old, but he was tough as boots, and he would have the door down in seconds.

Erik and Quinn ran toward Randall, but Jonas was puzzled. Whoever was in there must've heard them talking, and yet, hadn't called for help. There couldn't be much room inside, especially if there was still a desk, chairs, filing cabinet, and the usual associated clutter. Why stay hidden? As Randall continued pulling on the door handle, the group clustered around him. Jonas watched as Randall picked up a shovel and prised at the door's hinges. Then it struck him. If whoever was in there needed help, why was the door locked?

"Randall, stop," shouted Jonas, but it was too late.

As Randall managed to prise the door open an inch, a hand appeared through the slight crack, and then it burst open. Three zombies spilled out, one after the other, falling into a messy heap on top of Randall. The dead men were all dressed in work boots, jeans, and open-necked checked shirts. One still wore a yellow hard-hat, and clearly, the men had barricaded themselves inside. Unfortunately, one of them must've been infected, perhaps bitten, and it wasn't hard to work out what had happened to them. Jonas could hear grunting noises coming from the dead, and he hoped their teeth were well away from his friend.

Jonas watched as the group splintered, some running away from the zombies, some running to help Randall. He saw Erik drag Pippa away as Peter took Freya to safety. Quinn and Dakota practically threw themselves at Randall to help, and Terry jumped in as well, the knife in his hand plunging into a zombie's back. Outside the workman's shack, the pile of bodies grew, arms and legs tangling together as the dead and the living merged into a giant game of Twister.

"Hold still!" yelled Mrs Danick, as she trained her gun on the writhing pile of bodies. Her eyes narrowed as she concentrated her vision on the dead.

Jonas sprinted toward the chaos, determined that nobody else was going to die today. He could tell from the screaming and shouting that he was probably too late. A shot rang out, and one of the zombies fell away, its head exploding in a mist of red. Quinn and Erik pulled themselves up, dragging away one of the other zombies, and they grappled it to the ground. Quinn held it down as Erik lay into it. Using the butt of his Glock 22, he beat its head to a pulp, not stopping until all that was left was a pile of mush, its brains splattered across the ground. Jonas yanked Randall away, as Terry mounted the third zombie. He straddled it, and held it down with the shovel.

"Shoot it!"

Mrs Danick didn't hesitate and sent a bullet through an eye socket. The zombie stilled, and Terry slipped off it, exhausted.

"Jesus Christ," said Erik. "What the fuck was that, Randall? What were you thinking?"

"I...I thought they needed help. I..."

Jonas could feel the man trembling in his arms, and they slowly sunk to the ground. Randall suddenly arched his back, and let out a cry of pain.

"Randall, what is it?" Jonas lowered the old man to the ground, looking him up and down. Randall abruptly slipped into unconsciousness as the group gathered around him in a circle. Jonas examined the man's neck first, but there was no sign of any injuries. He patted him down, but he seemed fine.

"Jonas, you might want to step back," said Erik quietly.

"God damn it," said Jonas as he stood up. He stood by his wife and took Dakota's hand. Looking down he could see Randall's left hand had been almost chewed off. One of the zombies must've gotten a good bite as soon as they'd attacked. Randall was missing three fingers, and blood oozed out slowly from the stump. Jonas felt angry that he hadn't acted more quickly.

Terry knelt down and shook Randall's body. "Randall, wake up, man. Randall?"

"I think he's in shock," said Quinn.

"What can we do for him?" asked Terry. "Do we have a first aid kit with us?"

Peter had been rummaging around in his rucksack, but he was shaking his head. "We've got nothing. Just a couple of paracetamol, but..."

"Mrs Danick, give me your shawl." Terry held out his hands to her. "Well come on. We need to bandage this wound and stop the bleeding."

Mrs Danick drew her shawl tighter around her shoulders and stepped back. "I'm sorry, Terry, but you know we can't do anything for him. Not now."

Terry's eyes scanned the group. "Will someone help me? This is Randall, not a stranger. Erik, Pippa - he looked after Freya for you. You can't just leave him."

"Sorry, Terry, but Mrs Danick is right," said Jonas. He crouched down and noticed Randall's chest was moving up and down, but slower than before. It wouldn't be long now. "I'm sorry, Terry, but we need to go." Jonas slid an arm around Terry's shoulders. "Randall's not coming back from this. Even if he comes round, how long has he got?"

"You don't know," said Terry. "We haven't had to deal with this before. None of us have been bitten."

"Terry," said Jonas firmly, "those things are only just over the hill, and undoubtedly heard the gunshots, if nothing else. You know as well as I do that Randall won't recover from this. He *can't*. We've seen it before. You're bitten, you die. We saw it countless times at the start. It's no good pretending this isn't happening. I don't like this any more than you, but…"

Terry shrugged off Jonas and stood up. "So you're just going to leave him? Leave him out in the street to die like a dog? You're going to leave him to come back as one of those zombies, one of those disgusting things?"

"No, we're not." Erik stepped forward and cocked his gun. "He won't feel a thing. It'll be quick, I promise you."

Terry muttered something under his breath and marched toward the main road.

"You'd better go," said Jonas to the others. "Quinn, make sure Terry doesn't do anything stupid?"

Dakota nodded to Jonas, and then followed the group back to the road, leaving Jonas and Erik alone with Randall.

"It's not fair. What did Randall ever do to deserve this? He was only trying to help." Erik looked forlorn. "Randall helped me and Pippa a lot. Freya was a handful. Well, you remember what she was like at the start."

"I know, but Terry's right, we have to end it for him," said Jonas.

Jonas looked into Erik's eyes and wondered if his friend was feeling the same. Shooting one of the dead was easy. Shooting a friend was altogether different. Even though Randall had a death warrant, it still felt like murder. It still felt wrong.

"Do it quick," said Jonas, "and then we get the hell out of here. That pack will be back any minute."

As Jonas walked toward the group, he tried to find Dakota's eyes. Brimming with tears, she was staring into the distance, back at Jeffersontown. A single gunshot rang out, and Jonas didn't look back. He knew Erik would do what had to be done. When the time came, he could be counted on to step up. Jonas wondered what he would do if it had been Dakota. Shuddering, he pushed the thought from his mind. The day was far from over, and they had lost nearly half a dozen of their group already. The alliance they had formed was teetering on extinction, and if they didn't find somewhere safe soon, it was liable to get much worse.

Passing the group, he could feel Terry's eyes burning into his back. Jeffersontown lay before him, and a horde of dead were at their back. Where could they go? Realising the only sound he could hear was his own footsteps, he turned around. Everyone was looking at him, their faces a mixture of sadness, fear, and anger.

"Well, what are you waiting for?" he asked.

"Shouldn't we say something?" Quinn was standing by Terry who was ashen and shaking. He kept wiping his face, as if trying to hide his tears. "A prayer, or…"

"There's no time for that now," said Erik as he took Pippa's hand. "They're coming. I can smell them."

Jonas opened his mouth to speak, and then suddenly the first of the dead were in sight: runners. Six or seven of them came over the top of the hill. Arms swinging loosely, their loping zigzag run suggested a lack of cohesion, a lack of understanding of how the human body worked, but the dead were mobile and focussed, and the group of living were within sight now.

"Run!" Jonas shouted, and the group forgot clean about Randall and prayers. They ran back toward Jeffersontown, running for their lives.

CHAPTER FOUR

Javier left the house, trotted down the steps into the yard, and started the bike. Rose looked at him expectantly.

"Nothing," he said. "Just a dead dude and some empty cupboards. Someone's already ransacked the place."

When they'd seen the house from the main road, Javier had hoped they would find something of use, anything, and more than anything, he'd wanted to find the farmer's shotgun. Rose had taken out a couple of runners who had veered into the road, and they were down to their last clip. The bike was running low on gas too, and if they didn't find somewhere to fill up soon, they were going to be on foot. That was a prospect he didn't relish, especially with such a lack of firepower. Rose embraced him as they took off, leaving the deserted farmhouse behind them.

After leaving Jeffersontown, they had ridden around, not really knowing where to head. Using the sun as a compass, they tried to go north, only to find the roads blocked. Even on the Yamaha, trying to navigate a path through a mountain of burnt out cars was impossible. All the lanes across the highway, including the emergency shoulder were blocked, and they were forced to turn back on several occasions. Eventually, he headed to what he thought was east, and found the farmhouse. It was useless, offering nothing at all. Now that it was after noon, he was getting thirsty. He constantly had to wipe his visor. With so many dead around, the flies were not just annoying, but a menace. Swarms of them flew through the cities and towns, and Jeffersontown was no exception. Javier's gloves were covered in the remnants of dead, black flies, and his visor was smeared with their blood. Turning onto another road, he was feeling uneasy about the day ahead. Rose had been complaining about a headache since leaving Jeffersontown, and she was trigger-happy, too quick to shoot whenever they saw a zombie in the road. At least it appeared they'd now found a way out of the city, and the roads were slightly clearer the further out they got.

As they drove, he saw Rose raise the pistol out of the corner of his eye, and he brushed her arm down. "No need," he shouted back to her, "it's too far away. Save it."

The regular zombies couldn't keep up with the bike, but the runners were lethal. They were the only ones Rose was allowed to pick off, the ones who suddenly appeared in front of them. A collision with one of them could bring the bike down, and they so often appeared at the last second that driving around them was tricky. Back outside of Baton Rouge, they had almost come unstuck when a runner had appeared in front of them, and Javier had swerved around it, only to drive straight into another. Luckily, the zombie was old and fragile, and it had exploded into a storm of blood and guts on impact. Javier had lost sight of the road as his visor was smeared in gunk, and only narrowly avoided driving them straight into a ditch. After that, they had agreed to shoot the runners, rather than take any chances. Rose seemed to take it as a green light to shoot anything that moved though, and Javier's patience was wearing thin.

The road they travelled now was refreshingly clear of traffic, and he spotted only a few zombies away to the side, in the fields and side-roads. He knew he was going to have to siphon some gas out of one of the abandoned cars soon. It was a nasty job, and he hated doing it. The taste was foul, but he was more concerned about the dead. Rose did her best to cover him, but he would rather not put all his trust in her. She was too easily distracted, and whilst lining up a kill, another zombie could be headed right for them. Other than complaining of a headache, Rose had been quiet ever since they'd left Jeffersontown. She'd been quiet since they'd left Noah. He wondered if she felt sorry for the boy. If so, she could soon drop that attitude. The kid was done for, a lost cause, and no way was Javier going to let them be dragged down by helping the boy.

As they wound their way up a hill covered in shadows, Javier slowed down. He didn't want to run into any surprises at seventy miles an hour, particularly ones with teeth. At the crest of the hill though, the afternoon sun suddenly came back into view, temporarily blinding him. Using one hand as a shield, he looked at the road ahead. It was packed full of zombies. At least thirty were gathered in the road, and still more off to the side. He slammed on the brakes, and as one, the zombies looked at him. He swore he could feel their dead eyes on him, telling him exactly how they were planning on eating him. The bike ground to an abrupt halt, and instantly, the zombies were running toward them. There was no time to turn around, and if they ran for it, eventually, the zombies would catch them. They were running on fumes, and he wasn't sure how much juice the bike had left in her. The farmhouse was too far back, and they had barely a handful of bullets left.

"Shit," said Javier as he dismounted. "Fucking runners." He grabbed Rose's hand. "Go for that diner. Quick."

He could see the fear in Rose's face, and he sprinted ahead of her to the only place that might be able to offer them somewhere to hide. The diner seemed to be in good condition. The windows were not broken, and there were still some cars in the parking bays outside. If they were lucky, they could hide inside until the zombies found someone else to chase, and then try one of the cars. The bike was nearly done for anyway, so a fresh pair of wheels wouldn't go amiss. The diner was some sort of cheap fried chicken place, the sort of establishment that never tried to be anything more than it was. A large sign out front read 'Captain's Bucket only 9.99!' and the door was plastered in stickers announcing 'hot wings from 99c,' and 'AC seating for paying customers only.'

"Rose, hurry up," demanded Javier.

As they reached the diner, he didn't need to turn around to see what was behind. In the reflection of the large glass frontage he could see a crowd of dead running for them, their dead arms waving, and rotted teeth gnashing. He pulled on the door, but it was locked.

"Of course it is," said Javier, ruing his luck he had run into the only place left in Kentucky that still had a locked door.

Rose screamed as a runner reached her. Javier watched as it grabbed her hair, and she fell to the ground with the zombie on top of her. Realising she still had the gun, he hesitated. If he went back to help her, they were both liable to be swarmed by them, buried beneath a pile of moving corpses, and he had no intention of dying today. He wasn't quite ready to abandon her yet though, and looked around for a weapon. Before he found anything he heard the gunshots, and whirled around to see Rose pushing the dead body off her. She ran toward him, her face covered in gore.

"Round the side - the door's locked," he shouted, pushing her ahead of him. Rose thrust the gun at Javier, and he took it, tucking it into his pants. He prayed there was a side door, or a back entrance, otherwise, they were history. The zombies chasing them sounded like a pack of hungry dogs.

The roadside diner was a small building, and it didn't take long to realise there was no way in. Both side doors were locked, and the rear entrance was boarded up. For once, Javier began to doubt they were going to find a way out of the mess they'd gotten themselves into. The diner was being surrounded by the dead, circling it, and in turn, circling Javier and Rose. Punching a whole through the zombies seemed like a long shot. He might be able to take a few down, but there was no way they could both get through. As much as Rose was only an accessory to his life, like the bike, Javier wasn't quite prepared to abandon her just yet. He needed time to think.

"Help me," he said to Rose. Grabbing the side of a dumpster, they began pushing it toward the wall of the diner. It stank of rotting meat, and the metal sides were filthy, covered in flies that swarmed over something sticky. They quickly pushed it into place, and Javier gave Rose a boost up onto its lid. They made it up on top of the dumpster just in time, and the nearest runners ran straight into it, moaning in frustration as Javier and Rose kept their feet and legs out of reach. More zombies clattered into the dumpster, rocking it as they slammed into it. Looking around the parking lot Javier could see vehicles, but getting to them was a suicide mission. There was no way of knowing if any of them would even work, or had the keys still in them. There was no time to hot-wire them, so they were going to have to find a way into the diner. He looked up at the roof, about five or six feet above him. There was a gutter around the edge, and if he could get them up, there might be another way in, perhaps through a skylight or ventilation shaft.

Javier jumped, his fingers fleetingly touched the guttering, but failed to get any purchase, and he fell back onto the dumpster. He barely managed to stay upright, and Rose pulled him back before he fell into the mosh pit of zombies waiting below.

"Give me a bunk up," said Rose. She handed Javier the gun, and put her hands flat on the diner's wall. "Look, I can't help you, but I'm lighter than you, so give me a lift up. I pull you up when I'm up there."

Javier was reluctant to let Rose go ahead of him, but he knew he had little choice. He clasped his hands together. Rose put one foot into his hands, and Javier turned up his nose as his hands were coated in blood from her grimy sneakers.

"Go," he said, as he took her weight in his hands.

Rose jumped up and easily grabbed hold of the guttering. Within seconds she was up, and climbing onto the roof. She looked back down at Javier.

"Fuck, you should see it from up here. They're everywhere."

Javier could see her looking around the diner, but he wasn't interested in the view. The zombies were clawing over each other, and getting closer to reaching the top of the dumpster. He needed her to hurry. He reached an arm up, and looked into Rose's eyes. "Get ready to grab me."

Suddenly, Rose disappeared from sight, silently sinking back onto the roof without saying a word.

"Rose? Rose, what are you doing?"

Javier felt a hand around his ankle, and he looked down to see one of the dead had managed to clamber over the others to get within inches of him. Whipping his gun out, he put a bullet in its brain, and then shoved it back off the dumpster into the melee beneath him.

"Rose! What the fuck are you…"

Suddenly, she appeared back above him, smiling. "Look what I found. This'll make life easier."

Rose slowly lowered a plastic summer chair down to him, its green canvas back held together with thin metal legs. Javier took it, and planted it firmly on the lid of the dumpster. He used it as a springboard to get onto the roof, and the extra few feet enabled him to get a good grip on the guttering. Rose helped to pull him up, and then he was safely out of arms reach of the dead.

"Next time you feel like doing your own thing, maybe let me know, yeah?" Javier wouldn't admit it, but he had been scared back there, wondering if Rose was going to abandon him.

Javier watched as the zombies who had been piled up against the dumpster got on top of it, only seconds after he had escaped it. Clumsily, they staggered about, and the chair was trampled on before it was knocked off to the ground. There was no way the dead were getting any further.

"Shit, that was too close," said Javier. He stood and looked around. Rose was right. They were everywhere. The diner was totally surrounded, and they were effectively trapped.

"I found the chair over there," said Rose proudly. "Looks like someone used it as a breakout area."

The roof was almost flat, sloping slightly down from a central point. In the middle of the diner lay another chair and more importantly, a skylight. Javier smiled.

"Perfect."

Javier examined the skylight, and knew they had gotten lucky. It was still unlocked, and he pulled it open to reveal a step ladder beneath.

"Ladies first," said Rose as she kneeled down besides the opening.

Javier put an arm across her, barring her way. "Not this time. We don't know what's down there. I'll go. You come down when I give the all clear."

Javier was soon down the step ladder, and found himself in what was apparently an office. At one point, the manager had probably used the room to run the place, but it had long since lost its primary purpose. Javier noticed that someone had been staying in the office, using it as a bedroom. Crumpled, dirty sheets lay in two corners of the room, spread out like beds, and in another, the desk had been turned over onto its side, as if to give the occupants privacy. The room smelt funky, like a fifteen year old boy's bedroom, and the room's solitary window clearly hadn't been opened for months. Javier listened, but couldn't hear any noise from inside the diner, only the clumping, thumping noises from outside as the zombies tried to get in. Perhaps their luck was holding. If the diner was empty they could search around, maybe even find some food. Javier looked up at the skylight beckoning Rose to join him.

Once she was inside, Javier opened the office door to find a narrow hallway. The grey walls were adorned with menus, and certificates of hygiene that had faded over time so as to barely be legible. The corridor had two more doors. One led into the diner, the other apparently to the bathrooms judging by the outlined pictures of a man and woman on the exterior. Their way was dimly lit by a small, square glass window in the door to the diner. Javier nodded in the direction of the window, and Rose followed him. They went quietly, keeping their footsteps light, just in case the dead were inside. Javier drew his gun, and indicated to Rose he was going in, but she should wait again until he had given the all clear.

Pushing back the door slowly, Javier waited for the inevitable creak as reluctant hinges sprung to life. Instead, the door opened quietly, without the slightest squeak, and he took a step into the room. The diner was deserted. He saw rows of chairs and tables, food wrappers and napkins scattered about the floor, and a faint smell of burnt chicken. The diner's frontage was still intact, and the dead were pressed up against it, unable to get in. Javier smiled. They were safe.

"Okay, let's…"

The back of a frying pan smashed into Javier's face, and he screamed out in pain. As he staggered back from the blow, he saw a man rushing him, swinging the pan back toward Javier's face.

Without thinking, Javier fired the gun, and he succeeded in hitting the pan which flew from the man's hand. It skittered away to the floor, crashing around and around until it came to a stop. The man stood before Javier, his face showing nothing but pure surprise. The man looked at his empty hand, which moments before had held the frying pan. Javier screwed up his face in anger, and fired again. The gun clicked empty.

The stranger seemed to regain his composure, and realised he held a large knife in his other hand. Raising it slowly, he pointed it at Javier.

"You'd b..b..better get out of here, Mister, or so help me I'll..."

"You'll what?" asked Rose as she slid into the room and brought her own knife around the man's throat.

The man dropped his knife as Rose wrapped an arm around his neck. Javier quickly scooped it up.

"Sorry, I didn't hear you," said Rose. She whispered into the man's ear, and his eyes and mouth closed. He was like a statue, too scared to speak or move, his feet anchored in concrete. "You'll what?"

"Please, don't." A woman's voice came from deeper inside the diner. Javier realised the door they had come through had brought them into the main dining area, and he hadn't checked out the serving area, or kitchen.

Rose was pressing her blade hard against the scared man's neck, enough to draw blood, and Javier told her to stop.

"Just wait, Rose," he said firmly. "Wait."

Her eyes told him she didn't want to, but she also knew better than to disobey him, and she relaxed her grip on the man.

Javier took a step toward the serving area. He saw the counter, and its row of empty tills, but no woman. Above the counter was an unlit display of the Captain's meals 'available *all* day, *every* day,' alongside lurid pictures of buckets of fried chicken, and even bigger buckets of coke. Just behind lay the kitchen, but there was no sign of the speaker.

"If you come out now, I'll spare him."

Javier's voice echoed around the diner, but there was no reply. The woman was probably scared too. Still, that wasn't Javier's problem, and he couldn't wait all day. He also couldn't go charging back there, in case the woman was armed.

"I'm not going to ask again. Whoever you are, just come out. If you don't, your friend here is a dead man. I'll give you five seconds. If you're not out by then, I'm going to let my girl slit his throat, and then we'll come back there for you. Do you understa..."

"Yes. Please, stop." A slim woman stood up from behind a counter. She was petrified, and looked to be half the man's age. She wore a pretty blue sleeveless top over skinny jeans. Long, brown hair hung by her shoulders, and Javier had to admit he was attracted to her. Whether it was her appearance, or her easy submission to him, he wasn't so sure. The woman looked like she was about to break down. There was no confidence when she spoke, and she hugged her arms to her chest defensively.

"Come on out, sweetheart," said Javier as he picked the gun up from off the floor. Javier patted Rose's ass, and he felt the final clip he was looking for. This was the last of their ammo, and Javier suspected he was going to need it. As the woman slowly walked out from behind the counter, Javier reloaded the gun. This was it. He was going to have to figure something out, and he didn't want to waste their last precious bullets on these two, if he could help it.

Javier ordered the couple to sit on the floor, their backs to the counter, so that they were all in full view of the zombies outside. He wanted them on their game; he wanted them scared, desperate, and freaked out, to know there was only one person in charge now, and they had to cooperate, or face the consequences. There had been enough surprises, and he was not going to be caught unaware again. If the man had been carrying a gun, Javier knew he'd be dead now. The frying pan had left him with a ringing in his ears, and a dent to his pride, but luckily, nothing fatal.

"So, where shall we begin?" asked Javier. "How about some introductions? I'm Javier, and this is Rose."

Rose deftly bowed, and let a salacious smile escape her lips. She was tossing her knife from side to side, eyeing up the couple, deciding who she was going to kill first.

"Those people outside are no friends of ours. I'm very sorry to tell you this, but, well, they're dead." Javier sniggered. "Sooo…"

He looked expectantly at the couple on the floor, but neither of them said a word.

"Fine. You. What's your name?" Javier asked pointing the gun at the woman.

She looked at Rose, and then to Javier, before answering. "Cindy. Cindy Constance. Look, why don't you...why don't you just fuck off, and leave us alone."

Javier admired Cindy for trying at least, but her words carried no conviction. "Tut-tut. Such foul language from someone so pretty."

Rose crouched down beside the scared young woman. "Let me do her, Javier. I'll kill the bitch first, and then do the fat man. What do you say, fat man, fair deal?"

"Shut up, Rose," said Javier, annoyed that she was trying to butt in. He could sense she was itching to use her blade, but she had to have some patience. Rose shot him a glare, but he ignored her.

"You. Fat man. Your name?"

"I'm D..D..Derek," he stammered.

"Your name's D..D..Derek?" laughed Javier. "Well, D..D..Derek, I think it's about time for you to man up. You must've heard us out there. You must've heard the gunshots at least. You were just hoping we'd pass on by, huh? Just skip the diner, and leave you two alone? Thought you'd get cosy with Cindy I suppose. Can't blame you for that, she's not a bad looking woman."

Rose yawned. "Let's just get this over with and kill them." She drew her blade across Cindy's top, letting it pause over her breasts, but Javier stopped her.

"Not yet," he said.

Rose looked disappointed, but she stopped. Her knife was inches from Cindy's face, and Rose was aching for action.

"We've got a problem here, and these two lovebirds are going to help us out," said Javier reclining against the side of a table. He pointed the gun squarely at Derek who visibly shook. "You, Derek, how long have you been here? There much food left?"

Derek shook his head. "No, sir. We been here 'bout a w..w..week."

"A week?" Javier looked at the mess the place was in. Discarded cartons and tins lay everywhere, covering the floor and any available surface. From the smell of the back room, they had been living in the diner a lot more than a week, and the sheets he had seen had weeks of scum on them, not just a few days. Javier also noticed how Derek was clean-shaven. With so many knives in the kitchen it would be easy to keep a beard from growing. Javier looked at the dark kitchen, and saw how dirty it was. The floor was littered with discarded blue plastic bags, and the stovetops were filthy too, but not from food cooked recently, from weeks ago. Food scraps and baked oil were stuck to the top. Javier crouched down so he was at eye-level with Derek. Without taking his eyes off him, he told Rose to cut Cindy.

"Just a friendly warning, Rose."

Rose grinned. "Stick or twist? Hmmm. I haven't played in *such* a long time. I think...twist." Needing no second invitation, Rose drew the blade sharply across Cindy's cheek, carving a jagged line across the woman's face. The woman gasped, and then began crying. It wasn't a deep cut, but enough to warn Derek they were serious.

"I don't like liars, Derek. How long have you been here?" Thoughts of self-preservation and fear were gone now. Javier was in his element, enjoying the power he held over them. "If you don't tell me the truth this time, I'll have Rose cut off an ear."

Rose put the blade to the woman's face and smiled. "Oh, please. Lie again, Derek."

"Wait, wait! Okay, we've been here a month. Least I think it's a month, it gets hard to t..t..tell anymore. We stumbled upon this place by chance, and it seemed like a..a..good place to stay. Momma's place got burned down, and there was so much food here. You can have some. Take it, go on, we don't mind, do we Cindy? Just don't cut her no more, p..p..please, sir, just leave her be. She ain't done nothin' to nobody."

"Sorry, Rose, he's telling the truth this time." Javier could see Rose was annoyed. Playing games with people was more than a hobby for her; it was like a full-time job. Since the appearance of the zombies, finding idiots to play with had proven hard. Javier stood up. "You got wheels, Derek?"

"No, sir, I promise. I never learnt to drive. Cindy can, but, well, we crashed our car out there. On account of all them z..z..zombies, you see? We ran in here, and over the past few weeks they f..f..forgot about us. I knew they were out there in the woods, but I figured we could wait them out."

"Breaking news, Derek, your friends are back."

Javier tapped the gun against his temple, wondering what they could do. The bike was irretrievable. No way was he going to be able to blast his way through a hundred zombies with one clip. "Derek, you brought anything with you? You got any guns stashed away?"

"No, sir, nothing."

Derek answered quickly; too quickly for Javier's liking. He stared at the man, and noticed he was sweating. Hardly odd considering he had a gun pointed at him, but he looked more than nervous. His eyes were darting back and forth around the room.

"Derek, you know I don't appreciate it when you lie to me. You wouldn't be hiding anything from me, would you?"

"No, sir. There's n..n..nobody else here. Why don't you just take what you want and go? Take what you want, please. It's fine."

Javier looked around the diner. There was nothing particularly unusual, but Derek had definitely given away that he was hiding something. Javier wondered about the bathrooms. "Derek, I think I need to educate you. You see, I don't need you to tell me what to do, what to take, or what not to take. What I *do* need you to do is realise that I have a fully loaded gun pointed at you, and I *will* use it if you don't play ball." Javier looked at Rose. "Again," he stated.

Rose was like a trained soldier, just desperately waiting for the order, and now she had it. She plunged the knife deep into Cindy's shoulder, careful to avoid the heart and ribcage, but enough to make Cindy scream in pain.

"Stick," giggled Rose. "Definitely stick that time." Warm blood trickled down the shaft onto Rose's hand and she smiled. "I love it when they bleed."

"No!"

The diner's door exploded open and a teenage boy ran out, charging straight for Rose. Javier had suspected someone else was hiding, and he sent two shots at the boy. One missed the target and shattered a microwave above Cindy's head. The other didn't, and the boy crumpled into a heap. Now Derek and Cindy were both screaming and shouting, pleading for mercy, but Javier was ignorant to their pleas. He rolled the boy over to discover he had only wounded him. He dragged the helpless boy over to Derek and sat him upright, leaving a trail of blood on the kitchen vinyl. The bullet had entered the boy's gut, and his skin was a sickly pale. He was shaking and struggling to breathe. To his credit, the boy didn't shout, or scream. He simply murmured as Javier dragged him across to Derek.

"Shut the fuck up, all of you," demanded Javier. "Jesus, I can barely hear myself think."

The diner suddenly seemed very cramped. It was more like a prison than a safe house. Javier did not want to spend the next few weeks trapped inside like these three hicks, eating stale junk food, and stinking of shit.

Cindy stifled her cries enough to speak, her hands held up to her cut shoulder. "Please, sir, he's just a boy. James is only fifteen. We picked him up outside Saint Paul's. He..."

"James?" Javier watched the boy struggle to raise his eyes. He wouldn't last long, not with the amount of blood he was losing. "That was very noble of you, but very stupid. Unfortunately, Derek should've been honest with me, and I might have spared you. You can thank Derek for your untimely demise."

The boy drew in a weak breath and spoke. "Please, God..."

"Oh, James, I'm not God. I'm just *your* God," said Javier coldly. He pulled the trigger again, and blew James's head apart. Hair and blood splattered over Javier while Derek and Cindy began screaming again. Javier asked Rose to pass him a cloth, and he wiped James's brains off his hands. If he let the boy bleed out, he would've turned, so he chose to end it quickly. Really, it was the only humane thing to do. Javier regretted wasting the bullet, but under the circumstances, he didn't see as he had any other choice.

"Shut her up, will you?" Javier said to Rose as he threw the bloody dishcloth into a sink full of mouldy pots and pans.

Rose smashed a fist into Cindy's face, knocking her out and sending the room back into silence.

"Oh Jesus, oh Jesus, s..s..save me," muttered Derek. "The Lord is my shepherd, and...and..." James's body was slumped against Derek, and his mangled face was resting on Derek's shoulder. Derek vomited as Javier watched. "Jesus, save me." Derek began crying as vomit and spittle dribbled down his chin.

"Now, where were we? Oh yes, I was about to educate you, Derek, on the benefits on being truthful. The reality of lying to me is currently soaking into that nice plaid shirt you're wearing, although I doubt James appreciates it. I don't appreciate having to waste bullets, so you are doing a grand job of fucking everyone quite frankly. It seems that you are incapable of realising just how much of a world of shit you are in. So, here's what's going to happen. You and me are going to have a little chat. An intervention, if you like. Then I'm going to set you free."

Derek looked up at Javier. "Free?" he snivelled. "You'll let me and Cindy go?"

"That's not exactly what I said. Listen up, Derek. This is the situation. Your hitchhiking buddy, James, is toast. I had to put him out of his misery. He would've bled to death. I took no pleasure in doing so, but it was better to put him down now than let him take hours to go. Plus, he would've come back, and that's no way to be.

"I have plans for Cindy, so to answer your ridiculous question, no, you are not both being *set free*. I'm not running a damn shelter, so wind your head in and listen. I can see that you've made yourself a little home here. You've got four strong walls to keep the dead out, a nice woman, and plenty of food, but your time is up. Understand? It's over. I am leaving, and I'm taking Rose with me. Which means we are going to be opening those doors, and your house is going to come tumbling down like a pack of cards. The difference between you and me, Derek, is that I am telling the truth."

Derek's lips were trembling, and covered in spit. James' warm blood was splashed across his face. "You're s..s..sick. He was only fifteen. What did he do to deserve that?" asked Derek. There was no animosity in his tone, no suggestion he could fight back, just a weary resignation that he was next to bite a bullet.

"He came at me like a bull. What was I supposed to do, stand back and let him hit me?" asked Javier. "Look, Derek, that's not important. The past is the past; all that matters now is what you do next. Your future is in your hands."

Javier pulled Derek up to his feet, making sure Rose kept an eye on the unconscious Cindy. She did so with a questioning look in her eye, but said nothing. She knew better than to question

Javier. Cindy was cut, but not too badly. The wounds were only superficial, and certainly nothing that would cause her any significant problems.

Rose was feeling dissatisfied though, and wanted to get stuck in. It had been too long, and Javier was having all the fun. With any luck, he and Derek would go deal with the zombies leaving them alone. All she wanted was five minutes alone with this bitch, and she would rearrange her face with nothing more than a six inch blade, and a whole heap of enthusiasm.

Javier shoved Derek over to the doorway. Beyond the upturned tables and chairs were the glass doors. Dozens of zombies were now blocking the exit, pounding on the glass, and shuffling around the walls trying to find a way into the diner.

"There's the door, Derek, all you have to do is walk out, and you're a free man." Javier pushed Derek forward.

"Are you insane? I'm not g..g..going out there. They'll rip me to pieces in s..s..seconds." Derek began heading back to the kitchen, but Javier raised the gun and pointed it at him.

"Tut-tut, Derek. You take another step toward me, and you're dead. I'll just make Cindy go out there. This way, you have a chance. There's a truck outside. No more than, what, fifty feet? See that tow-truck with the red lettering on the side? You're going to find out if it has any gas in it. If it does, you have a choice. Get back here, and we can all leave, or take it. Take the truck, and just go. Leave Cindy with us. It's your call, Derek." Javier smiled as he pointed the gun at Derek's head. "Time for you to leave."

CHAPTER FIVE

The run down the hill was far from easy. Weak and disoriented, Jonas felt like breaking down with every foot he planted on the hard ground. Following the centre line, he knew it would be pointless breaking into one of the buildings at the roadside. The dead could see them, and they would only end up trapped. Instead, he followed the road until they reached the bottom, and then took a hard left, running alongside the municipal swimming baths which offered a little protection by way of its high walls. Opposite it was a row of shops, all decorated with a large canopy that ran the length of the street. The shop windows were dressed for summer, with mannequins dressed in a variety of shorts and swimwear. Besides the clothing stores, Jonas noticed a bathroom supply store, a drycleaners, and a coffee shop. It appeared to be quiet, and so he paused by the baths, crouching down by a graffiti covered wall. He asked if Dakota was okay, and waited for the tail end of the group to catch up. He heard a single gunshot, and then Tyler rounded the corner with Mrs Danick just ahead of him.

"We don't have long," said Tyler breathlessly. "I just took out one of the runners. I don't know if it's them or us, but something is drawing more out. You can see them coming out of the buildings and cars."

"Mrs Danick, how're you doing?" asked Jonas. He could see from her face she was having trouble keeping up the pace.

"Fine. I'd rather die of a heart attack than be eaten by one of those fuckers." Mrs Danick rubbed Freya's head, and the little girl snuggled into Pippa's arms saying nothing. "Sorry, Freya, I didn't mean to use a bad word."

Jonas heard Dakota let out a yelp, and her hand gripped his arm. A runner had found them. Emerging from the plumbing shop opposite it came straight across the street toward them. Tyler raised his gun, but Jonas waved him down. "Save it," he said as he brandished his axe.

As the zombie got close enough to take a chunk out of his arm, Jonas swung the axe and smashed it into the zombie's head. Spinning out of control, the runner fell to the ground. Jonas was on it instantly, smashing the axe into its skull once more. Shards of bone splintered as the axe chopped its way through the zombies face, and blood spattered Jonas's shirt. Once the dead man had stopped moving, Jonas faced the group.

"Let's move."

Quinn and Dakota began jogging away from the marauding dead, and found themselves dodging more than abandoned cars. Past the swimming baths was a school, and the road was littered with corpses. Most of them were half eaten. Many of the bodies had severe head wounds, suggesting someone had shot a lot of them, and too many of them were children. There were girls and boys still in uniform, and the sickening sight brought Dakota to her knees. So many of the bodies had begun to rot, and several had been reduced to skeletons, with just flaps of tissue caressing the yellow bones.

"Dakota, we can't stop. We can't do anything for them," said Jonas as he helped her up. Pulling her up, he tried to catch her eye, but she refused to look at him. Her face was drawn, and she stumbled along blindly, not answering his questions or responding to his pleas to talk to him. Walking through the street, he could understand why she was withdrawing into herself. It was horrific to see so many dead. As they neared the school's entrance gates, there was a charred pile of what used to be children. Someone had torched them, and over the last few months, the sun and the rain had melded the burnt bodies into one massive structure, like some kind of twisted monument to what the school used to be.

It was as if the unburied bodies had a disheartening effect on the group, and they slowed down by the gates, eventually coming to a standstill beneath a dying willow tree. Beneath its low branches they stopped, and fell silent. Jonas looked at Dakota, knowing she wouldn't be able to carry on much further. Terry too looked as though he was about to give up, and the others were hanging on by a thread. It wasn't so much the physical effort in running, but the mental aspect of seeing so much death, so close. It was draining. It wilted all their hopes, all of their energy, and it felt like they were running nowhere. Jonas felt it too. Every corner they turned, every doorway they ran through only led to more death. He could see Erik and Pippa trying to protect their children from the carnage, but they couldn't run with their eyes closed, and whilst Peter was old enough to understand, Freya was not. She didn't look so much scared as comatose. It was as if her brain was tuning out, refusing her mind permission to process the disturbing images she was being forced to look at. Jonas looked down at his feet, and noticed he was standing in a bloodstain. Tracing the dried river of blood back to its owner, he looked at what was once probably a pretty young girl. With a satchel around her shoulders, her face had collapsed in on itself when the bullet had passed through her jaw. She looked more like an old woman now as the weathered pale skin had stretched itself tightly around her bony face. Her once blue eyes, so full of life, were now gone, plucked out by greedy hands, and the sunken sockets were a nest for crawling maggots. A spider ran from the girl's mouth and rested on her chin briefly before scuttling down her neck and into her ripped blouse. The breeze fluttered her long hair across her forehead, and the ripe smell of death reached Jonas's nose. Something had eaten away at the rest of her body, and he could feel something building up inside of him. It took a moment to reveal itself, and at first, he wasn't sure if he was going to cry or scream. His gut ached, his head was like a washing machine on full spin, and his hands were curling up into fists, desperate to hit something. He wanted to find the person responsible for this innocent girl's grisly death and deal out some retribution for her.

Jonas suddenly felt energised. No way was he going to die like that. No way was he going to let Dakota, or any of the others be left out in the street to die. Randall had been unlucky. Jonas refused to accept the others were going to die like him. He had to do something, to find a way out of this mess.

"Erik, this is Jeffersontown Junior, right?" asked Jonas as he approached Erik.

Through bloodshot, tired eyes, Erik looked up. "Yeah. So?"

Jonas needed to try something, and Erik was his best shot at galvanising the others. "So, at the end of this road is Tucker's alley, right? From there we take a short cut into Abramson Memorial Park. Try and put some distance between ourselves and the dead chasing us. If we can slip into the park, we might be able to take a breather, maybe give us a chance to figure out where we're going instead of running around in circles."

Erik looked at Pippa holding his daughter. He looked back at Jonas and nodded. "The more obstacles between them and us the better. If we take the next right we can cut down Sycamore Street, and across the park," said Erik.

Quinn joined them, hearing the plan, and was grateful to be able to take her mind off their surroundings. "If we cut through the park we might be able to get to the Interstate. Maybe hitch a ride out of town?"

"I don't think the buses are running. You know how to hotwire a car?" Erik asked.

"It doesn't matter," said Jonas. Knowing that Erik was a cop, Quinn didn't answer, and it was obvious that she was holding back. Jonas didn't want them to stop and get into anything. Their individual histories were irrelevant now. The zombies were still after them, and they only had a moment to decide where to head. "Look any vehicle we come across, I expect the batteries are probably dead, and I'm sure the I65 is closed anyway. They were setting up roadblocks when it started, and it's likely to be one giant car park right now. Our best bet is through Abramson Park, and hope they lose us in these buildings. Erik, remember how we used to cut through the back of Joe's bar? Instead of Sycamore Street we should go down Tucker's alley, sneak through the bar, and into the park that way. They couldn't possibly all follow us if we took the scenic route."

"Let's do it," agreed Erik.

"Sounds like a lot of dark corners and risks to me," said Quinn. "You sure it's safe?"

Jonas looked at Erik. "It's been a while. You want to take point?"

"Gotcha. Everyone follow me. Any trouble, yell. Quinn, you mind tagging along beside me? I could do with a spare pair of eyes. Tyler, you bring up the rear, you have the only other gun, and yes, Mrs Danick, I know you can shoot better than any of us, but we can't risk you slowing us down. You can cuss me out later. Terry, I need you to help her, okay, buddy?"

Jonas watched the group settle into their roles with ease. Mrs Danick eyeballed Erik, but she said nothing. She could nail a fly's ass from fifty yards with her pistol, but she wasn't quick on her feet, and Erik was right. Terry was subdued. He had been close to Randall, and was feeling his loss more than anyone. With the zombies on their tail, they had hardly stopped to think about what had happened. Peter held onto his younger sister, Freya, and Pippa stuck close to Quinn. Jonas rubbed Dakota's back, and then they were off. He knew that Erik would lead them to the park. It had been so long since Jonas had spent any time in the area, that he trusted Erik more than himself.

As they left the school behind, Jonas saw the dead. They weren't far away, and their numbers seemed to have swelled. Tyler was right. The noise they were making was only drawing out more. They made it to the end of the street, and Jonas saw Erik turn them down the alley, ignoring Sycamore Street. A dead policeman lay in the middle of the road, and Jonas quickly checked him over. Ignoring the stench, he took a gun from the dead cop's hand. Running to catch up with the rest, he checked and found the gun still had four in the chamber. Better than a kick in the nuts, he thought, and he rushed to the head of the group to join Erik.

As they jogged down the alley, Jonas half expected something to jump out at them from the shadows. He was on edge, and his stomach was churned up. If he had anything to throw up, he would've done so, but like everyone else, his stomach was empty. He saw Erik slip through a wooden gate that led to the back of Joe's bar, and remembered doing the same thing when he was fifteen. He and Erik would sneak into the back yard, steal a couple of beers, or crates if they could handle it, and then head to the park to drink them under the moonlight. Joe's bar had been around forever, and the security was non-existent. The rusted, iron railings behind the bar had been twisted and turned almost inside out, so they had created a hole just big enough for them to get through. He didn't know who Joe was, or who owned the bar today, but it looked from the outside as if nothing had changed. The faded welcome sign was still there, and the exterior of the building clearly hadn't been painted since prohibition had been repealed. Jonas crept through the gate, and found himself looking at Erik.

"They fixed the damn railings."

Jonas looked and saw that the rusted iron that had separated the bar from the park for all those years was now a high brick wall. There was no way through it.

"Oh crap." Jonas handed the cop's gun to Dakota, and looked at the wall that was barring them from the park. "What about the bar? We could force a way in, hide there a while?"

"No good," said Peter as he pulled on the door to the rear of the bar. "It's locked."

"No telling what might be waiting inside, plus they know we're here. How long before they get in? It's too damn risky to stop now," said Erik.

Two gunshots rang out as Tyler fired back through the gate they had just come. "Two runners," he said. "Got them, but we need to hurry. I'm out of ammo." Frustrated, Tyler pocketed the gun hoping to find more ammo later.

"Steady, Tyler," said Mrs Danick, as she stepped up to the gate. She drew her gun, and aimed it between the gate posts in case of more runners. "You go help fix a way out of here."

"Tyler, come help," said Jonas.

Peter was looking after Freya, while Jonas, Erik, Quinn and Pippa were dragging empty beer barrels over to the wall. Tyler grabbed another, and in a minute, they had a dozen lined up, forming a makeshift step. It was just about enough for them to get over.

"Peter, you get over first. Then you can help Freya and Mrs Danick down, okay?" Jonas took Peter's hand and helped him up onto the barrels. "If you see any trouble on the other side, holler."

"Don't worry, you'll hear me yell if I see anything," said Peter as he clambered up onto the top of the wall. Sitting astride it, he announced that the park looked clear, and then he dropped down on the other side. There was a soft thud, a grunt, and then Peter shouted that he was okay. Erik and Pippa helped the silent Freya up and over, and then Mrs Danick left her post to go next. She closed the gate behind her, and one by one they filed up over the wall, until just Erik and Jonas were left.

"Go man, I'll watch your back," said Erik. "When you're up top, just give me a pull up and we're home free."

Jonas shook his head. "No offense, but I'm not going to be able to pull you up. You go first and pull me up."

"Shit," said Erik smirking. "Just because I ain't got sparrow's legs like you. Never did carry much weight, did ya?"

"The way I remember it, you'd usually eaten my meal before I could even smell it cooking." Jonas held out a hand so Erik could get a boost up over the barrels.

"You snooze, you lose," said Erik as he hoisted himself up. Once he was sitting on the wall, he looked down at Jonas and held out his hand. "Come on then, Hamsikker. Let's get your bony ass...watch out!"

Jonas whirled around and saw a zombie forcing its way through the gate into the yard. Fumbling for his axe that was laid on the ground, Jonas picked it up to find he was too late. The zombie was already towering over him, its rancid rotted face blocking out the sun. Yellow teeth lined a purple mouth, and Jonas smelt death as the diseased body prepared to fall upon him. With a deafening roar, the zombie's head exploded, and Jonas was showered with gore. The dead body fell to the ground, and Jonas stood in awe, the axe in his hand now idle and useless.

"Hurry it up," said Erik as he holstered his Glock. "I've got a couple of bullets left, but then I'm out too."

Jonas looked at Erik's outstretched arm. As he wiped the gore from his eyes, and ran bloody fingers through his hair, he thought how easy it would be to ignore the hand of help. Just sit down and let it go; let himself slide into oblivion, and not have to deal with this shit anymore. Then he remembered the schoolgirl, her body left to rot in the street, her eye-sockets full of maggots, and he knew that he could never give up. No matter what, he wanted to live. It wasn't even a choice. He wanted more than anything to win, to beat this, to beat the dead; to show the world that life was the most important thing on Earth.

Grabbing Erik's hand, he hoisted himself up and both men dropped down into the park. Jonas found himself being helped up by Dakota whose face was set, and he knew he was in for it.

"Jonas Hamsikker, what the hell? I thought you...I thought..."

As Dakota melted in his arms, Jonas embraced her. "It's all right, honey, I'm fine."

The expected admonishment never materialised, and Dakota kept quiet. Jonas knew she was mad at him for putting himself at risk. Her silence was unsettling, and he wished she would argue with him, hit him, kiss him, and just do anything except give him the silent treatment. He wasn't sure if it was anger, or simply a weary acceptance of the inevitable. One day she expected to find her husband dead. He wasn't about to make promises he wasn't sure he could keep, so he settled for a kiss. He pecked her cheek as she sighed, pushing him away and shaking her head. She was pissed, but she'd come around, she always did.

Making their way across the green grass of the park, they put some distance between themselves and the back yard of Joe's bar. They could hear clattering and banging sounds from behind the fence, but it seemed like it would hold, and Jonas doubted the zombies would figure out how to climb the barrels over the wall. At least it would take them some time. Surrounding the park were scarlet oaks, illuminated by the afternoon sun, their leaves glistening as they bathed in sunlight. A few birds flew overhead, flitting from tree to tree, Jonas noticed that the further away they got from the bar, the quieter it became. He could see the edge of the town over the tops of the trees, and a plume of smoke still rose over the northern perimeter, probably from some burning gas station, or buildings that continued to smoulder with nobody left to put the fire out. Set against the charred city, the park was peaceful and tranquil. The grass, whilst long, was still a bright green, and it felt soft beneath their feet. Jonas was grateful that the immediate trees circling them, a mixture of American beech and black oaks, were tall and still thick with leaves to hide the ruined city. A cardinal flitted between branches overhead as Jonas slowed down, and he wished they had time to stop. He imagined the park was an island, a lake of serenity in amidst a burning city of the dead. Pausing by a large trunk, he let the others catch up. Nobody spoke as they collapsed at his feet, and he knew they needed to rest. Mrs Danick in particular looked to be struggling. Her face was beetroot red, and she'd even loosened the shawl around her shoulders.

"One minute," said Jonas. "One minute, and then we have to keep going. We don't know if they're still following, and we can't risk staying out here in the open."

He looked around the park and spied a children's play area. There was a large, orange swing above a ten by ten square pit of chipped bark, and a rusted, blue climbing frame set beside a sandpit. Several benches surrounded the playground, and on one lay three small bodies. He didn't need to go any closer to know that they were children, or that they were dead. Not the sort that got up and walked, but truly dead. The bodies had been left where they'd fallen, and over the last few months, the strong Kentucky sun had damaged them. The stomachs had blown apart, forcing the bellies to extend beyond their natural capabilities, and bloated intestines lay pooled around the children's legs and on the ground beneath the bench. He could see movement on one of the children, just something small wriggling around, and he guessed they were maggots. The skin had burned and rotted away, and in places, he could see sheer white bone sticking up where rats, or some sort of vermin, had chewed away the meat. What kind of God would let this happen, he thought.

Dakota brushed up against him, and seemed to know what he was thinking. "Don't look at them," she whispered. "They're in heaven now. They're safe."

"Heaven? I'm not so sure anymore. I think God's on vacation," said Jonas wearily.

Dakota stroked his hair and wiped the sweat from his forehead. She looked up at him with piercing blue eyes. "Honey, trust me when I say God is still looking out for us. I don't claim to know how He works, but I can tell you that He is still looking out for us. You of all people should know that."

"If this is His work, then I'd hate to see what the Devil has in store for us." Jonas kissed his wife. He picked a piece of rough, black bark from a tree and crumbled it between his fingers. The texture was dry, brittle, and he realised that summer was over.

Assuming they survived the fall, winter would be on them in no time, and then they would have a whole heap of different problems to contend with. "Sorry, baby, I don't mean to snap. I'm just...I love you."

"Love you too," she said sighing. "You'd better stop holding out on me though. First the garage, then back there at the bar. What were you thinking?"

A lone black crow perched atop the oak tree above them suddenly flapped its wings and took off. Jonas watched it fly over to the dead bodies in the playground. It landed on one clumsily, dancing from side to side until it found purchase on a rib cage. Its beady eyes darted around, and it casually began pecking at the meat before the crow plunged eagerly into the raw flesh with surprising ferocity. Its frantic attempts to eat dislodged the body, and a floppy arm fell down to hang loosely above the ground. The small fingers were broken, and blood smeared the pale flesh of the arm. The crow pulled at a piece of stringy meat, straining at it with its beak until the tissue broke, and then it flew away, its prize firmly clamped in its mouth.

Disgusted, Jonas turned away, and looked around the group. He saw broken people, disillusioned, bereft of hope, and with barely enough energy to stay awake. Could they do this? Could *he* do this? Dakota never lost her faith, yet, his wavered from minute to minute. He had to find strength somewhere, and if it couldn't be from God, he would have to find it within himself. Before all this started, before the dead walked, it was his love for his wife that drove him on to work harder, to provide for her, to make their lives as content as possible, and to make a safe home. Dakota was his everything, and he drew upon his deep love and admiration for the woman who stood beside him now. Even now, when they were lost, she still stood by him, and never lost her faith. He would do it for her. When he was at a low all he had to do was look into her eyes, and it was like looking into another world. Nothing else mattered when he was looking at Dakota.

"I wasn't thinking about anything. I just did what I had to do. You know I'll never leave you, Dakota. It'll take more than a zombie to keep me apart from you."

Jonas heard a rustling sound coming from somewhere within the treeline. He heard branches breaking, and leaves being crushed underfoot. There was a faint moaning sound, and he knew they were still coming. Maybe they had found a way over the fence, or maybe there were stragglers in the park. Either way, they couldn't stay any longer.

"Time to go," Jonas said lifting Dakota to her feet. He pulled up Terry, and then approached Erik who was examining his Glock.

"I'm almost out. We need to find somewhere safe to go, and fast." Erik looked at his wife, and then to Peter who was strapping on the backpack as he helped Freya to her feet. They looked shattered.

Jonas nodded in agreement. "How are they holding up?" he asked quietly.

Erik shrugged. "Peter's got more strength than most people I know. He's still a kid, but anything I ask of him he does without question. He looks after Freya like she's part of him. I just wish this was over."

They began walking through the park, deeper into the trees. On the far side lay the Interstate, and from there they hoped to find a vehicle, or somewhere to at least stay a while and rest up. No one was thinking long-term at this point. When they had set off in the morning, they had assumed they were moving to the garage. It was a well-stocked secure place that Cliff had supposedly checked out beforehand. Instead, they were running from place to place without any sense of direction, or any plans beyond the next five minutes. Jonas asked Quinn to take the lead, as she knew the area well. He needed to talk to Erik.

"She said anything to you?" Jonas looked at Freya. The girl was like a ghost, her skin pale and her movements slow. When she walked, it was as if she floated just above the ground instead of trod on it. She was clinging to her brother's side, and Jonas could see what Erik meant. Peter let his sister hold his hand, and from the whiteness of her knuckles, she was gripping his hand tightly.

"She hasn't said a word," said Erik. "It's been months now. She used to be such a happy girl. Always laughing and playing. She didn't have a care in the world, then this. It's like she's shut down. Pippa tried talking to her last night. We thought if she realised it was going to be her last night in her own bed that she might open up, but all she did was run for Peter. I'm glad she feels like she can trust him, but it makes me feel so useless. All I want to do is look after my family. You can understand that can't you? I see how you and Dakota are, how close you are. I miss that closeness that I used to have with my daughter. I thought we had a special bond, but now...well it's gone, and I'm not sure it'll ever be back. She doesn't speak at all, and she constantly looks scared. Hell, she *is* scared. What can I do? I've talked to her, Pippa and Peter too, we all have, but at the end of the day, she's just a kid. This is too much for her."

Jonas felt in his pocket for his keys. He'd kept his car keys on him, a relic of the past, of a life now gone that would never return, and he couldn't explain why. They were never going to be useful again. He decided to give something to Freya, and slipped a keychain off. He let Peter and Freya catch up, and bent down to her.

"Hi, Freya. How are you? Look, I was just talking to your Daddy, and I wanted to let you know that we're all here for you. I want you to have something. Here." Jonas held out the keychain to her. It was a metallic square, with a picture of a hand-drawn building in green, set inside a golden yellow circle. There was an inscription on it that read Fort William Historical Park. He could see Freya sizing it up, but she refused to take it.

"The thing is, Freya, this is really important to me, and while I'm fighting off the bad men, I don't want to lose it. Fort Williams is in Canada, and it's close to where my sister lives. She has three young boys, and they sent this to me after they visited. Can you please help me, and look after it? I promise you can give it back to me when we're safe, away from the monsters and mad men. Okay? What do you say? Can you help me with this?"

Freya looked up at Peter who returned her gaze with an approving nod. She reached out and plucked the keychain from Jonas's hand. She looked at it, before stuffing it into a pocket. Saying nothing, Peter just smiled at Jonas, and they trudged on in silence. Erik silently acknowledged Jonas's gift, and then headed off to walk with Pippa.

The trees were thick, but there was a dirt trail leading them through the copse toward the edge of the park, and then the road. Jonas began to believe that maybe they could find a car. Maybe they could actually find a way out of Jeffersontown, somewhere far away from this hellhole. The moaning sounds had receded, and the zombies that had been following them seemed to have disappeared. The axe in Jonas's hand was heavy, and slick with blood. He longed for the day he could put it down, and never have to pick it up again. His thoughts were shattered quickly, and he realised that day was a long way off, when from up ahead he heard Dakota scream.

"Peter, keep Freya back. *Stay here*." Jonas brandished the axe in both hands as he ran. He ran toward her, towards sounds of gunfire, splintering wood, and shouting that filled his ears.

"Please, God, not Dakota. *Not Dakota*."

CHAPTER SIX

Abramson Memorial Park was fenced off from the highway by a thick concrete wall, designed to hide the usually busy road from the quiet park. A ring of black oaks surrounded the brick wall, and low to the ground were a variety of thick bushes and common flowers. There was an exit leading to a public footpath outside the park in two corners. These exits were now as useful as a blindfold in a fist-fight.

When the zombies first appeared, they sprang up all over the city, and inevitably, some of them strayed onto the Interstate. With the authorities and the public caught unaware, there was a multitude of crashes throughout the whole country, and many cities were reduced to gridlock. Louisville's trunk roads quickly snarled up, and outside the park, a large trailer jack-knifed. The resulting pile-up involved twelve cars, a postal delivery van, and a police car. The fatalities were high, made even worse as one truck involved was on its way to deliver high octane gas. The resulting explosion left a blackened sump in the middle of the road, and blasted a huge hole in the wall surrounding the park, scattering bricks like leaves. It was this hole that Jonas could see through the thinning trees, and zombies had found their way through it with ease. The gunfire he heard stopped, replaced by shouting, and the guttural cries and grunts associated with hand to hand combat.

Quinn was hacking away steadily with her knife, assisted by Terry who was fighting them off with a thick branch. Pippa had taken refuge behind a pile of bricks, whilst Erik used his bat to fend off their attackers. Sickening thuds repeatedly sounded as he caved in heads, sending the zombies hurtling back. If they came again, he simply stood his ground, defending his wife, and struck at them until their heads were nothing but mush, their bodies falling to the ground at his feet. Jonas saw Mrs Danick and Tyler pistol whipping more, and then he finally found Dakota. She was literally punching a zombie, kicking wildly at it, pushing it, shoving it back with all her might to keep it at bay. The gun he had given her lay at her feet, empty.

Jonas charged and raised the axe above his head. With a scream he swung at the zombie attacking Dakota, and the axe whistled through the air. The blade landed in the zombie's neck and near took off its head completely. The dead man's head flopped to one side, and his neck was ravaged, dead tissue and blood splashing over the axe. It was enough to make the zombie stagger backward, but not stop it entirely, and as Dakota fell to the ground she crawled away. Jonas retrieved his axe, and swung again, aiming at the gaping wound on his attacker, this time succeeding in severing the man's head altogether. The zombie's head rolled away coming to a stop by a tree stump, and the decapitated body staggered forward before slumping at the base of a gnarled witch-hazel bush. Dakota screamed again as another zombie appeared beside Jonas.

Swinging his axe around, Jonas smashed the axe-head into the torso of a huge zombie. The man looked like he had been burnt alive. The skin was blackened, and the body completely hairless. Its clothes had been fried too, and stuck to the dead man's thick body. As the axe ripped into the man's chest, flayed pieces of crispy, black skin came free and fluttered to the ground. Jonas jerked the axe out, pulling a couple of ribs free with it. The man was huge, at least a foot taller than him, and the arms were reaching out for him. Crisps fingers, like burnt sausages, reached for him, delicately brushing against Jonas's face as he recoiled.

"No fucking way am I dying today," said Jonas as he swung the axe again, plunging it deep into the dead man's head. The axe split the man's skull neatly in half, and shattered the zombie's jaw. With the zombie scalped, its eyes and brain gone, and only its broken teeth exposed, it tottered on its feet unsteadily. As if unsure what was happening, the zombie stayed there, reaching for

Jonas, but making no movement or sounds. Like a headless chicken, its body seemingly refused to accept it was dead, and the body kept twitching. Jonas heaved the axe one final time bringing it down in a neat vertical line, aiming a direct strike onto the man's bloody lower jaw. This time the sheer weight of the axe made it sink straight through the jaw, into the neck, and it only came to a stop when it hit a bone. Jonas was weak, unable to hold onto his weapon as the zombie fell, and the lumbering giant took the axe down to the ground. The axe was firmly lodged into the man's shoulder, nestled between a shoulder blade and collar-bone.

Looking around, Jonas saw the fight was over. What had taken mere minutes had felt like hours. The zombies were dead. It had been a relatively small group, thankfully free of runners, and they were spread out thinly. Peter and Freya had joined their parents, who were all hugging beneath the frame of an old oak tree, and Jonas was pleased that Erik's family was safe. Quinn and Terry were sitting by the feet of a dead zombie, their red faces evidence of their exertions. Mrs Danick stood at the park walls, looking out at the road, and Tyler was approaching Jonas, his face sweaty, his palms bloody.

"Dakota. You okay?" asked Jonas as he turned to his wife. He got down on the dry ground beside her, reaching out to her, offering his hand. She looked up at him, her eyes wide, her expression one of shock and fear.

As he drew Dakota to him, he could feel her shaking uncontrollably. He stroked her hair, matted with dirt and tangled with leaves, and she clung to him as if he were a lifeboat on a stormy ocean. Dakota buried her face in Jonas's neck, and he knew that she was in shock. He had never seen her strike anyone, and being reduced to batting away a zombie with her bare hands must have been terrifying. He was the only solid thing around her, an island surrounded by death and doom. Her warm breath caressed his neck as she drew air in and out quickly, and he waited for her to calm down. He whispered reassurances to her, telling her he loved her, and that she was okay now. He gradually became aware the others were talking amongst themselves, sizing up the situation, and wondering what to do next, but his priority was Dakota. He looked her up and down as best he could, noticing the skin on her bruised hands, and her grazed knuckles.

Then he looked closer.

There were scratches on her forearms, and a deep welt on her left wrist. Something sharp had gouged out her skin, leaving a fresh trail of blood. The wound was healing, the blood clotting, but it left him feeling cold. Cuts and scrapes had become commonplace, yet, this was different. If she had been bitten by one of them, or even just scratched, then she couldn't be patched up with a Band-Aid. Jonas studied her face, looking for something that told him she was okay, *would* be okay.

She *had* to be.

"Hey, Jonas," said Tyler, "you all right, man?"

Jonas ignored him. "Dakota, honey, look at me." He slowly brought her face up to his, ignoring the numbness in his right hand that had been wielding the heavy axe. Her eyes told him everything he wanted to know. Before she looked away, in that split-second that their eyes locked, he thought that the gates to Hell had been opened, and all the vicious, nasty monsters that lurked beneath the souls of Men had surfaced. His heart was pounding so hard he thought that it might burst.

"It was just the bush," Dakota said as she pressed on the cut. "I cut myself on the witch-hazel when I fell. I'm fine. I'm going to be fine, honey. Are you okay?"

As the horrible thoughts and nightmares swam from his mind, he realised he had been about to go into full panic mode. His heart continued to throb, pounding like a sledgehammer into hard concrete. Storm clouds swept over the flat, grassy plains of peace, and darkness approached. Tornados of doubt guzzled every rational thought in his mind, sweeping up logic, and spitting out dire warnings of doom, disaster, and death. Jonas blinked, banishing the storm. Dakota was his guide through all of this, his light, and while she was here there was no reason to succumb to the power of those dark thoughts. He smiled at her as he brushed the dirt from her cheeks.

"I'm fine."

"You should get Pippa to look at that," said Tyler noticing the cut on Dakota's arm. "Don't want to get infected."

Dakota nodded. "Not now though. Later. I'm not staying here a second longer than we have to."

Jonas watched as she gently squeezed her fingers together, ensuring she still had full use of her hand. There was no serious damage, and the cut had missed her tendons. He wasn't sure he still believed in God, but he said a silent prayer anyway.

"Hey, Jonas, you okay, man? Is everyone all right?" asked Erik.

They gathered by the hole in the park wall, and everyone confirmed that they were okay. Nobody had been bitten. They all had a few cuts and bruises, but no major damage had been done, and Dakota had come off the worse. Peter got out some bandages from the rucksack he'd been carrying, and wrapped them around Dakota's arm to stem the bleeding. As they all discussed their situation, they soon realised that things were progressively getting worse than they thought though.

"So, you too? Damn it." Jonas saw Tyler put the gun back in his pocket, but it was useless. He was out of ammo, as was Erik, Dakota, and Mrs Danick. Their entire arsenal had been depleted, and all they had between them now was an axe, a baseball bat, and a couple of knives. If they faced another attack by a large number of the dead, it was going to be difficult to repel them.

"We need more guns," said Quinn, "and quick."

"You think?" Terry paced back and forth. "We're screwed. We are so fucking screwed."

"Hey, Terry, calm down for a second, we just need to think this through," said Jonas. The embers of the afternoon sun cast an orange glow over everything, and Quinn was right about needing guns, and needing to do it quickly. Jonas estimated they had a couple of hours of sunlight left, no more than that. If they hadn't found somewhere safe by then, they were in big trouble. The night was worse than the day, and no sane person ventured out after sundown.

"Look at us," said Terry, "we have nothing. The only thing separating them from us, are our morals. Now we have to kill, to butcher our way through these poor people, just so we can live another day, and for what? To scavenge like rats for food? To die one by one? Like Anna? Like Randall? We have nothing."

"We have resilience," said Jonas firmly. "We don't kill, we fight. We don't murder people, we defend ourselves. I'm proud of every single one of you. We have a lot more than so many other people, and I'll be damned if I'm going to let that slip away from us."

Terry was usually the calm one, but this latest attack seemed to have unnerved him. Jonas could tell he was scared, they all were, but panicking now was not going to help them one bit.

"Terry, just cool it, okay? We'll figure it out. These things aren't people anymore, and killing them is nothing like killing a real person. Come on, we're all on the same side here." Jonas held out his hand and Terry looked at it before shaking it.

"Sorry, I just..." Terry turned away and leant against a tree. His eyes glazed over, and the last time Jonas had seen a man look like that was at his mother's funeral. His father wore that same expression on his face when they had lowered her coffin into the ground. It was a face full of grief, devoid of hope, and yet an awakening of sorts: a knowledge that death was not just inevitable, but horrible and cruel and dirty, and it was coming for them.

"Um, Jonas?" Mrs Danick had so far remained silent. She had been watching the sun slowly set, turning the road into a corridor of shadows. "We may have to do a lot more fighting before the day is over, and I'm beat. We also have to go, like *now*. There are more coming. I can see them."

They all peered at the road, looking west along the highway in the direction of Louisville, and saw movement in the distance. Between the jammed cars was a sea of heads, bobbing up and down, but definitely moving their way.

"The gunfire would've drawn them at least." Erik picked up a brick from the smashed park's walls, and gave another to Peter. "Better than nothing, right?"

"Everyone happy to head east?" asked Jonas. Without waiting for an answer, he jumped over the wall into the road. The median was just as clogged as the main highway with destroyed vehicles. He wasn't happy about having to navigate a way through the littered cars, knowing they could contain hidden dangers, but they had little choice. They couldn't head back into the park the way they had come, and if they went west, they would only be marching straight into the army of zombies coming out of the city.

"There's an off-ramp about a quarter mile that way," said Quinn. "I would suggest we take it. If we stay on here, we could get trapped. Better to get off and back into Jeffersontown where there are more places to go."

As they crept through the highway, skulking between the cars, putting more distance between themselves and the dead, Jonas couldn't help but think about Janey. He had been fooled into thinking everything would be fine, and that if they stayed holed up inside long enough, eventually the problem would just go away: except it didn't. The zombies were still around, and their numbers only seemed to swell every day. Now that they were out on the streets, he was beginning to realise just how tough it was to survive. Janey had three kids to look after, and their father wasn't on the scene. The gutless bastard had left her after little Mike was born, without so much as a goodbye. Now she was facing this? He knew he had to get to her. As soon as they had regrouped, he was going to have to go. She told him she would stay put, and wait. She told him she had enough food to last a few months, and she lived right above a grocery store, but what if she was forced out? What if one of the kids got sick? What if their house was attacked? What if…

Up ahead, a car door rattled, interrupting his thoughts. None of the others seemed to notice it. Despite the long shadows, he could see it moving, just an inch or two, but definitely moving. There was no wind to speak of, so it wasn't being blown open. It could be an animal, a wild dog perhaps, scavenging for food. As Jonas got nearer to the car the door opened further, and the pent up air inside was released. He was hit by a wall of fumes, of heat, and of putrid stale air that smelt rotten. Whatever had been inside had been done no favours by the Kentucky sun, and had probably been baking for some time. There was nothing good that could come from that car, but he couldn't leave it. What if he ignored it and a runner came out behind them? Cast beneath the giant dark shadow of a delivery van, he couldn't see inside the car. There didn't appear to be anyone inside, but he wasn't going to take any chances, and he readied his axe as he approached the beat up old Chevy. On the dash a Hula girl swayed her hips silently, her smiling plastic face at odds with the stench of death coming from the car.

A palm stretched out from the slowly opening door, before smacking flat onto the tarmac. Jonas watched as another arm appeared and a second palm did the same. Nothing followed, and he looked around the door, curious to know what was behind those two frail arms. The rotting face of a dead woman looked up at him through pale, lifeless, unblinking eyes. The skin had turned a purple-brown colour, and grotesque holes had been torn into the woman's neck by her now long-gone attacker. The zombie's jaws opened, showing off two rows of yellow teeth and a swollen, black tongue. The woman reached for him, but her body was stuck in its seat, still tethered in place by the seatbelt. A faint moan escaped her lips, and as Jonas got closer, he could sense the eagerness to free herself reaching a crescendo. The zombie was pulling and twisting at the strap that held her in the car.

Jonas felt disgusted. He wanted to be rid of this thing. It was no longer a woman, no longer a human, just a disgusting sack of maggots. He put his hands on the top of the open car door, and swung it closed. With an audible crunch, the woman's head was pinned between the door and the framework of the car. One arm snapped instantly, its fragile bone snapping like a twig, and it hung uselessly from her shoulder. Bringing the car door back and swinging it hard, he smashed it into the zombie's head again. One eye plopped out, but the creature kept moving, kept flailing its one good arm, kept moaning and hissing and drooling as Jonas remained tantalisingly out of reach. Again and again, Jonas brought the door flying into the zombie's head, over and over until his arms ached. The dead woman's skull finally caved in as brown goo slopped from her broken head, oozing out onto the street and splattering his feet. Finally, the zombie stopped moving. Jonas peered in through the open door, but there were no more inside. There didn't appear to be much of use either. The woman's handbag was still on the passenger seat, but getting it would mean having to reach over the dead body. He knew she was dead, but he couldn't bring himself to do it. He couldn't reason there was much point in getting close to the body just for a bag that was likely to contain little they could use now. Lipstick, cigarettes, and even money were all worthless now.

Relieved he had been able to dispatch the zombie relatively quietly without causing too much commotion, he continued on, mindful there may be more surprises in the traffic ahead. Dakota had watched him, waited for him, and said nothing as he joined her. He said nothing either, eager to move on. What was there to say? Killing the dead had become de rigueur. They walked on, on the lookout for trouble, but only coming across a few bodies. They were the sort that couldn't return, truly dead, truly at peace. Jonas noticed how Dakota whispered something as they passed each body, and he thought he caught the odd word. It sounded like a prayer. In fact, it sounded more like a plea, a request for God to end the suffering and take them into His arms. Jonas had once been like Dakota, but with every passing day, he found himself becoming more disillusioned. He didn't begrudge her faith, and when he thought about it, he was a little jealous. The only thing he believed in now was his love for her, and the knowledge that he had to get to Janey. He'd promised her he would come. Family was all that mattered now. It was real, and it was something he could hold onto. Divine beings seemed a long way off, more like a fantasy that served little purpose in their efforts to survive. How Dakota held onto her beliefs staggered him. The moment his dead father had gotten up and walked again had been the last time he had thought he believed.

"Jonas, get down," Quinn hissed, signalling for everyone to stop.

Freezing where he stood, he looked up. The off-ramp was just ahead, and they were almost clear, except for a school bus blocking their way. It had been left right across the road and its open door was facing them. To get around it would mean having to get very close to that door. There was movement inside, but whoever was in there was doing a good job of staying concealed. All he could see was the top of a head in one of the seats. Occasionally, it moved from side to side, indicating they were still alive, but other than that, he couldn't see what was going on. Jonas crept forward to Quinn, dismissing his rambling thoughts, pleased to be able to focus on something else, something that actually led somewhere. Once they were downtown again, off the highway, they could find somewhere to stay. Even if only for one night, they needed a place to rest.

"What do you think? We could just run for it. We could probably be past it before they heard us," Quinn said.

"Maybe," said Jonas. He doubted they would all get past though, and whoever was last, was likely to be faced with whatever was on that bus. "What if there are more inside? We could try to sneak past, but if they cotton on to us, we might have a whole heap of runners on our tail, and we're not equipped to deal with that. It's too risky."

"So what then?" asked Erik. He had joined them, also seeing the bus that was blocking the road down into Jeffersontown. "What if it's a kid, Hamsikker? What if it's just some poor kid who's been living out here alone? We can't leave without knowing for sure."

"God damn it," said Jonas. They had been lucky so far, finding a way through the vehicles without a single zombie emerging from the wreckage. The only one had been the woman trapped by her belt, and she had been easily dealt with. Now, just as they were almost clear, they had this to deal with. As unlikely as it was, Erik was right. There was a chance it was some kid hiding out, and he had to know. He had to know for sure. Jonas looked across at Dakota, wanting to get her opinion, to seek reassurance he was doing the right thing, but she was side by side with Mrs Danick, staring at the ground, and occasionally looking over her shoulder behind them. Was she avoiding him, or just avoiding having to make any decisions, to take any responsibility?

"Right, I'm going in," said Jonas resolutely. "The best form of attack is to use an element of surprise, right? Erik, you follow me, and guard the door. If anything rushes me, I'll hold them off. Quinn you stay here. If I don't come back out, take the rest of the group, and get them out of here."

"But..."

Quinn's words were lost as Jonas charged at the bus. He ran silently, but quickly. He was rapidly getting fed up of the highway, and wanted off. Keeping low, he clambered up onto the bus. The stench wasn't unfamiliar, reeking of death just as the car had done half a mile back that had housed the dead woman. He crouched down and looked down the aisle, seeing nothing but a mouldy piece of fruit that had stuck to the floor. It was so far gone he couldn't even tell what it had once been. He climbed further into the bus, looking for the person they had seen from outside. Whoever it was must've slunk down low in their seat, as he couldn't see anyone. Maybe they were trapped by their seatbelt too. Maybe they needed help.

"Hello?" Jonas put on a brave voice, but the truth was he was scared. The bus was silent, and eerie. Dakota and his friends seemed a long way off as he stood alone inside the bus. He looked around at the doorway. Erik was there, his back to the bus, his eyes scanning the road for trouble. No voice answered Jonas, and he turned around, knowing he was going to have to go further into the bus. If it was someone hiding, especially if it was a child, they could be scared. Maybe they were injured and couldn't walk. He took a step forward, and then froze. A child appeared at the end of the bus. It stepped out into the aisle, facing Jonas.

"Hello? Are you okay?" Jonas's voice echoed around the bus, and the child said nothing. It was dressed in a faded, green school uniform, and from the long, strawberry blonde hair, Jonas guessed it was a girl. "We're here to help, okay? What's your name?"

The afternoon sun was fading, and in the gloom, it was hard to see if the girl was injured. She would be scared at least. This bus had been her home for a long time, and now she was looking at a strange man. He could understand perfectly why she didn't answer. Just like Freya she was scared witless. It didn't look like she was carrying anything, and her arms hung down by her sides. Jonas took another step forward. He lowered his axe, not wanting to frighten her any more than he knew he already was, and put it on an empty seat, sending dust cartwheeling into the air. The little girl was probably six or seven, just a fraction shorter than Freya. He wished she would say something, but she just stood there, in the darkness at the back of the bus. Jonas held out his hands and knelt down, hoping his non-threatening posture would encourage her to come forward. If he rushed her, she was liable to get scared and scream or do something stupid. The last thing he wanted was for her to start screaming and bring a thousand zombies their way. If she did have a weapon, things could get tricky in the close confines of the school bus.

The girl slowly took a step forward, and then another. Her feet scuffed the floor as she walked, and she mumbled something that Jonas couldn't hear. As she approached Jonas, she began to speed up, and Jonas was grateful she was finally coming to him. In the middle of the bus a thin strip of sunlight illuminated everything, and as the girl stepped through it, Jonas saw her face. All hope suddenly vanished, and he was gripped with panic. With her teeth flashing in the sunlight, the girl broke into a run, her dead fingers reaching out for him, and her eyes were locked onto his. Jonas desperately fumbled for his axe as the dead girl bore down on him. He knew he had no time to reach it though, and he thought of Dakota briefly before the girl's teeth were in his face, and he was suddenly fighting for his life.

CHAPTER SEVEN

Derek kept telling Javier he wasn't going to do it, he wasn't about to kill himself, and pushed back every time Javier nudged him closer to the exit. It was a fight Derek was destined to lose. Javier had shed his old skin like a rattlesnake, growing up quickly, leaving childhood behind in a flash. Threats meant nothing to him anymore, and he was not one to back down from a confrontation. He had been involved in more than a few fights in his time, and Derek was just another boy trying to be a man, playing a part, but with no conviction. They both knew how this was going to end. Javier ended the short-lived quarrel by punching Derek on the nose, and Derek reeled backwards. He collided with a chair leg, and skidded to the floor. Blood spurted from his nose, and Derek sat looking at the bright red blood dripping onto his hands, his eyes glassy and wide, as if he were looking at a miracle.

"Get up," Javier said. The bloody nose was enough to shock, but he knew he hadn't hit Derek hard enough to do any real damage.

Javier closed his eyes, counted to three, and then told Derek to get up one final time. Derek was neither deaf nor dumb, but he was trying to waste time. All he was succeeding in doing though was trying Javier's patience. "Don't test me, Derek. I won't ask you again."

Derek sat on the floor in a stupor, and Javier snapped. "Right." He kicked Derek over and over, lacing the man's kidneys with boot prints, and only stopping when Derek was by the glass doors. Pleading and crying had never worked when his mother had done it, and it never worked now. Crying was a sign of weakness, giving your enemy a clear sign he had won. Derek had lost, and they both knew it.

Javier reached down and picked him up, shoving Derek's face up against the glass. He was staring right at the zombies, only inches away now, and they bit at the glass trying to get to him. It was smeared with blood and skin, and Derek whimpered like a wounded dog. Javier knew the front doors to the diner were locked, and he unloaded a couple of bullets into the lock, smashing them open. He carefully pushed one door open, just an inch, and he looked Derek in the eye. "Don't let me down, D..D..Derek. Cindy's relying on you. Remember what I told you."

Javier pushed the door open a few more inches, and then squeezed Derek through the doorway. He watched the fat man barrel through the zombies, into the parking lot, his survival instinct kicking in just in time. With the zombie's attention drawn to Derek, Javier was able to close the door, and stepped back, interested to see how far the fat man would get. Javier chuckled. Judging by the zombies that had hold of Derek's arms as he tried to run, it was not going to be far.

"Honey, what are we doing?" Rose was pouting, and her voice sounded like a child's. "Derek's never going to make it to the tow-truck."

Javier walked over to Rose who stood above a still unconscious Cindy. "I know, he's just a decoy."

"Yeah?" asked Rose. She relaxed, smiling, as if she was in on the plan all along. She looked up at him as if he was the king of the world. Her blue eyes sparkled, and Javier was so drawn to her that he almost forgot Derek's screams outside, so captivated was he by her.

"Yeah." Javier wanted to take Rose into the back room, throw her down onto the dirty sheets, and fuck her senseless. He wanted it so badly that he actually contemplated if there was time. Rose had a certain way about her. Somehow, she always looked sexy. Maybe it was the way she held her blade, the way she eyeballed him, or maybe the way she curved her full lips up slightly when she spoke. Maybe Javier was just feeling horny. He tried to push away the thought of Rose's naked body writhing on top of him, and concentrated on the plan.

"While Derek keeps them busy, he's going to get all their attention around the front of the diner. Meantime, we're going out the way we came in." Javier bent down to Cindy, and grabbed her arms. "Get her legs, Rose, we're taking her with us."

Sighing, Rose took hold of Cindy's ankles, and they slowly began carrying her toward the back door, back to the office where they could access the roof. "Why? We don't need her. I don't see why we don't just leave her here."

"Because," said Javier as he struggled to open the door, "I have a plan."

They put Cindy down on some of the sheets, and Javier noticed she was stirring. He told Rose to go up on the roof, quietly, and check the back of the diner. When the zombies had thinned out, she was to whistle, once, and then Javier would come up with Cindy.

"So, now it's just you, and me," said Javier, as Rose disappeared up the ladder to the roof.

Cindy opened her eyes, looking around the room, and she slowly woke up as Javier held her hand. He caressed it gently, like a father soothing a crying child. Cindy's skin was pale, and her eyes hazy.

"It's okay, we're getting out of here," said Javier. "Any second now, in fact. Are you okay to walk?"

Cindy struggled to her feet, and let Javier lead her over to the ladder.

"But...I...where's Derek?" asked Cindy. She was dazed, and weak. The cut on her shoulder was deep, and blood still seeped through her shirt. Javier could see Cindy's skin was sallow, and she wobbled when she walked.

"He's gone ahead of us," said Javier. "Look, Cindy, you don't need to worry about any of that right now."

Rose had only been gone a minute, and there was still no whistle. Perhaps Derek was taking longer to die than expected. Javier stifled a laugh, picturing the bleeding fat man running around the parking lot as the zombies chased him.

"What? What's funny?" asked Cindy. She looked Javier up and down, noticing the gun in his hand. It was as if she wasn't afraid anymore. She was calm and composed. Javier knew she was in shock though. Her eyes moved across him slowly, and she spoke in a hushed voice, as if reading a bedtime story to an infant.

"You're cute," said Javier, stroking away the hair from Cindy's face. He cupped her chin in one hand, pressing the gun against her belly, and leant forward so he could feel her against him. His lips were millimetres from hers, yet she did not flinch or back away. She maintained eye contact with him as he kept the gun pointed at her belly, and he let his free hand drift down her neck. The skin there was cool and soft, and he felt her shiver as his hand carried on down to her collarbone. He slipped his hand inside the opening of her shirt, letting his fingers trace the outline of her breasts. A whistle sounded from the roof, and Javier brought his hand up again to Cindy's chin. The thought of fucking Rose still lingered in his mind, and he found he couldn't switch off. She got in his head, and coiled around his brain like a snake wrapping itself around its prey. In a different time, in a different place, he would've fucked both her and Cindy in this cramped room. Shaking it off, he waved the gun at Cindy's face.

"Another time, maybe."

As Javier backed away, Cindy closed her eyes. He gave her credit for not begging for her life, for not crumbling under pressure like Derek did, but ultimately, he was going to do what he wanted, whether Cindy accepted it or not.

"Right, Cindy, get up that ladder. I'll be right behind you. I'm going to help you, okay? It's time to get out of here."

Cindy obediently began climbing, and Javier followed her up. Out on the roof, he saw Rose crouched down where they had come up. She signalled him over, and asked him what to do next. The zombies had thinned out dramatically. As Javier predicted, most of them had been drawn around to the front of the diner.

"Derek stopped shouting a few seconds ago. I think he's gone," said Rose. She looked at Cindy with disgust. "I still don't think..."

"You're not here to *think*, Rose. Just listen. There are half a dozen vehicles down in the yard. We need to check them over, quickly, and we'll go with whichever one still has the keys in. We can get past these zombies easily. The runners are gone, and if you need to take one down, use your knife." Javier looked down at the dumpster. The chair had been knocked off onto the ground, but the jump wasn't far. "Rose, you check that green Honda, the courier van, and that battered old white thing next to it. I'll go to the motorhome first, and then there are a couple of cars on the other side of it. We do this carefully, quietly, and we'll be fine."

"What should I do?" asked Cindy nervously.

"Stick by me," said Javier. He could see jealousy flaring in Rose's eyes, but didn't have time to argue. It wouldn't be long before the zombies got through Derek, and then they would be back for more. They needed to get off the roof, and away from the diner before their voices brought the dead back around. "Yell if you get lucky, Rose," said Javier.

Rose slipped off the roof, and sprinted over to the Honda, easily dodging the few dead that still shambled around the yard.

"You next," said Javier. Cindy slipped off the roof, lowering herself gently over the guttering until she found herself dangling above the dumpster.

"I can't find it," she said. Panic welled up in her eyes.

"Just drop. It's right beneath you," hissed Javier. "Hurry up."

Cindy let go and fell onto the closed dumpster, yelping in pain as she landed. Javier was beside her in seconds, dragging her onto the ground, and then they were running for the motorhome.

The doors were locked, and he decided to try a different vehicle. Cindy stuck to him like glue, preferring to find safety in the company of a murderer than face a zombie. Javier ran over to the next vehicle, a red saloon with one window half down. The doors were locked which was probably a good thing. The back seat was a festering pile of gore and bones, the only clue as to what was once there now a shiny, blue dog-collar adorned with the name 'Jeff.' Javier almost burst out laughing when he read the dog's name. What kind of mutt was it that it had been given such a bad name? He moved onto the last vehicle, noticing Rose hadn't had any success either. She was running over to a brown four-wheel drive, and he hoped it worked. He would much prefer a solid vehicle like that to some family hatchback that would crumble as soon as he hit a zombie.

Cindy screamed, and it echoed around Javier's head, the shrill pitch grating on every nerve. She screamed again, and he realised she was freaking out. A wave of zombies was coming from the front of the diner, pushing and fighting over one another, emerging from both sides, and filling the yard quickly. Javier told her to shut up. The zombies needed no help in finding them, and the screaming didn't help anyone. She quietened down, but held onto his arm as he approached the last vehicle. It was a minivan with seating for eight people, and down the side, it read, 'Charlie's Motel - your home away from home.' The side was scratched and dented, and one side window was shattered. The passenger door was locked, but Javier noticed the driver's side was wide open. He scurried around the back of the vehicle, and found a lone zombie staggering toward him. The zombie was an old woman, already frail before she died, and he had no trouble in taking it down, swiftly stabbing it through the head. He shrugged Cindy off as he approached the open door. On the ground beneath it lay the carcass of a man, only a few bones remaining of his skeleton. There was a navy cap on the ground covered with blood and black hair, and Javier tried to ignore it as he leant over to look inside the van. There were no keys in sight, and he pulled down the shade to find nothing but a mirror.

"These any good?"

Javier turned back around to find Cindy kneeling on the ground, holding up a set of keys. Her hands were covered in blood, and the keys were attached to a hunk of pink meat.

"You just have to know where to look," said Cindy staring at the body of the dead man at her feet. "I'm guessing the driver didn't quite make it."

Javier held out his hand. "Pass them to me. I'll check the engine before we…"

"No. I'm driving. I'm not stupid. You'll leave me here." Cindy kept the keys in her hand as she got to her feet, trying not to faint. "I can do it. I'll get us away from here fast. I don't want to hang around this place."

"You know I could just shoot you, take the keys, and leave the dead to eat you," said Javier. The woman was in no position to barter with him, and they didn't have time to discuss the point. Still, there was something about Cindy that amused him.

"You could," said Cindy. She took a step toward Javier, stepping onto the bones of the dead driver, not caring what she trod in, ignoring the pain in her shoulder. "But surely you can find a better use for me than to make a meal for the dead?"

She smirked as she spoke, and Javier knew she was playing games with him. Cindy would no more sleep with him than she would marry him. She thought she could tempt him, and it was her only real chance of staying alive at this point in time. He wondered if she had used the same ploy with Derek. She knew she was beautiful, and she used it to her advantage. Well, you had to use what you had, and Javier decided he would play along, for now, and see what else Cindy might do to survive. He stepped out of the doorway.

"Be my guest. If the engine turns over, honk the horn so Rose knows we're good."

As Cindy climbed into the driver's seat, Javier looked across to the diner. The dead were rapidly gaining on them, and he waved at Rose who was sitting inside the cab of the four-wheel drive, slamming her hands on the dash. Evidently, she had not found the keys. Rose looked up toward Javier as the minivan rumbled into life, and Cindy sounded the horn.

"Scoot over," Javier said.

Cindy shook her head. "No way, José. I told you, *I'm* driving."

"Look, Cindy, you're in no state to drive. We need to get out of here fast."

"Fuck you. You want a ride? You'll have to climb over me. Or shoot me. Either way, I'm not moving from behind this wheel."

Javier toyed with the idea of shooting her, but it was too easy. Besides, Cindy would make an awful mess of the van, and they really did need to get a move on. She was not going to back down, so he reasoned that he would let her drive until she was on the verge of passing out. Then he would take control of the wheel, and control of the two women he now had in his company. Looking at the state of her, it probably wouldn't be long before she slipped into unconsciousness again.

"Rose, hurry up!" Javier shouted, watching her knife one of the dead on her way across the yard.

As Javier climbed into the van, Cindy stayed in her seat forcing Javier to slide across her. He expected her to flinch away as he crossed her, to try to sink back into the seat, but she stayed perfectly still. Her eyes followed his as he mounted her, and the thought of Rose writhing on top of him fleeted across his mind once again. Ignoring his feelings, he swiftly fell into the passenger seat and opened the door for Rose to climb in beside him.

Wasting no time, Cindy slammed the van into gear. As they drove through the yard, she avoided most of the zombies, but a few collisions were inevitable. The dead slammed into the side of the van, and a few bounced off the front fender, but Cindy was true to her word, and she got them out of their as fast as she could, weaving between the dead. Javier was surprised she managed the van so well. She clearly was a good driver, and in her condition, he was impressed. Perhaps he had underestimated her. His plan had been to use her as another decoy. He had intended to leave her in the parking lot, a bullet in her gut, screaming her head off as he and Rose made their escape, and the zombies feasted on Cindy's body. If she hadn't lost too much blood, she could prove to be more useful though, and he decided she could stick around a bit longer.

"Why the fuck is *she* still here?" asked Rose when they were out on the road. "Why the fuck is she driving? Where are we going? Are you *trying* to piss me off, Javier? Do you..."

Javier slapped Rose on the cheek, and she glared at him. Javier held her gaze, fed up with her constant biting. This eagle was about to go solo. Usually a gentle slap was enough to quell any uprising, but Rose was in no mood to quieten down.

"I asked you why's she still here, Javier? She serves no purpose. What, we can't bring a young boy along, but we'll bring along some slut just because you want to fuck her?"

Javier went to slap Rose again, but she blocked his hand with an arm, and she began to squirm in her seat.

"Let me at her, I'll kill the bitch," said Rose.

"Calm down." Javier tried to get Rose to sit still, but she was too worked up, and there was no way he could get enough leverage to make her shut up. All he managed to do was slide his arms around hers, and stop her from getting to Cindy.

Cindy simply drove on, ignoring the argument, and she looked across at Rose. "Don't worry, Rose," Cindy said smiling. "I'm sure once Javier's done with me, you can have him back."

"Shut up, and drive," said Javier. He looked in the rear view mirror, noticing the diner was behind them now. They were heading away from Jeffersontown, but he had lost his bearings, and the low sun meant long shadows split the road into varying shades of golden white and murky black. The darkness hid their path, and he was going to have to make a decision as to where to go. They had lost all their gear, and picked up a stray. Finding somewhere to bed down for the night wouldn't be a bad thing. Rose needed to calm down, and he was growing tired of the bickering between the two women. He knew they had a couple of hours before nightfall, but sleeping in the minivan filled him with dread. If there was any kind of attack, they would have little option but to run, and running in the dark was a bad idea.

They passed an open field full of dead sheep and goats. The farmhouse was burnt to the ground, and the smell of cooked flesh made Javier's stomach turn over in both sickness, and hunger. A large, white swan crossed the road up ahead, as if it were a normal day, followed by a cygnet. They meandered into the farm's driveway, and then disappeared underneath a large bush. Javier didn't care much for animals, but he was surprised to find himself smiling. The cygnet couldn't be much more than a few weeks old, and yet, there it was: life. Perhaps all was not lost. Perhaps his brother was all right, still waiting for him. He realised he hadn't thought about Diego all day. There was just too much to do, and too many other things and people clamouring for his attention. He was beginning to lose sight of the long-term plan.

Rose stopped struggling, but Javier held her in his arms, reluctant to let go. Part of him suspected she would just start fighting again, but part of him didn't want to let her go. Her presence was reassuring and irritating in equal measure, and he found himself letting up the pressure on her arms slightly. He took a hand and she squeezed it back.

"Honey, I'm sorry," said Rose. "Honest."

Javier let Rose go, and she looked out of the passenger window, resting her hand on his thigh.

"I'll make it up to you later. I know I lost it, but...well, it's just hard, you know."

Javier looked out of the passenger window, leaning across Rose so his arm touched her breasts. He knew exactly how she would make it up to him, and he found himself growing hard again. Why he was suddenly feeling so hot for her he couldn't quite understand. He put his forehead on her shoulder, and kissed her neck. He brought his lips slowly up to her ear. "Question me again, and I'll kill you."

Rose shivered, and squeezed Javier's thigh. She remained still, her face pressed against the window.

A moment passed, and when she didn't answer, Javier knew she had got the message.

"Look at that," Rose said as they slid around a curve in the road. "There's a fence over there. It looks intact. Perhaps we could..."

They were so lost in their own world that neither Javier, nor Rose, noticed the minivan start to drift. It was barely noticeable, but they started to veer from the left lane across the centre to the right lane. It only took a few seconds, but they were suddenly in the wrong lane. Cindy had started to feel nauseous, and then faint, and she had been unable to keep her eyes open. Like the sun setting, the light in her eyes dissipated as she fell unconscious behind the wheel, the blood loss and shock telling her body to rest. As her hands fell from the steering wheel, her head fell back, and Cindy slumped in the seat as the minivan lurched to the right of the road.

Javier felt the van start to spin out of control, and he whirled around to see Cindy unconscious. He grabbed for the wheel, shouting at Rose to put her belt on, but when he looked out of the front window, he knew there was no time. A small SUV had been left in the road, abandoned when the driver had succumbed to the bite on his left arm, and was unable to continue driving. Javier was able to read the SUV's bumper sticker, something witty about Jesus driving their other car, and then they were airborne. The van smashed into the back of the stationary SUV at high speed, instantly sending the SUV into the roadside ditch. The van flipped over, and Javier saw the ground flying beneath him. Cindy's lifeless arm slapped him in the face, and Rose screamed, before suddenly, the van hit the ground. It rolled over and over, crashing loudly as metal scraped along the tarmac, and the windows all shattered.

Javier tried to hold onto something, yet was unable to do anything but go with the flow. The front windscreen caved in, showering him with glass, and as the van rolled over, he only saw glimpses of what was happening, scenes flashing in front of his eyes, blinding him like flashbulbs, as they destroyed his plans. How had he been so stupid to let this happen? He saw the steering wheel break in two as the dashboard collapsed. He saw Cindy flying through the now empty front of the van head-first, disappearing through the hole where the glass should've been, one leg being torn open as her flesh caught on a piece of twisted metal. He felt Rose being banged up against him, but she was silent, and he knew she was either unconscious, or dead. He saw a brief glimpse of the blue, evening sky, before suddenly the grey tarmac was coming rushing up to meet him. There was a sickening thud, and Javier's head smashed against something hard. He blacked out, and saw nothing more, as the van came to rest in the middle of the road, upside down, its underbelly split open, and the engine dying as the van began smoking. The reanimated corpses in the vicinity turned their attention to the noise of the crash, and the van's occupants were silent, unconscious and unaware of the zombies that were closing in on them.

CHAPTER EIGHT

Jonas could hear Erik shouting, but was concentrating on holding off the dead girl. For her size, she was surprisingly strong. Or maybe he was just weak, having not eaten a decent meal for weeks now. He was unable to reach his axe, and caught the girl as she fell on him. He managed to get his knees up in time, forcing her body up and over his torso. Now her face was directly above his as they lay in the aisle of the bus, her jaws snapping continually at him. He tried to wriggle free, but it was impossible with her on top of him, and with the seats so close, he had nowhere to go. Already his arms were being sapped of what little strength he had left, and the weight of the dead body was pinning him down.

He so much wanted her to be alive. At first, he thought she was, convincing himself she was another survivor, when all along he should have realised she was just one of them. He knew he had been foolish in putting his weapon down, and now he was about to pay the price. Grisly gore fell from the dead girl's mouth, and splattered his face as they struggled. The smell coming from her mouth was repulsive, not unlike the stench of the garage from earlier that morning, and it was hard not to be sick. As he fought to keep her off, he noticed her attention begin to wane. Her eyes looked up, and then her whole head followed. Her grip on him relinquished, and he wondered what had drawn her away. With her head above him, Jonas watched in disgust as it was suddenly thrown to the side and smashed into the side of a seat. Her head blew apart instantly, and great dollops of congealed blood and tissue fell onto him. It felt like someone had thrown jelly and soggy pastry over him, but tasted far less appetising, and Jonas spat out the grunge from his mouth. He saw the bat come around again, and he held the dead body up that was still somehow holding onto him. The head was split right open this time. Crushed against the seat back, the girl's face shattered, and Jonas was covered in her brains. They slid from her cracked skull slowly, dripping onto him like clotted lumps of cottage cheese. The body slumped on top of him, and he quickly cast it aside, rushing to his feet.

"Fuck, Hamsikker, you okay?"

From the expression on Erik's face, he knew he must look a sight. Jonas wiped his face, trying to erase the sticky fluids and blood that covered him, and he spluttered out an answer. He couldn't really think straight. All he could see was the girl's face exploding.

"She didn't...get you?" asked Erik. He was still holding the baseball bat aloft, its rounded tip covered in gore.

Jonas could see that Erik had adopted a defensive stance. He was ready to strike, and this time the bat would be aimed at Jonas's head. It was fair enough. The man had a family to protect. If Dakota was in trouble, he knew he would do the same thing. He wouldn't let anyone hurt her, including his friends.

Jonas picked up his axe. "I'm fine," he grunted.

Erik looked at Jonas from head to toe. Jonas felt like he was under a microscope, being scrutinised in case he was lying.

"I said I'm fine. What, you want to take me in for questioning, *officer*?" said Jonas brusquely as he wiped his brow. "Let's get out of here. I need to get this shit off me."

Jonas attempted to push past Erik, to get out of the bus into the open air, but Erik didn't move. He didn't lower his bat either.

"Listen, Hamsikker, and listen up good. You got lucky. What the hell were you thinking, dropping your weapon like that?" Erik's expression had turned from one of sympathy to anger. "You get yourself in a situation like that again, and you're likely to end up losing more than your dignity. You understand?"

Jonas thought about answering back. He thought about shouting Erik down, telling him to back off, to let it go, to forget it, but he was too tired, and he didn't want to argue. Nothing had happened, not really, at least nothing that warranted getting into an argument. He just wanted to get out of the bus, away from the stench of death, and to wipe the girl's innards from off him. "I'm cool." He sighed. "I just...I just hoped she was...you know."

Erik lowered his bat, and shrugged his shoulders. When he spoke next, he had softened his tone. Jonas wondered if it was a technique he had learned in the force. "All right, buddy, no harm done. I know that we're all wound up right now. Just don't take any chances next time, okay?"

"Next time?" Jonas smiled. "Next time, *you* go in first, and *I* stand guard."

"True that," said Erik.

Jonas smiled at Erik, and Erik smiled back, but both were forcing it. It was as both men wanted to prove they could handle it. Neither wanted to think about what might happen the next time one of them was cornered.

"Right, let's go," said Erik clearing his throat, back in police mode. "The others are outside, but it won't be long before those critters catch up."

They filed out of the bus, and Dakota ran up to Jonas. "What happened? You look terrible." She began to wipe at his face and neck, dabbing at him with a handkerchief.

"I'm fine. Just a little trouble - nothing we couldn't handle." Jonas hated lying to Dakota, but she didn't need to know the truth. He knew that if Erik hadn't been there, he might not have been walking out of that bus alive. He began to wipe his face. "How're you doing?"

"As well as can be," said Dakota as they followed Quinn down the off-ramp. "I just wish this was over. My head is killing me, my feet are sore, and it's so damn hot, I think my sweat has sweat." Dakota wafted her shirt, letting some air up underneath the loose cotton.

"We can't stop just yet, honey," said Jonas. "They're not far behind, and it's not safe here. We have to keep going, just a bit longer until we find somewhere to rest up." Jonas looked around at the streets as they reached the bottom of the off-ramp. "I remember this area. That cafe over there, that's where we used to hang out after school sometimes. Janey would usually go for a chocolate milkshake, and I would have a ginger beer."

"But you hate ginger beer."

"I know, but I thought it looked cool."

Dakota smiled. It was a rare thing these days, and Jonas savoured it. As soon as the smile had come, it was gone though, flitting across her face like the shadow of a bird. Janey used to smile like that too, back when their mother was alive and they could claim to be a happy family. Remembering Janey only made him realise how much he missed her. He had only met her kids, his three nephews, via Skype, and right then he would've given anything to see them all in person. He had wanted to talk to Dakota about heading north again, yet, time seemed to be at a premium, so he attempted to broach the subject again as they walked. It was no good putting it off until later. He wasn't sure there would be a later the way the day was turning out.

"I've been thinking," said Jonas. "We need to get back on track. I really need to get to Janey. Tomorrow, I want to get going."

"To Canada? You realise how crazy that sounds? I'm not sure we can find a way out of Jeffersontown, let alone get across three states, *and* the border to another country. "

"I know, but I have to try, I really do. I can't let her down." Not again, he thought, but he didn't say it. "After tonight, I'm going to tell Erik and Quinn. If they're on board, I think the rest will come with us. Safety in numbers, you know? I'd rather we stuck together. I don't like the thought of leaving them, especially Erik, but I can't just keep waiting. Things aren't getting any better, and Janey's on her own."

"And if they won't come? What then?" asked Dakota.

"Then it's you and me. Okay?"

"She might not be on her own. She might have friends with her."

Jonas hoped she did, but he doubted it. The last time they had spoken, it didn't sound like Janey had anyone with her except the kids. He told her he would come. He promised he would come for the children, for Mike, Chester and Ritchie, and he told her how much he loved her and wanted to put things right. It was when he started talking to her about the funeral that she had begun crying. She hadn't cried when he'd told her their father was dead, but she cried that night on the phone. She cried and poured her heart out about how difficult it was on her own, how she missed Jonas, how cold she was, and how scared the kids were. He promised her again he would come, and then the line had gone. He couldn't leave her like that, he just couldn't. He couldn't let that be the last conversation between them.

"Look, Dakota, I don't think this is the time to debate it, I just wanted to tell you."

"But don't you think…"

"*It's happening.*" Jonas cut Dakota off and strode ahead, aware that Dakota was falling behind him. He instantly regretted snapping at her, but there was no way he was going to get into an argument about it. Janey needed him, and Dakota had to realise that. It wasn't like they could stay in Jeffersontown forever. The town was dead, and he could see little point in staying. Erik would surely agree. They had more chance if they headed north. Get away from the big cities, away from where the population had been, and find Janey. She lived in a small, quiet town, only just over the border. She'd asked him to visit so often, and there had always been an excuse. He realised now he had just been putting it off. He hadn't seen his sister in person for years. They frequently talked on the phone, and he'd Skyped last Christmas, but actually seeing Janey in the flesh scared him. He wasn't sure how Janey felt about their past, or if she expected anything now their father was gone. She said she didn't hold grudges, but she sure as hell held one for her father, and he couldn't blame her on that one. The question was did she hold one against Jonas? Maybe that was why she never pushed him to visit. The past was never an easy place to go, and the distance between them somehow made it more bearable. It wasn't exactly the sort of thing he wanted to talk about on the phone, so he kept their conversations light, discussing the news, how the kids were, and how their jobs were going. There was only one thing he could do now to make up for his failings, and that was go to her, to tell her how sorry he was, and to make sure she was surviving. A promise was more than words, and he was going to fulfil it, no matter what fate put in his way.

"We need more guns," said Jonas as he caught up with Erik.

Erik looked at him. "I hear you. There's a station a couple of blocks from here. We could try it, but to be honest, I think it's a waste of time. Any cop with a brain would've taken what they could. It's likely to be empty."

"We can't keep defending ourselves with bats and knives. They're getting too close. Any gun stores around here? I don't remember."

Erik shook his head. "No. This is a pretty boring neighbourhood. Nothing much has changed in the last twenty years, except the usual. You know, retail stores closing down, more boarded up, and more gas stations opening. No, if we wanted to find a gun shop we'd have to head south, and that's quite a task. It would take us close to the park, and back to…"

"Right, gotcha." Jonas was still feeling irritable from his brittle conversation with Dakota. "Any *useful* information, you can depart with?"

"Yeah," said Erik, "wind your head in, otherwise, it's likely to get bitten off. I'm not stupid. I know we need weapons. We also need food, water, and a place to stay for the night. You think I haven't thought about that? You think I haven't thought about how I'm going to protect my wife and kids?"

Jonas saw Pippa looking over at them, and wished Erik would just stay quiet. Her eyes were accusing, and he wondered if she was angry with Jonas for questioning her husband, or more annoyed with her husband for raising his voice. He was about to answer Erik when they came to a halt. Quinn was standing in the road, one hand clutching her knife, the other held up as if she were a cop directing traffic.

"Enough. I've just about had enough of you two bickering. In case anyone needs reminding, we have more pressing matters to deal with," said Quinn.

Jonas glanced around and saw everyone looking at him. Pippa and Dakota were throwing him icy stares, while Terry, Tyler, Peter and Freya kept their distance. They didn't get too involved in what went on with the group. Jonas almost snapped back at Quinn, but he fought the urge to answer back. She was right about one thing; they had more important matters to deal with.

"You said we wanted guns, right?" asked Mrs Danick standing shoulder to shoulder with Quinn.

Jonas replied with a nod. He raised his eyebrows expectantly. "You stumble across an AK-47, Mrs Danick?" It had sounded like a joke in his head, but it came out deadpan, and he instantly regretted his choice of words. As Mrs Danick shot him one of her withering looks, he could practically feel his balls shrivel up. He wasn't intentionally trying to piss everyone off, but somehow today he was messing everything up.

"No, but if you care to take your head out of your ass, you might want to look in there." Mrs Danick pointed across at two large, white tents straddling the road ahead. They were barricaded by makeshift gates and white CDC vans.

Jonas took a step forward, forgetting the conversation. His attention was now fully drawn on the tents and what might lie within. Two police cars parked outside hinted that they might not find any help inside the tents. Jonas saw one had smashed into a tree by the roadside. The front windscreen was gone, and the hood was smeared with blood. The other had taken on a fire truck, and neither had come off well. With their crumpled bodies and broken glass, they looked more like a piece of modern art with the way their twisted metal frames had melded together. Under the fire truck was a body, its legs still twitching. The head was hidden from view, and one of the huge wheels sat on the body's midriff. Jonas didn't need to go looking under the vehicle to know it was a zombie, trapped forever, destined to twitch its legs until time finally decomposed it and its dusty remnants were carried away on the breeze.

"What do you think?" asked Erik as they slowly neared the scene.

His question was meaningless. Jonas knew Erik wanted to explore the tents, to see if they could find any information, or get their hands on any useful supplies. The truth was so did he. There was a risk involved, but when wasn't there? Randall had already paid with his life, and standing still wasn't an option. They had to investigate the tents. If the CDC had set them up, there could be useful information inside, maybe even medicine or information that could help.

"You take that large front opening," said Jonas, "but be careful. Could be anything in there. Quinn, you stay with the group, in case...in case we don't come out."

Erik nodded.

"I'll go in from the rear. There should be a way in around the side there. That way we have the entrance and exits covered. I don't want any surprises, so wait until I'm in position before you go in, okay?" Jonas squeezed Dakota's hand and turned to her. "I'll be back in a second."

As he walked away he regretted his choice of words. Wasn't it bad karma to say 'I'll be back,' right before going into a dangerous situation? He could have told Dakota to stay safe, or that he loved her, but no, 'I'll be back.' The words played on his mind as he slid between two wooden gates, and slipped quietly around the side of the tent. There was complete silence, and no sign of anything moving inside, yet he gripped the axe so tightly his hands hurt. He did not want his last words to be anything as stupid or pithy as 'I'll be back.'

He heard a zipping noise, and knew Erik was about to enter the front. Jonas approached the flapping tarpaulin doorway, and with one hand he slowly drew back one side of the entrance. Peering into the gloom, he saw a tangle of wires, some chairs and tables, and a mountain of paperwork scattered about the floor. Nobody came out to greet him so he slunk through the opening, the axe raised to head height. Looking further around the first tent, he guessed it might have been some sort of checkpoint at one time. The road leading out of Jeffersontown was probably overrun with people trying to get away. By the time the CDC had set up shop, most people would've left anyway, been infected, or turned. Still, the illusion of safety had helped the great populace before, and perhaps the government thought they could pull it off again.

Too little, too late, thought Jonas as he cast his eyes over the desk to his left. A mug of curdled coffee sat by a blank computer screen, and mould grew over the lip of the mug. He was tempted to stick a finger in and suck on it; to taste coffee again would almost be worth the undoubted sickness he would suffer arising from touching that dirty mug. Seeing nothing of use, he carried on and ventured toward the next doorway. There was a lone bloody handprint on the ground, and he ignored it. Blood was such a common sight these days that unless it was pouring from a fresh wound, it was of no more significance than the sun rising. Besides, the blood was old and dry, and whoever had left it there was no longer around. He poked the axe head through another opening, and saw a room similar to the one he had just been in. This one was a little different though, as there were two dead bodies curled up in a corner. He knew they were dead; their corpses were little more than skeletons, and they had been left to rot. A few rags still covered them: tattered pieces of clothing stuck to yellow bones, and the group had no use for them. He looked across the room and noticed another figure, this one under a table, laid out flat. It was clothed in a grey Hazmat suit, and still wore protective boots and mask. In one hand was a revolver, and the man's head was in bits. It looked like the man had blown his brains out, but that didn't mean he couldn't help now. Jonas bent down and read the name badge stuck on the dead man's chest.

"Sorry, Di Maria, but I need this more than you do." Jonas took the gun. He checked and found there were still four bullets inside. Pocketing it, he saw more guns beneath the table. He didn't know much about guns, and didn't recognise them, but he would take anything he could at this point. Erik could look over them later, when they had time. Left behind in the rush to leave, the guns were going to be useful, and Jonas scooped them up in his arms. Feeling pleased they had finally come across something useful, he turned to the doorway he had come through and saw a figure stumble toward him. Its eyes were gone, nothing but shallow bloodied pits, and its jaw hung open. Strands of grey hair flew around its face, as the zombie lurched toward Jonas. Surprised, Jonas dropped the guns quickly, and raised his axe. Before he took aim, Jonas noticed the creature had something in its hands. Something red and juicy was clutched in its gnarled fingers, and Jonas thought he saw a scrap of hair protruding from its teeth. It looked like it had fed recently. The thought that there might be other survivors out there rushed over Jonas, renewing his energy, and it urged him on to take down the monster approaching him.

With one clean blow, he felled the zombie quickly and quietly. The zombie's face was cleaved in half before it even hit the ground. Jonas scooped up the guns, and decided to leave. Where there was one, more usually followed. Quinn and Tyler were more than capable of handling the odd one, but if they were suddenly surrounded, Jonas didn't like to think of the consequences. He was about to leave the way he'd come in, when he heard a scream. It was cut short abruptly, and then he heard more noise coming from the next room. A clattering sound, as if someone was banging pots and pans together erupted. He didn't want to risk leaving the guns again, in case he couldn't get back to them, but there was no way he could fight off anything while holding them all. He looked around and found a briefcase lying askew beside a bare desk. He raced over, tipped out its contents, which proved to be nothing more than a collection of old files, and a mouldy apple, and placed the guns inside. With the case in one hand, his axe in the other, he felt better equipped to deal with whatever was going on. There was another short scream, but he couldn't tell who it was. It was coming from outside the tent, but first, he had to deal with the noise in the next room. Erik might be in trouble.

Pushing aside the tent flap, Jonas strode in with his axe raised, and found Erik on the floor wrestling with a dead man. The room was trashed. The fight had taken them all around the room, and what appeared to be some sort of triage room had become a chaotic mess with medical equipment scattered everywhere. Erik was broad shouldered, and as tough as they came, but the zombie on top of him was just as large. Evidently a construction worker of some sort, judging by the yellow vest he wore, and solid work boots over dirty jeans. Jonas could tell Erik was struggling to push the dead man away. Dropping the case, Jonas immediately brought the axe down on the dead man's back. They were rolling around too much for him to risk aiming for the head, and he buried his axe deep between the zombie's shoulder blades. There was no cry of pain, or shock, but it must've been enough to alert the zombie to Jonas's presence. It turned its head, and Jonas was struck by how normal the man looked. If it weren't for his ashen skin, and a gaping hole in the dead man's neck, he could've passed for a normal, living human being.

Jonas grabbed the dead man by his feet and began pulling him off Erik. With an audible sigh, Erik succeeded in wriggling free from under the beast, and jumped up, out of reach of the zombie's snapping teeth and clawing hands.

"Mother-fucker surprised me," said Erik reaching for the Glock tucked into his belt. Without hesitating, Erik put a bullet between the man's eyes, and the huge body slumped back, the zombie still at last.

Jonas tugged on his axe, slowly freeing it, and then picked up the case full of guns. "I heard screaming from outside."

Erik nodded in confirmation. "Me too."

Both men ran, and as they left the tent Jonas noticed the rest of the rooms all looked the same as the ones he had been in. There were a couple of dead bodies, most of the meat having been eaten, and one was completely headless. Otherwise, there was nothing of use, and Erik clearly hadn't found anything. The checkpoint or whatever it was had been messed up long ago. If it wasn't for the extra weapons Jonas had picked up, it would've been yet another waste of time.

As Jonas pushed back the final flap of tarpaulin, and emerged outside into the glare of the low afternoon sun, he saw Dakota, Tyler and Mrs Danick crouched over someone lying on the ground. There was a zombie a few feet away, with a knife sticking out of its head. Erik rushed over to Pippa, who was comforting Freya.

As Jonas strode over to them, Peter approached, his eyes staring at Jonas's chest, as if afraid to make eye contact.

"What is it? What happened?" asked Jonas.

Peter stopped in front of Jonas, and slowly drew his eyes up. He spoke in a flat, monotone voice. "It caught us by surprise. It just came out of nowhere. There was nothing we could do, it was so fast, and..."

Jonas brushed past Peter and ran to Dakota. She was kneeling over Terry who lay prostrate on the ground. She was tenderly wiping his forehead, while Quinn rubbed his hands. It looked as if Terry was asleep. His eyes were closed, but he appeared unharmed.

"What happened?" asked Jonas again as he knelt down beside Dakota, dropping the case of guns. His axe clattered noisily on the ground, and he stopped himself from reaching out to Terry. If the man had been bitten, he was dangerous. He didn't have long left either, and the best thing they could do would be to leave him.

"Dakota?" Jonas wanted answers. How could one zombie do this? Terry should've been more careful. "Dakota, if he's bit we should leave him. You should get away from him." Jonas pulled at Dakota's arm, but she resisted.

"What?" Dakota looked at her husband with disdain. "Terry's not bit. He just fainted. Probably the shock."

Jonas relaxed slightly, but was puzzled. From what Peter had said, he thought someone had been hurt.

"Dakota? Was that you I heard scream?" asked Jonas. "I thought maybe... Look, like I said, if Terry's been bitten, he's a dead man. You know that. There's nothing we can do for him now."

"Jesus, Hamsikker, just give us a fucking minute," said Quinn. "God damn it."

As Terry stirred, he mumbled, and Quinn stood up. She walked over to Erik, leaving Jonas alone with Dakota and Tyler.

Dakota bit her lip, and then looked at Jonas. "You can be such an asshole."

"What did I do? Look, I found guns, ammo, we can do this. We can..."

"Jonas, just shut up will you? Terry's not been bitten, and it wasn't me screaming." Dakota pulled her arm away from him, and marched away to join Quinn.

Jonas rocked back on his heels, as Terry came around. Jonas looked up at Tyler who so far had said nothing. The young man had a smile on his face.

"You're okay, Terry, you'll be fine." Tyler looked across at Jonas, and together they helped Terry up.

"Sorry, I just...I don't know what happened. I heard Pippa screaming, and then I saw it, the zombie, the dead woman so close to me, that...I'm sorry. I guess I'm just weak. I blacked out."

Terry saw the concern on Jonas's face. "Is everything okay? Is everyone all right?"

Jonas patted Terry on the back. "I'm glad you're okay, Terry. We're all fine, in fact we..."

"No," said Tyler sighing. "We're not all fine, Hamsikker." Tyler held out his arm and showed them the back of his hand. A deep cut ran down the back of his palm, and blood oozed from it slowly.

Jonas looked at Tyler as an icy fear washed over him. "Not..."

Tyler nodded. "It's just a scratch, but I know what it means. It was a runner. Like Peter said, it came out of nowhere. Before I knew it, it had grabbed me. I managed to push Terry out of the way before Quinn took it down. But..." Tyler looked at his bleeding hand and shrugged. The smile disappeared from his face, and he looked at Jonas. Tyler's cheeks were flushed, and his eyes sparkled. "Well, Hamsikker, I guess you'll want to get away from me now."

CHAPTER NINE

As the town edge became more apparent, the roads became clearer, and the dead thinned out. Jonas knew they were still being watched, but the zombies were trapped in shops, or fenced gardens, and only the odd one reached them. When they did, they were quickly and efficiently dispatched with by Jonas, Erik, or Quinn. The axe, the aluminium baseball bat, and the claw hammer were invariably coated with blood, brains, or both, permanently. They didn't want to use their guns in case the noise drew more. There was a limited supply of bullets too, and there was no way of knowing when they would need to rely on them. Jonas insisted they only use them as a last resort. In the back of his mind, he knew he might need one for Tyler, not that he dare suggest it to any of the others.

They'd been walking barely an hour, but Tyler was obviously tiring. Randall had been different. He'd been old and weak, and he'd lost a lot of blood. With Tyler, it was barely a scratch, but it was still enough. They weren't sure how long he had, but it was decided that he would stay with them as long as possible. Jonas wondered if it was the best idea, to keep an infected among the group, but discussing it with everyone was a sure fire way to get a bullet himself. Tyler was popular with everybody. He was kind, and smart, and he'd saved Jonas's ass back at the garage. So Jonas kept quiet, and vowed to keep a close eye on him. He couldn't afford to let his guard down, no matter what. Tyler had taken it in his stride. He'd said he was going to fight the infection; that he refused to succumb to it. His body was not in accordance with his brain though, and his face had already turned a sickly pale colour. He was starting to lag behind the others, and Quinn kept him moving. Jonas saw her pass her knife to Erik, and she put an arm around Tyler's waist, helping him to walk.

They proceeded through the town in relative silence, only calling out or speaking when they were attacked. Once the zombies had been dealt with, they resumed their morbid silence. Jonas didn't need to know what was on their minds. Nobody wanted to face the reality of what was happening to Tyler, and it was as if they were all hoping the problem would just go away. Jonas was concerned about where they were heading to. In an hour, it was likely to be dark, and they still had no place to go. As they left Jeffersontown, the attacks began to become more sporadic, until finally they stopped completely. He hadn't found anywhere that could house them for the night, and was beginning to wonder if they might be sleeping out in the open. As the town buildings gave way to hills and trees, there was an increased sense of safety. The sky was darkening, but the aura of death was no longer there. At one point, a flock of starlings flew overhead. Jonas thought they might just be able to get out of town, and not look back. Perhaps it was better in the country. Perhaps there were areas clear of zombies?

"Hamsikker, hold up a second."

Erik trotted up to Jonas, and fell into step with him.

"Erik." Jonas was in no mood for another lecture, and was sceptical of what Erik wanted to talk to him about.

Erik looked about, to make sure no one could hear him speak. "Hamsikker, we need to find shelter. It's dark and quiet in the woods. Maybe we should camp out for the night. It'll be cold, but we can make it work. I don't think there are many of those things out here. We can't keep walking like this. At some point, we just have to try somewhere. One of these..."

"Erik, we can't stop now. The more distance that we put between ourselves, and Jeffersontown, the better. Who knows how many are following our trail. You want to bed down under the stars and wake up to find your arm chewed off? No, we go on. We'll find something suitable soon."

"Like what? You think we're going to stumble across a bus with a full tank of fuel? You think we're just going to walk into a nice warm home, find grandma baking fresh bead, and poppa stoking the fire? Get real, Hamsikker. Look around you. Look at Dakota. Look at Mrs Danick. Look at Tyler, for Christ's sake. They're dead on their feet."

Jonas shot Erik a look. "You think I don't know that? You think I don't care about my own wife?"

"That's not what I'm saying. Jesus." Erik sighed. "Since we left my place, things are different. Maybe it was the garage, I don't know, but whatever happened in there... I know we lost some good people. Anna, her poor girl, Mary, Cliff..."

Jonas gritted his teeth, but said nothing.

Erik continued. "We're still on the same side, you know. We all want what's best for our families, and I know you want the best for the group. Problem is, Hamsikker, the best doesn't exist anymore. You have to compromise. Make do with what you got, and right now, we're out of options. We have to stop." Erik leaned in close and spoke in a whisper. "Look, Tyler doesn't have long. I'm not going to leave him, not like this. I vowed to serve and protect, and that's what I'm doing for everyone. Not just Pippa and Peter and Freya, but everyone, including you. You're a pig-headed bastard, but you're my friend, and I can tell when you're in trouble. You're shattered."

Jonas rubbed his eyes, trying to wipe the gritty feeling away, wishing that Erik wasn't right, but knowing that he was. Erik wasn't a cop for nothing. He could cut through the bullshit in a second. He was right about Tyler. Jonas casually looked over his shoulder, and could see even Quinn was struggling to carry him now. Tyler wasn't going to last much longer.

"I just wanted to find a place that was safe and secure," said Jonas. "Somewhere we could truly rest and not have to sleep with one eye open. Walls and doors can be broken. The zombies can find a way in, slip through the cracks, and then we'll all wake up in Hell. We need a fucking castle, but there's nothing like that around, is there?"

Erik shook his head. They'd turned a corner, and suddenly Jeffersontown was out of sight. All around them were trees and fields, dotted with wooden outhouses and barns. "There's nothing around here but old farmhouses and fields of dying corn and wheat. Of course, there is the famous..."

"Wait," said Jonas, "look over there."

To their left lay a gate, and beyond it a single lane track. A few feet to the side, in a field of overgrown, dying wheat, there was an empty byre. What really intrigued Jonas though was the farmhouse that sat at the end of the track. It was two storeys high, made of red brick, and with a wooden porch where a rocking chair sat idle. The windows were dark, and no smoke came from the chimney.

"You want to see if grandma's fresh bread is as good as you remember?" asked Jonas.

"Bound to be," said Erik. "Let's check it out."

They told the others that they needed to check out the farmhouse, to see if it was a viable option to spend the night. Erik and Jonas would go investigate it, while the others hung back in the barn. It was too dangerous to all go in there. The group were too weary to answer back, and all of them happily headed to the byre to wait where they could rest out of sight from the road. They left Quinn in charge, under no illusion that were there to be any sign of trouble in the house, that she should get everyone out of there. She was not to wait, but take the guns and head back to the road. Jonas and Erik took one gun each, but they preferred to be quiet, and would only use them as a last resort. If there was any shooting done, it would only draw in the dead, and then the farmhouse would be compromised.

Jonas quietly asked Dakota to keep an eye on Tyler, in case Quinn was preoccupied, but as he prepared to leave, he could see it was irrelevant. Tyler was lying on a stack of hay in the centre of the barn, and everyone else was sitting about him. Pippa and Terry sat near the doorway, so they could keep an eye on the farmhouse from a safe distance, while Peter kept Freya occupied away from everything. He showed her the various tools hanging on the walls, but she said nothing as he pointed them out. The byre was dry, but no good to spend the night in. It was too exposed, and offered no protection should anything come their way in the night. The rusted tin roof was full of holes, and if it rained, they would get soaked through. Jonas knew the house was their best bet. Holding his trusty axe, Jonas strode out onto the dirt track, and Erik walked beside him armed with Quinn's knife. Both men kept their guns tucked in their belts, hoping they wouldn't need to use them.

Jonas took a last look at Dakota. She was bending over Tyler, soothing him with quiet words of reassurance, and wiping his brow. It was like a scene from the Bible, and Jonas could picture Tyler as Jesus, the animals and visitors around him. It seemed slightly surreal given the circumstances, but it was the first thing he thought of when he looked at them all.

"You think God's looking out for us?" asked Jonas to Erik as they walked toward the farmhouse. "I mean, Dakota's adamant, but..."

"Sure I do. No matter what He throws at us, you can't doubt Him," said Erik. "Don't get me wrong, I'm not about to lie down and ask Him to protect my family from all this. I have a Glock 22 for that. If you're asking me if I still believe, then yeah, I do. Your faith can be tested, but it's how you deal with it that matters."

Jonas grunted. Years back, Erik's family had gone to church with Jonas's, almost every week. At first, just their parents, but then the children joined in. It had started out as a chore, but soon became just another thing they did together, and Jonas remembered fondly the two of them sitting in the back of the church, laughing every time the priest mentioned the Virgin Mary. As they had grown up though, they had started taking it more seriously. It was never going to be more than what it was, but back then, in Jeffersontown, it meant something. It meant something to all of them, and he wasn't sure exactly when he'd lost his belief, but Jonas knew he'd lost it. The things he'd seen today, the people they had lost, the people who had died: they were all part of a jigsaw that led him to believe he was on his own. If Dakota ever ended up like Tyler, Jonas knew his world would fall apart. It felt like his grip on reality was nothing more than a thin wire, being stretched with every minute, and every dead body was just itching to snap it.

A crow circled overhead, and as Jonas walked up the dirt road that led to the farm, he noticed how the farm had been left to ruin. The field of crops had withered and died, and the track had been churned up badly. It seemed that a lot of feet had been up and down the road, turning the mud into a thick chunky soup. Garbage was strewn over the yard, and as they approached the farm, it began to look more like a wasteland. It had been neglected, left to rot, and Jonas began to think there was little point in even going any further. The house was in a poor condition. As he neared it, he could see the windows broken, the glass cracked, and the wooden slatted frames hanging askew. The front door was hanging off its hinges, and a cold wind was ushering him toward it, like an open mouth to Hell.

There was a garage to the side, and they crossed the yard to it. Cautiously, he opened the door, and it swung back with a large creak. The inside was gloomy, but empty, and he ventured in with Erik behind him. There was an old tractor in the centre of the garage, rusted and stripped for parts. Shelving and tool boxes covered the walls, and Jonas's feet scuffed against a dead bird as he walked around the garage examining things. Looking around, he saw nothing of use, and was about to leave, when a glint of light reflected back at him. A single jar sat perched on one of the top shelves, and he reached up to grab it. Ignoring Erik's questions of what he'd found, he dusted off the lid and opened it. He knew instantly from the smell what it was. The last time he'd drunk moonshine was with Erik. They were only fifteen. One of the older kids brought it to school one day so they snuck out of class early, and they all had a taste. The same smell reached his nostrils now, and he sipped from the jar. It was still disgusting, and he coughed as the foul liquid burnt his throat. He wiped his mouth before offering it to Erik. Silently, the big man drank, and then drank some more before passing it back to Jonas. The burn made Jonas feel alive, and they quickly finished the jar.

Leaning back against the rusting red tractor, Jonas wished he could just stay in the garage. His legs were heavy, and it would be so easy just to crawl into a corner and sleep. The others were grown adults, they could handle themselves. Erik could search the house, and he could rest, just for a little while. If only he could close his eyes and sleep. When he did close his eyes though, he kept seeing terrible images, a slideshow of horrible things that he couldn't forget. He saw horrible things that he'd done, and wished he could change things, but there was no going back. Perhaps when Tyler passed, he could move on. It wasn't like he wanted the young man dead, but he was a reminder. He'd hardly spoken to him since the morning. Perhaps it was better that way. Perhaps it would be better if Tyler were dead, before they got back.

"Come on, Hamsikker, we need to check out the house," said Erik standing in the garage doorway. The man's face was flushed, and he looked embarrassed.

"Don't worry, Erik," said Jonas. "You're allowed. You're not on duty anymore."

Jonas walked over to the doorway.

"Are you kidding? I'm always on duty," said Erik.

Together, the men approached the farmhouse.

"So, now what?" asked Jonas. "It looks quiet, but…"

"Let me go first," said Erik. "I've done enough house searches to know how to handle this. We go in through the front door, quietly. If it's clear, I'll go on upstairs and check around while you check the ground floor. Sweep the rooms first. Once we're in the clear, we can see if there's anything useful, and get back to the others. If we're lucky, we may just be able to bunk here for the night."

Jonas nodded, and followed Erik, not for one second believing they were going to get lucky. He saw Erik take up position by the front door, his back flat against the wall. He held his knife out ready, and then stepped inside quietly, motioning with a deft flick of his hand for Jonas to follow him. Jonas could see that Erik had lost none of his expertise. All his training was kicking back in. It was as if he was back at work, doing nothing more than going on an everyday drugs-bust. There was more than likely worse inside the farmhouse than a bag of weed though, and Jonas held his axe in both hands firmly. The moonshine had made him feel relaxed, but the feeling was gone so quickly. He was on edge again, worried about what they might find inside. Was it too much to ask for that it was deserted?

Floorboards creaked and groaned as he followed Erik inside. Jonas saw movement. It was as if the very walls were alive, and when he looked closer, he saw bugs. There were hundreds of bugs everywhere. Cockroaches and beetles scuttled up and down the walls, ants and spiders scurried over each other, and moths and flies flew around the ceiling lazily. Jonas put a hand over his mouth to try and keep the stench out. He could smell it, taste it, and feel it washing over him like a wave of death. Jonas looked across at Erik, but if he'd smelt it too, then he was not showing it. The farmhouse had seen death, and it had not let go.

Erik was scanning the foyer carefully, his eyes looking up at the grand staircase in the middle of the room, then back to the doors that lay on either side. There was a dusty fake chandelier hanging above them that seemed to be swaying slightly in the gloom, as though someone was pushing it. The air was stifling, and the house reeked of death. Jonas tapped Erik on the shoulder and whispered to him that they should leave.

"Stick to the plan." Erik shook his head. "From the state of the place, I'd say there's one dead body in here, if not more, but that's no reason to bolt now. We need to check it out."

Erik placed a foot on the first step, and began stealthily to creep up the stairs. Each foot he took left a print behind, and Jonas wasn't sure if the steps were covered in dust or blood. The house was dark. Even though there was still a semblance of light outside, it was as if the house was forcing it away, revelling in the desolate gloom, embracing its new found evil. The building seemed unsteady, as if it has given up on living and wanted to go to the other side, where no one comes back from.

Jonas crossed the floor to a closed door, and pushed it open. The wooden door swung back slowly, a faint creak echoing throughout the room as it did so. Jonas could see a living room of sorts through the doorway. Everything was coated in a fine layer of dust and dirt. He saw two lazy-boys, a silent TV set with bent rabbit ears, a sideboard adorned with photo frames, and a dark green couch that was stained with something orange and sticky. Jonas wandered around the room, seeing little of interest, and purposely ignored the photographs. He didn't need to know who had lived here. Whoever the occupants were, they were evidently long gone. The fireplace sat cold and empty, but it could be started again, and Jonas saw a pile of kindling next to the hearth, clearly collected and stacked up ready. Whoever had lived here probably thought they would need it to get them through winter. Perhaps, if it wasn't damp, Jonas thought, they could use it now and get some warmth in them tonight.

He crossed to another door on the far side of the room. This one was already open, and it led to a kitchen. The room was small, but practical, with a square window perched above a stainless steel sink, still full of dirty crockery. There was a small table in the middle of the room, and the chairs were still neatly tucked under. He began to search through the cupboards, looking for food. He brushed aside the centipedes and spiders that hid in every corner, hoping to find something he could take back to the others.

"Not even a damn tin of tuna?" he said as he rummaged through the kitchen. Drawers were slung aside as he searched for any food, but he drew a blank. The house had already been emptied, and anything useful had been taken. There was nothing. Even the fridge was empty. Cursing, he looked out of the window, into a small garden surrounded by ash trees. There were three bodies on the lawn, laid out in a row beneath the twilight and a weeping willow tree. They weren't moving, or breathing. Jonas decided it didn't warrant investigation. It could be the family who had lived here, it could be the dead, it could be something, or it could be nothing. As long as they stayed out there, they were nothing to him. The garden was off limits for now anyway. They were checking the house out, and if the dead were in the garden, who cared. He wasn't looking for more dead bodies. He'd seen enough of those today.

Jonas retraced his steps back to the foyer, hearing the occasional creak and groan from upstairs as Erik went from room to room. Jonas saw another door, nestled under the staircase, and pulled open the door. The room was tiny, cold, and had been some sort of bathroom-cum-storage closet. There was a toilet, a cracked dirty sink, and mirrored cabinet above it. Opposite the toilet, there was an ironing board, a mop, and a collection of cleaning materials. One look at the scuzzy toilet was enough to tell Jonas he didn't want to stay in the room for too long. It was blocked, and the white porcelain now stained with a hue of rich colours that defied logic. The floor around his feet was sticky and wet. The smell was only worse in here, but he knew he had to look in the cabinet. Tyler was in pain, and if there was any medicine inside, Jonas had to get it.

He wiped the dust coating the cabinet mirror, and rested his hands on the sink. His reflection surprised him. He felt tired, and knew he looked far worse. The dark bags under his eyes were a clear indication of how weary he felt, but he actually looked older. It was as if the last six months had aged him six years. Just the last six hours were enough to send him over the edge. Stubble grew over his chin and neck, as shaving was a rare occurrence, not to mention painful without water. His greying hair was shiny and flecks of blood covered his skin; washing away the evidence of the day's bloody work was a tricky business, and going for days without washing at all was now the norm. He turned the tap, but nothing came out. The pipes groaned and ached, sending wailing sounds around the house, but no water came.

Jonas turned the tap off, frustrated, and pulled open the cabinet on the wall. The three small shelves contained within it were all near empty, but coated with an inch of dust and yet more spiders. There was a half empty roll of toothpaste, some cotton swabs, and a couple of vials of unmarked pills. Shoving them all into his pockets, he left, pleased to be out of there. The confines of the small bathroom had given him the shivers. The house was turning out to be a dead end. They might be able to spend the night, but with the doors and windows broken, it wasn't very secure. As he crossed the foyer, he looked up the staircase, wondering how Erik was getting on. Jonas thought about calling up to him, but it was too risky. Better not to startle him, or let anyone hiding know of their presence. Jonas kept quiet, and tried the last door. As it swung back, if creaked ominously, sending something small and furry scurrying for cover. It ran over Jonas's feet as he stood in the doorway, and he almost brought his axe down on it. It would've been a sure fire way to lose a couple of toes, and he managed to get a grip on his nerves. The rat, or whatever it was, had run off, and Jonas was left with nothing but the sound of his own beating heart thumping loudly in his head. He took a step into the room, a sort of dining room and office combination, and the smell hit him. It was far worse than the foyer, and Jonas put his arm across his face to mask the stink. An armchair sat facing the doorway, and the body slumped on it had been dead a long time. Buzzing flies swarmed the air as Jonas approached slowly, his axe raised, his eyes watering as the smell permeated his clothing, and soaked into his skin. The identity of the dead body would forever be a mystery. Jonas guessed it was a man, probably the farmer who lived here going by the work boots and dungarees on the body, but even if he had looked at the photographs in the other room, he still wouldn't have been able to recognise him. The man had blown his head off. A shotgun still lay nestled in the man's arms, its barrel pointed upward where the man's face should've been. Splattered on the wall was dried blood, traces of it arcing all the way from the floor to the ceiling. Chunks of brain and skull still stuck to the flocked wallpaper like crude decorations. The ceiling was flecked with blood too, and matted hair adorned hunks of flesh. Jonas saw writhing maggots crawling around the man's neck, swimming in his death. The body had decomposed, and must've been dead for some time. Yellow skin was stretched tightly across the man's bony fingers, and the clothes were loose, as if the man had shrunk into the chair.

Jonas's hands were shaking, and he couldn't take any more. He turned to leave, but as he planted a foot on the floor, he trod on a sizeable piece of skull that had come from the dead man. Jonas's feet slipped from beneath him, and with a crash, he landed flat on his back, his axe falling from his hands as he hit the hard wood flooring. His eyes flickered shut, and his brain thought about shutting down. Pain coursed through him, and he knew he had to get up. There was a creaking sound from above his head, and Jonas lifted a hand to feel his head. There was no cut that he could find, but as he felt around, he kept touching the feet of the dead man. The creaking sound grew, and Jonas could sense what was happening before he could do anything about it. His fall had dislodged the body, and slowly it was tipping out of the chair. Jonas opened his mouth to shout, but it was too late, and the body of the dead farmer fell forward. It tipped out of the chair and landed right on top of Jonas. Dead fingers caressed his face, as the surprisingly heavy body covered him. Maggots showered down over Jonas, obliterating his vision. Thick, juicy, crawling maggots fell down the collar of his shirt, wriggling into his hair and nesting in the crook of his shoulders. Jonas kicked himself free, pushing aside the bloated body, spitting and shouting as he scrambled to his feet. He ripped open his shirt, brushing frantically at his chest, pulling the maggots off him, and all the creepy crawlies that had been living on the body. Jonas's mouth was dry, but he summoned up enough saliva to spit again, desperate to make sure he didn't swallow anything.

"Fuck this." Jonas swore as he buttoned his shirt back up. He was shaking, cursing, hopping from foot to foot, and frantically shouting to Erik to hurry up and come down. This place was a death trap. What were they thinking? As he began to calm down, he realised the farmer's shotgun had fallen free, and he picked it up. If they could find some shells, it would be very useful. The door creaked open, and Jonas felt a little embarrassed about how he had reacted.

"Sorry, Erik, I didn't mean to shout like that. This fucker caught me by surprise." Jonas examined the shotgun in his hands. It was cold, but with a little cleaning, it should work fine.

There was no reply from Erik, but Jonas heard the footsteps cross the room, each one causing the floorboards to creak.

"Look, Erik, I said I'm sorry." Jonas turned to face his friend, to rebut another lecture, but discovered that Erik wasn't there. A woman faced Jonas, long blonde hair wrapped about her face, hiding her eyes. The woman was tall and thin, her arms hanging slack by her side. She wore a blue dress covered in white flowers, and her feet were as bare as her arms. As she walked toward Jonas, she said nothing.

"Say, are you..." Jonas wanted the woman to speak, but she said nothing, and kept walking toward him. "Look, lady, we don't want any trouble."

Jonas raised the shotgun and pointed it at the woman. She was only a few feet away from him, and still shuffling toward him. The dead farmer lay at Jonas's feet, and Jonas felt uneasy. What if this woman had been hiding inside the house, waiting for help? What if she was the farmer's wife, or daughter, and she thought Jonas had killed him? He was holding the shotgun, and it looked to all intents and purposes as if he was guilty.

"I'm sorry," said Jonas lowering the gun, "it's just..."

A low moan escaped the woman's lips. She raised a hand and leant forward. Beneath the shaggy fronds of hair hiding her face, Jonas could see her mouth open, or at least what was left of her mouth. Her lower jaw was gone, and she had only a row of neat teeth along her upper jaw. With one more step he could see more, see her dead eyes and the bruising on her skin. As the dead woman lunged for him, he quickly raised the shotgun and pulled the trigger. Nothing happened, and the woman knocked it aside easily. Jonas felt around for his axe, but remembered he had lost it when he'd fallen to the floor. He could smell the woman now, only a foot away from him. Months of decay and rot were billowing out to him, and he knew the zombie must've been hanging around the farm somewhere. She'd probably snuck through the open doorway whilst they'd been looking inside. The woman raised her other hand and the fingertips touched his chest. There was no way past her, nowhere to run, nowhere to hide. He had to get rid of the zombie approaching him, and fast. The woman's upper jaw was moving, and she might not be able to bite him, but he knew that it only took one scratch from those teeth on his skin, and he was done for.

Jonas reached behind him, pulled the gun from his belt, and fired three times at the woman. The force sent her spinning backward, tripping over the dead farmer, and crashing into a small wooden desk. A computer and lamp rolled off, crashing to the floor, and the woman staggered to her side before finding her composure and resuming her hunt for Jonas. He had punched three bullets into her chest, one right through the heart, but she'd been too close for a head shot. This time though, he aimed, and pointed at her face. Her greasy blonde hair was swept back around her neck, and he could see her eyes. He used them as a focus point for the gun in the gloomy room. As a beam of light caught her eyes, he remembered the last time he had pointed a gun at someone. That person had been living, breathing, and moving. He remembered the last time he had killed someone. Was that why was it so hard to pull the trigger now? The woman was going to kill him if he didn't, but when he saw those eyes, he hesitated. It was so final. The woman, whoever she was, had been living once. She had loved and cared for someone, been someone's daughter, perhaps someone's mother. Maybe she was the farmer's wife. Jonas felt sick. She had taken time one morning to put on that nice blue and white dress, to choose it, perhaps thinking it brought out the blue in her eyes, only to die that day. Now he had to put a bullet in her brain, and end it. His hands shook, and sweat dripped down his face as he aimed between her eyes at the top of her nose. Any second now, she was going to take a chunk out him He knew he had to pull the trigger.

Shoot her.

Kill her.

Kill the dead.

A booming shot rang out, and the woman crumpled to the floor. Her head was ripped from her shoulders, and her skull was blown apart from the gunshot that Erik had put in her.

"What the fuck, Hamsikker? You got a death wish?"

Erik stood in the doorway to the room, his eyes taking in the dead farmer on the floor, the blonde woman who had now joined him, and Jonas.

Erik looked at Jonas as if he were mad. He knew he was covered in blood and gore from the farmer, but he had brushed off most of it. He lowered his gun, and stepped toward Erik. The man was clean, calm, and Jonas noticed how thick his beard had grown. It was so thick and red now that Erik was beginning to look more like a Viking every day. They often joked as teenagers that Erik was descended from them, and his nickname had been Erik the Red. Erik the Angry would be more appropriate now.

"You need a shave," said Jonas. His heart was still beating wildly, but the danger had passed, and he was starting to calm down. With Erik at his side, he felt like they could accomplish anything.

Erik put a hand on Jonas's chest as he tried to leave the room. He leant his red face toward Jonas, so close that he could smell the moonshine still on his breath. "Hamsikker. What the hell was that? That bitch was about to have you for dinner, and you just stand there like a mannequin. Where's your axe?"

Damn it. Jonas realised he had almost left without it, and he retrieved the axe from where it had fallen. "Thanks, I almost forgot it."

Erik licked his lips. He checked behind him, making sure there were no more surprises. "Well?"

"Look, it's not a big deal. I just froze. I was about to shoot her. But after the damn farmer fell on me, I just freaked out a little. It's nothing." Jonas wanted out of the room with the two dead bodies, out of the farmhouse, out of Jeffersontown, and to get as far away as possible. A minute ago he would've gone anywhere with Erik, done anything for him. Now he hated him. If only he could click fingers and be in Canada with Dakota, Janey and the kids.

"Nothing?" Erik laughed. "You call that nothing? We were supposed to be doing this *quietly*, Hamsikker. I heard you clattering about down here, shouting your head off, shooting the place up, and then you make me fire my gun too."

"So fucking what?" asked Jonas. He could feel his anger rising, but couldn't stop it. "So fucking what?" he shouted. "This house is useless. It's completely fucking useless. There's nothing here, just a dead family and a world of shit. We have to move on. It's not safe to stay here, you must know that. The windows and doors are all broken. The place is empty, Erik. There's no food, no water, and no drugs for Tyler. We're way too close to town. Even if we stayed overnight, there's no defence. If the zombies from town found us, we'd have nowhere to go. You keep telling me to get my head together, but I think it's you who needs to get it together."

Erik laughed again, only this time it was deep and quiet. He took a step toward Jonas and raised his finger. "You're right, this place is useless. There's nothing upstairs, just some empty bedrooms, a bunch of kid's toys and a closet full of mouldy clothes. But it was quiet, and far enough from the road that we *could've* stayed here a while. Maybe only a few hours, but it would've been enough for us to get some rest. What with you shooting your mouth off as much as your gun, they'll be heading this way from miles around. Look, Hamsikker, from now on, *I'm* deciding what we do. We tried it your way, and it didn't work. I can't have Pippa and my children at risk, because of you. I don't know what's going through your head, but…"

Jonas charged at Erik and landed a punch on the side of the man's head. Together they fell to the ground, grappling with one another, trying to land punches, only failing because there was no room to swing. Jonas managed to hit Erik in the kidneys, before Erik retaliated, forcing Jonas back with a succession of quick punches to the jaw. It only took a few seconds, before Erik was on top, and had Jonas pinned down. He forced Jonas onto his back, and held his arms, causing him to squeal in pain.

"Get the fuck off of me," said Jonas through gritted teeth. "You're not a cop anymore, Erik, so back off. This how you treat your friends, there's no wonder you joined up. Typical cop, huh."

"You say one more word, and I'll break your arm," said Erik.

Jonas stopped struggling. He knew Erik was stronger than he was. Erik knew how to deal with fights too, and Jonas knew there was no getting out of the arm lock that Erik had him in.

Panting heavily, Erik spoke through deep breaths. "You're certifiable. You know that, Hamsikker?"

Erik paused for breath. He loosened his grip on Jonas slightly, enough to give him some freedom, but not enough to let him out just yet.

"I'm exhausted," said Erik. "I'm too fucking tired to fight you. So here's the deal. You want to stick with us, you stop going off gung-ho, trying to save the world with this macho bullshit, or whatever it is you think you're doing. This last twenty four hours, since we left my house, you're acting different. No, not since we left the house, since we left the garage. Whatever's eating at you, deal with it, and quickly."

Erik got off Jonas, and the two men sat up, looking at each other. They stayed in silence for a moment before Jonas offered an apology. He knew he had to, even though he didn't feel like apologising.

"I'm sorry about the cop thing. I didn't mean it. Look, don't worry about me, Erik. I just need some time to adjust. I need the world to get better, to be someplace safe for Dakota, and... Hell, I don't know. We'll do things your way."

There was a cough in the doorway, and both men looked up to see Dakota stood in the doorway. In the growing darkness, all Jonas could see was her red eyes. He wondered how long she had been standing there, and what she'd heard. When she spoke, her voice was sombre and quiet.

"When you two boys have finished playing, we need you to come help bury Tyler. He died a few minutes ago."

CHAPTER TEN

The fields of dead sprang to life, and from far around they came. A few here, a few there, all in varying states of decay, but all with one common goal; the noise had been tremendous, and amidst the quiet fields of Kentucky, there was now only one point of interest for the hundreds of zombies that had left the city. A lone, white van, sitting upside down and idle, promised more than field-mice and solitude; noises like that suggested the living were present, and the living meant food. A farmhand, Darron, once a young boy with a promising future, was first on the scene. He had died early on in the outbreak, having been bitten by his employer, who had returned from Jeffersontown earlier in the day from getting supplies. The farmer had been bitten by a crazy man on the street, but instead of heading to hospital for help, decided to head home where he could fix himself up and not bother anyone. Unfortunately, over the course of the day, the man had succumbed to the infection, and when Darron eventually found him, the dead man took a chunk out of the boy's neck. Darron had soon taken a chunk out of the next door neighbour's dog, and not long after that, nobody took much notice of who was taking chunks out of whom anymore.

Darron approached the van steadily. His body was in poor shape, having spent so many of the summer months in the open air, and he walked with a limp, dragging his left foot behind him. If it weren't for his broken ankle, he probably would've been able to achieve his goal, and would've found three warm, juicy bodies waiting for him. As it was, his foot scraping on the ground was enough to wake Rose, and he was to taste nothing more than the steel blade that entered through his jaw, and penetrated his brain.

"Fucking piece of shit," said Rose as she dropped the dead boy. He fell at her feet, and she looked at where the zombie had come from. There were more of them, out in the fields, and nothing was going to stop them now.

Rose turned to the van, and her knees buckled. As she fell to the ground, she felt her head spin, and she placed her palms flat on the ground as she waited for the dizzy spell to pass. She knew she'd been lucky to wake up when she did, and even luckier to find her blade resting right on her lap. At first, she had shouted for Javier to wake up, but he was motionless, bent over next to her, blood dripping from a fresh cut to his head. There hadn't been time to wake him up before she heard the first of the moans. Rose had pulled herself free of the passenger seat, fully aware that if she didn't take care of the zombies, she and Javier were as good as dead.

She sucked in a mouthful of air, letting the oxygen renew her senses, and then spat out a mouthful of blood. She'd felt better, but nothing was broken, and a few cuts and bruises were the least of her worries. She heard another scraping sound from behind her, and turned to face her attacker.

A thin woman approached, long grey hair sweeping over bare shoulders, and sunburnt arms. The woman was dressed in a brown tunic, covered in dirt and grime, and her shoes made scratching sounds as she shuffled across the road towards Rose. Heaving her weary body to her feet, Rose grabbed her blade, and made the first move, swinging the knife at the zombie's head. The blade struck bone and rebounded sharply, succeeding in only cutting a wedge of skin from the woman's face. It hung down like a slice of pizza, and Rose swung again as the zombie groaned. The blade struck true this time, slicing through the dead brain, and Rose staggered back out of reach as the woman fell down dead, the knife lodged firmly into the woman's skull.

There were more moaning sounds drifting over the breeze, and Rose realised she was going to have to work something out quickly. The sky was turning a deep blue, and the van was still smoking. They had to get away from the crash site, and find somewhere to stay the night. She didn't even know if Javier could walk. Leaving him behind never crossed her mind, and she retrieved her knife from the dead woman's skull. She looked around, and noticed the nearest zombie was a good two hundred yards away. Javier had not emerged from the van, so she was going to have to get him out. As she walked across the road, littered with glass, she heard a faint moaning coming from up ahead. She couldn't see anything, but it was unmistakeable. It appeared to be coming from the ditch, and she couldn't risk ignoring it. It was closer than the others were, much closer. She didn't want to be surprised whilst she freed Javier from the van, so she wiped the blade on her jeans, and walked up the road ahead, looking for the source of the moaning sounds.

No more than fifty feet away, Rose found a hand lying in the road. It had been sliced off with a precision cut, as if it had been severed in a hurry. What puzzled Rose more was that, whilst the hand was missing an owner, it was in an otherwise perfect condition; the skin was clean, and the fingers were only slightly grazed. A tiny pool of blood had formed around the severed wrist, and Rose saw something shining in the blood. One decapitated finger still wore a gold ring, and Rose tugged it off, putting it on her hand.

"One day, Javier," Rose said admiring the small diamond in the centre of the ring.

Rose looked to the side of the road for the hand's owner. A body lay submerged in the undergrowth, and Rose would have passed it by except a leg lay protruding from a bush. The moaning sound came again, and Rose stepped carefully over the ditch, parting the thicket to find Cindy lying on the ground. Her legs were shattered, and her face looked like it had been put through a blender. One eye had burst, and tiny shards of glass stuck from her arms and legs, making her look like a human pin-cushion.

Rose smiled. "Hi, Cindy."

A thin moan escaped Cindy's lips, and her one working eye looked lazily up at Rose. She tried to speak, but only a trickle of blood came from her blue lips as she wheezed.

"Hurt much?" Rose knelt down on the ground beside Cindy. "Well, that's not how I intended things to go for you, but I guess you never know what's around the corner. Poor you."

Rose stroked Cindy's hair back from her face, and then brought her blade out, dangling it in front of Cindy's eye. A lone tear fell from Cindy's eye and turned to orange as it mixed with the dried blood on her cheek.

"Stick, or twist? Stick, or twist? It's a little game I like to play, but then you know that already. Hmmm, stick, or twist?"

Cindy raised her arm to fend off Rose, but only had the energy to raise it a few inches off the ground before it fell back down again. Rose watched as Cindy's good eye looked away.

"What, I'm not good enough for you? You can't bear even to look at me? I'm helping you out here, Cindy. What do you say we go back to the van, and get Javier out together?"

Cindy didn't answer, couldn't answer, and Rose heard a faint moaning sound coming over the wind.

"I thought as much. Well, sadly, due to unforeseen circumstances and time constraints, I don't have time to play today. It's going to have to be stick."

Rose plunged her blade into Cindy's remaining eye, causing it to burst, and Cindy shuddered, letting out a squeal of pain like a stuck pig. Rose noticed Cindy didn't move much, and wondered if her spine had been broken in the crash. Rose retracted the knife, having only stuck it in far enough to blind Cindy, not wanting to kill her. Cindy managed to get her hand up to her face, and put it over her eye. Blood and slime coated her fingers, and Rose laughed.

"Enjoy being dead, won't you," said Rose as she got to her feet. "I was going to kill you, but I figure I'd rather you were eaten alive. Javier wouldn't have touched a gutless skank like you. I know your type. You're just a common whore who got what was coming." Rose spat on the ground. "Fucking bitch."

Rose left Cindy in the ditch to await her fate. Javier was still in the van, and she was going to have to get him out by herself. She quickly jogged back to the van, and crawled in through the front window, ignoring the glass on the ground that was tearing into her legs. Javier was out cold, and Rose wrapped her arms around his shoulders. Slowly, she inched him out of the cab, and pulled him free. He had numerous cuts to his face, and a particularly nasty looking bump forming above his right eye, but other than that, Rose had no idea if he was seriously injured. She gently shook him, aware that the zombies were getting closer.

"Come on, honey, please wake up."

There was no other vehicle on the road, other than the SUV they had smashed into, and it was now a useless heap of twisted metal. Wherever they were going, they were doing it on foot. Rose realised she might have to carry Javier if he didn't wake up soon. She could get past the zombies on her own, but carrying someone at the same time might be too much. What if she encountered a runner? What if she stumbled across a group of them? She was going to need both hands to defend herself, and if she had to, Javier was going to have to fend for himself, unconscious or not.

"Fuck." Rose sighed and stood up. She had her knife, but the gun was long gone. There might be something she could use in the van, but it was unlikely. It had seemed empty when they had climbed in back at the diner. She looked up and down the road, but there was nothing; there was literally nobody to help. To the east, across a field of rotting vegetables, was the fence she had seen earlier. It was intact as far as she could see, and stretched for quite some distance. Fences and walls were good. They kept the living from the dead, and whoever had erected it was probably still alive. It was her only chance. She stepped away from Javier and took a few steps into the field. Her feet sank into the soft earth, and she looked harder at the fence. Between it and the road, there were three or four zombies, but she was confident she could take them on. She could run to the fence, get over it, and hopefully get help for Javier. If he stayed unconscious, perhaps the dead would ignore him. She knew it was unlikely, but there didn't seem to be much choice. They'd had a good run, and she hated leaving him, but what options did she have? Stand and fight until it got dark? For all she knew, Javier might never wake up. Damn, that Cindy had fucked it all up. Rose was glad she hadn't killed her. Let her rot in peace.

"Right then," said Rose, summoning up the courage to head across the open field for the fence.

"Rose?"

Startled, Rose turned around to see Javier standing before her.

"Where are you going?" Javier asked. He clutched his stomach, and bent over in pain.

"Oh my God, Javier!" Rose ran to Javier, and embraced him. He winced in pain as she grabbed him, but she didn't care, he was alive, and that was all that mattered.

"What the hell happened?" Javier looked at Rose, studying the cuts on her face.

"We hit something in the road. Oh Javier, I'm so...so..."

Rose surprised herself when she started to cry. She held onto Javier, reluctant to let him go, squeezing his body and reassuring herself that she wasn't imagining it. Her eagle was still here, still breathing. It was so much better than being alone.

"Shit," said Javier looking at the van, "what a mess. Are you okay?"

Rose nodded. "I'm fine, but we need to get out of here. The dead are all over the place. Can you walk?"

Javier limped along painfully, but he reassured Rose he could walk. Rose helped him across the ditch into the vegetable field.

"That's where we're going," she told him pointing at the fence. "It's our best bet. Put a nice big barrier between them and us for the night. You need to rest up, honey, you don't look too good," said Rose.

"I've felt better," said Javier as they began to trudge through the field. Beneath their feet were the remnants of cabbages. Their sad, yellow leaves had large holes in them where bugs had fed. "Wait," said Javier stopping abruptly, "where's Cindy?"

Rose pulled Javier along. "She didn't make it," said Rose bluntly. "I found her body up ahead. She got thrown out of the van when we crashed. A piece of glass sliced her throat, and she was dead before I got to her."

"*Dead*, dead?" asked Javier as they continued walking. "You know, like normal dead, or like..."

"Don't worry, she's not coming after us," said Rose. She tried to keep the satisfaction from her voice when she spoke. "Her head was crushed. Her brain was splattered all over the road. She won't be going anywhere. She's *dead*, dead."

They walked on in silence across the field, dirt sucking at their ankles, and a cold breeze filling the evening air. Halfway across, Rose told Javier to sit and wait, and he did so without complaint. Up ahead were four zombies, close enough now to smell. Rose took them down one by one, slicing each one through the brain with her knife. Once they were down, she returned to Javier, and they carried on towards the fence, their path now clear.

"What do you think's on the other side?" asked Rose. They stopped on a wide road that ran the length of the fence. Several large oak trees loomed over them, and she knew they needed to get in as quick as possible before the daylight evaporated entirely. "I mean, there could be literally anything on the other side, right?"

Javier shrugged, and clutched his stomach. "Search me." He didn't see the point in conjecture. It would be what it was, and he examined the fence. Getting over wouldn't be easy. The fence was solid metal, and there were no gaps in it. On the top lay thick barbed wire. There were no doors or gates, and no signs marking an exit or entrance. "Come on. Let's try our luck down this way."

Javier took Rose's hand and they started walking south, away from the van and the zombies, away from Jeffersontown, and hopefully away from any more trouble. Javier hadn't felt this bad since he was fourteen. He had been sleeping rough behind the old downtown rail station in Austin, and woken up to find two men standing over him. They demanded that he go with them someplace warm, somewhere they could help him get off the street, but it was clear they weren't looking out for his welfare. Living on the streets, he soon became used to being approached for sex by older men. He refused, and told them that he would call the cops if they didn't leave him alone. One of them went to leave, but the other stayed, demanding Javier go with them. When he called the man a queer, he received a punch to the side of the head in reply. Before he could get on his feet, they laid into him, kicking and punching, until he passed out. He awoke the next day to find he was where they had left him, sheltering beneath an old arch, surrounded by rats and garbage. He took his beating, telling himself it was better than going along with what they *really* wanted to do with him, and it knocked him out for a week. Unable to scavenge, he lived on scraps of food, and waited for the bruising to fade before he could walk again. It was a wake-up call too though, and as painful as it was, it was a useful lesson. Since that day, he had taught himself how to defend himself properly, and he never backed down from a fight. Now he felt the same, as if his head had been used as a football, and his gut ached. The cuts would heal, but he had been stupid to let Cindy drive. He should've seen it coming, and known she wasn't up to it; it had cost Cindy her life, and almost cost Javier and Rose theirs. He was thinking with his dick, not his brains, and the price was a hefty one for his misjudgement.

"Could sure use a shot of Crown right about now," said Javier. He had not spoken a more honest word in days.

"Don't know about that, honey. Tequila maybe? Just a little something to see us right - to get us through the night."

Javier couldn't help but laugh. "I'm sorry, but that sounds like a bad country song. You just make that up?"

Rose laughed. "You know I ain't got a musical bone in my body. I couldn't tell you the difference between a piano and a pitchfork."

Javier laughed again, and creased over as a shot of pain coursed through his chest.

"Damn," he wheezed. "You know, I think I busted a rib. Sure does hurt."

"Look, there's a sign up ahead. Maybe it'll tell us a way in." Rose hurried ahead of Javier, skipping ahead like a schoolgirl going out to lunch.

They hadn't been in this much trouble for a long time, yet, they had managed to share a joke, and Rose was acting as though she hadn't a care in the world. Maybe she was finally getting it. Back at the diner, she had been a pain in the ass, and Javier was starting to remember the crash. Rose had been a handful in the van, and he remembered seeing the world upside down briefly, before he blacked out. Rose hadn't caused the crash, but her behaviour had distracted him from Cindy.

"Javier, quick, come look at this."

He took his place by Rose's side, and admired the huge sign that hung between two black, ornate lamp-posts. It was a little dusty, but otherwise, painted very neatly and sharply.

"Saint Paul's Golf Course. Welcome to the most prestigious PGA Championship Golf course in the USA."

Rose whistled. "Read that bottom part about intruders. Says they fenced off the course for member's privacy and protection.

Access is strictly limited and the public entrance can be found on the north-east quadrant, from Memorial Avenue only."

Javier and Rose looked at each other.

"You know, unless someone's punched a hole in this fence, we may just have a good bed for the night. These rich folk aren't going to do a half-assed job, and I bet this fence could hold out a small army." Javier strode over the small grass verge, and put a hand on the fence. The metal was cold, and no matter how much he pushed, the fence didn't move. It was solid.

"This doesn't change anything, you know," he said.

Rose frowned. "Of course it does. It means we have somewhere to stay. Assuming there are no zombies inside, then it's perfect. Safe, secure; it's just what we need, Javier."

Javier wasn't about to get into another debate with her about the merits of settling down. She had been itching to feather the nest for a while, and he couldn't take yet another argument about heading north to find his brother. "We can rest a while, maybe a few days, but no more. After that, we move north, as planned. All we need to do now is find a way in."

"I guess we have to go find the main entrance. I could probably get us past a few zombies, but it won't be easy the shape you're in," said Rose. "I hope we can find the public entrance soon."

Javier felt affronted by Rose's suggestion that he was weak, but the truth was that he was exhausted. He had no weapons, no idea where they were, and no idea if they would survive the night out in the open. Getting over that fence was priority number one.

"We don't need to," said Javier. "The main entrance is for show. All those rich folks want a fancy entrance they can drive their Jags and Limos through, so the press can get a good shot of just how obscenely rich they are. You think the cleaners use the same door? You think when they empty the garbage bags that they just throw them out the front door? No, we find the back door. There's always a secret door for the working schlepps. It won't be anything fancy, but it'll be there. Let's keep heading east, away from the main entrance. It might be well hidden, so we'll have to watch out for it. If they secured this place prior to the outbreak, they may have boarded it up, or disguised it somehow. Perhaps they covered it with something."

With the zombies at a safe distance, they began searching for a way in. With the barbed wire on top, there was no way of getting over the fence, and the low-hanging branches of the nearby trees had all been trimmed to avoid anyone trying to use them to climb up and over. As they walked, they talked. At first, about the diner, and how they had foolishly let their guard down and nearly been trapped. Rose had apologised for being so wild, for acting so crazy, and Javier apologised for letting things get out of control. After walking a while, and finding no way into the golf course, they found a quiet spot beneath a tall elm. It was well hidden from the fields, surrounded by overgrown brambles, and they took a few minutes to rest.

"What can I say, Rose, I'm a lone wolf, that's just my nature, and who I am. You know the first thing I do in any situation is watch my back. The second is to watch yours. It's just habit. Growing up as I did, you had to be like that, and it's difficult to change."

"I know, honey," said Rose. "I'm kinda the same. I wouldn't hurt a fly if I didn't have to. I like to stay in the background, let you do all the work, and I know that's not fair. I need to step up more. Unless I'm provoked, I guess I find it hard to hurt someone."

Both knew the other was lying, but they went with it. They had nothing to eat, or drink, so they held each other and chatted to pass the time. Javier was still in pain, and he needed the break, however short it was.

Javier was pleased to be with her, but he knew there would likely soon come a day when he might lose her. It seemed there was a thin line between living and dying. "When it happens, Rose, *if* it happens I mean, don't let me be like that. Don't let me turn into one of those things."

Rose looked at Javier, horrified. "You're *not* going to end up like that."

"Maybe," said Javier wistfully. "Derek and Cindy probably didn't think they'd die today, but they never even saw the sun go down."

"Javier, I'd do anything for you. You know I would. I am never leaving you, you hear me? *Never*. Don't talk about us like that, as if we ain't gonna be together forever. We are. I *know* we are."

As Javier stared into the distance, watching the sun sink over the horizon, and the night air fill with the moans of the dead, Rose slid her hand beneath his belt buckle, and began feeling for him. He let her toy with him as he waited for his body to reenergise. If Rose wanted him, she was going to have to do all the work.

"You're my eagle," Rose whispered to him. She kissed his neck tenderly. "Always."

Javier looked and listened for any of the dead, but they seemed to be far behind. The night air was cold and quiet, tinged with only the faintest of moaning sounds coming from afar. They needed to get into the golf course. Even if the place was overrun with zombies, which he doubted, it was somewhere they could stay a while. Maybe they would have water too. His mouth was so dry. He looked at Rose, and wondered why she did it. As she kissed him, and rubbed herself up against him, he realised he actually didn't care if she continued, or stopped. He was letting it happen, but ultimately, it made no difference to him. What she was doing to him wasn't sexual. It was just her way of forcing him to bond with her, and the kisses were a symbol of the trust she put in him. It was something she did frequently. She was confident when she wanted to be, but sometimes she reverted to her old self, acting as if he was her father. Just like now.

Javier thought about the future, a land without the dead. Could they one day live in peace? He wanted to be back in control, and have not just Rose, but others subservient to him. He imagined how it would be to be rich, to have others bring food to him, and to wait on his every need so he could truly relax. There could be a day when he had others, soldiers perhaps, to guard him and protect the new land. It was way off, but once he found his brother, anything was possible. There were a lot of desperate people in the world who would do anything to survive. Cindy had been playing games with him, but in the end, she would've done whatever it took to stay alive. He would've made sure of that. Now he was alone with Rose, a woman who felt nothing, who forced herself to love Javier. She said the right thing, did the right things, but all he had to do was snap his fingers and she would kill herself for him. He knew that wasn't power: it was pathetic.

Jeffersontown had turned out to be trickier to navigate than he had imagined. Even though they had avoided the main cities, it was looking increasingly difficult to find a way north. Even out in the fields, away from the towns, the dead were present. With or without Rose, it might be useful to have some help. Perhaps, if he met the right person, he could forge an alliance to get to his brother. Alone, with Rose, it was difficult. Despite the pleasure she gave him, she was a loose cannon. He was fed up of foraging like a hobo. He wanted someone else to do the hard yards for once. Rose was handy with a knife, but it was about time someone else had their backs.

When he came to after the crash, Rose had been in the field, walking away from him. Was she going to leave him and let him die out there? He was going to have a word with her about that. Later, when he had regained his energy and recovered, he would explain what true trust was. No doubt, she would resist, as she always did at first, but eventually, she would see sense, and when she had recovered, they would move on, as they always did.

A crack, like the snapping of a twig, brought them both back to the present, and Rose jerked her head up.

"What was that?"

"I think it was a signal we need to get a move on," said Javier getting up. He straightened himself up. "This way. Let's not wait to find out what's coming around the corner."

He looked back as they left the shade of the tree, noticing a zombie had gotten close to them. There were more behind, and those few minutes resting had let the dead catch up. The need to find a way into the golf course was getting more urgent every minute.

"Javier?

"Yes?" Javier snapped at Rose impatiently. Now was not the time for talking.

"Is that it?"

Rose pointed her knife at a gate in the fence up ahead. It was painted the same colour, and secured in place with a sliding bolt. The gate was only small. It was thin enough for one person to pass through at one time, no more, and probably just an emergency exit. There was a padlock too, but it wasn't locked, and slipping through the small gate would've been easy, except for the dead standing in the way.

The half dozen zombies blocking the way to the gate turned and faced them. Their hungry mouths opened, oozing groans and blood in equal measure.

"Shit," said Javier, as he instinctively reached for his gun, only to find it gone. It was left behind somewhere in the wrecked van. He heard more of the dead approaching from the road behind, and a wave of fear gripped him. "We're trapped."

CHAPTER ELEVEN

The soles of Jonas's feet were hot and sore. The sneakers he wore weren't suitable for hiking, and with every step, the blisters on his heels grew larger. The road was baking hot, and he felt like he was slowly being cooked alive. They had only been walking for half an hour, but already the morning sun had burnt through the crisp air and low clouds. He would give anything for a drink of water. Since leaving the farm, they had found nothing to eat, or drink, and their rations were all gone.

While Peter and Pippa kept a look out, Erik and Jonas had dug a shallow grave for Tyler. At the back of the byre, there was a small square plot of land that hadn't been cultivated. It looked like the farmer probably kept it clear for turning vehicles around, but there was no better area to use. The fields were overgrown, and nobody wanted to risk going around the back of the house to the lawn where the dead bodies were. So Erik found a pickaxe and a shovel at the back of the byre, and they dug a grave in silence. Two zombies stumbled across them as they worked, but Quinn dispatched them with ease, her knife easily sinking through the soft flesh at their temples. Once the grave was deep enough, they brought Tyler out. There was a blanket stowed behind the stacks of straw, and they wrapped him in it carefully, leaving only his face showing. He looked peaceful, wrapped in it like a baby, and once more, Jonas was reminded of Sunday school and the stories they were told about baby Jesus, wrapped in a protective swaddle.

Erik and Jonas worked together, saying nothing, and carried Tyler from the byre to his grave. They gently lowered him in, as Dakota watched on, crying softly. Erik planted the shovel into the soft earth, and threw its contents over Tyler's body.

"God bless, brother," he said as he passed the shovel to Quinn.

In turn, they took the shovel, every one of them saying their personal goodbyes to him. Only Freya did not take part. She stayed silent, constantly cowering behind her brother, Peter, or her mother. Mrs Danick recalled an appropriate passage from the Bible to quote. She joked that she'd been to so many funerals that she could remember whole verses by heart now. Nobody laughed. They were just grateful that she said something.

"The righteous perish, and no one ponders it in his heart; devout men are taken away, and no one understands that the righteous are taken away to be spared from evil. Those who walk uprightly enter into peace; they find rest as they lie in death."

Mrs Danick stood back, and Jonas watched impassively as Tyler was gradually covered in a mound of earth, his body sinking into the dirt until there was nothing left to mark he had been alive at all. Terry found some branches, and some twine in the byre, and made a small cross to mark the spot where Tyler was buried. He planted it into the earth firmly and whispered so nobody else could hear him.

"I'm sorry, Tyler. It should've been me."

They spent some time just sitting around his grave, as if his passing was a sign that they should stop. What seemed like hours was only minutes, but eventually, Erik suggested they be on their way. There would undoubtedly be more zombies coming, and they couldn't afford to stay still for long. Jonas tried talking to Dakota, but she pushed him away. She refused to meet his gaze, and that hurt him more than anything. He could deal with Tyler's death, he could understand why Erik was so affronted by Jonas's actions, and he could handle the constant menace of the dead. However, Dakota giving him the cold shoulder was unbearable. He tried a few times as they left to talk to her, but each time she rebutted him, either walking ahead, or dropping back to join Pippa. The most he got out of her was a shake of the head.

Jonas guessed she was not only upset about Tyler, but also angry about the fight. He knew he should make amends with Erik, but there was more to it than saying sorry. He had let them down, let himself down, and yet, explaining why was difficult. The reasons behind it were private. He couldn't possibly explain why he had done what he had done, and he had no choice but to move on. The others had no idea what it had been like. Seeing Anna and Mary die like that, being killed viciously by the zombies, was a reminder of how powerless they were. Anna had pleaded with him to help her daughter, but he was surrounded, unable to move, and he had seen Mary's throat torn out. He had seen James fight to the bitter end. Even when they had bitten him, torn off the flesh from his arms and face, he still kept kicking and punching, trying to take down as many as he could before they overpowered him. Yet, the death he most vividly remembered was the one he had truly been responsible for. He had murdered a man. He didn't think of himself as a murderer, but maybe he should. Hadn't he done what was right? Wasn't he just protecting the others, protecting Dakota? Or perhaps he was just searching for a reason to excuse what he'd done, when he had acted out of fear: a fear for his own life, and not for anyone else. He refused to accept it. He didn't want to let his thoughts dwell on the past, and tried to think of what they were going to do next. As much as Erik was angry with him right now, he knew he could rely on him, and the others, too. Mrs Danick and Terry kept to themselves mostly, and were a little slow, but they were dependable. Quinn was strong, as strong as Jonas, and he was thankful she was there. She rarely passed judgement, and had been the only one to speak to him after the burial. She told him how she had made sure that once Tyler had passed, he wouldn't be able to come back. A quick flick of the knife, incapacitating his brain, and he stayed dead. It looked like he was asleep, and she hoped he was dreaming of something when he'd gone. The last few minutes had been painful for Tyler, but he refused to cry out, not wanting to compromise the safety of the group. He was stoic in death, and deserved more than to come back as one of the undead.

After Tyler was buried, they packed up, taking with them what they could. The pickaxe and shovel were in Quinn's hands now, as Peter still carried their rucksack. Terry and Mrs Danick passed the case of guns out, and even Dakota took one. She had been reluctant, but knew she had to. She was useless in combat, and openly admitted that if she carried the axe or baseball bat, she wouldn't have the strength to use it. The evening had turned to darkness as Tyler was laid to rest, and they had walked on in silence in the darkness.

After trudging wearily for a short while, they came across an abandoned truck. Erik and Quinn scoped it out, and decided it was safe. The front cab was exposed, and covered in blood, but the rear doors were open, and inside, there was nothing but two empty boxes. It smelt vaguely of fish, but its cargo had long since disappeared, and now the truck was just a box on wheels. It was parked up by the side of the road, and there was really nothing else around so they hopped inside, closed the doors, and tried to sleep.

It wasn't the easiest of nights, but they were at least able to sleep in fits and starts. Freya's nightmares kept Jonas awake for a while. She said more at night than in the daytime. Her occasional cries for help as she slept were the only words she ever said now. Dakota still refused to speak to Jonas, and she slept by Pippa and Peter. Mrs Danick and Terry grumbled, but accepted their lot, and finally fell asleep. Quinn and Erik told the others they would sleep by the doors, just in case anything disturbed them in the night. Jonas found a quiet corner to himself and hoped he would get some much needed rest.

At first, he lay there, remembering the day's events, remembering those who had passed, but eventually, his tired body demanded rest, and he fell asleep. He didn't remember his dreams, but was quite sure he dreamt about something. Sometimes he was woken by Freya, and sometimes he woke himself in a sweat, his hands clenched and his heart pounding. At one point, there was a banging on the side of the truck, and he sat upright, looking for the source of the noise. It was coming from outside, somewhere near the rear doors. It was an irregular sound, as if someone was walking into the side of the truck repeatedly, like a bumblebee banging its head repeatedly against a window. Jonas looked over and saw Erik and Quinn awake too. Erik raised a finger to his lips, indicating for Jonas to be quiet. When Jonas reached for his gun, Erik frowned and shook his head. After a few minutes, the banging stopped, and whatever was outside continued on its way. After that, Jonas tried to sleep, but with the constant interruptions, no matter how hard he tried, it was impossible to drop off fully.

He was woken in the morning with sunlight on his face. Erik and Quinn opened the rear doors, and everyone was filing out. Jonas had no idea how long they'd been inside the truck, but he was pleased to be back outside. He stretched and looked around, as the others yawned and gathered themselves together. Peter handed out rations, and everyone took a sip of water. When Peter handed Terry an empty bottle, he announced that they'd just had their last meal. The food and water was gone, and the rucksack now had just a few medical supplies, and some of the guns and ammo that Jonas had retrieved from the CDC tent yesterday. As of now, they were homeless, and had nothing to eat or drink until they found something.

They had been walking the road since then, and Jonas was obediently following the rest of the group. Dakota still ignored him, and he had given up trying to talk to her. She clearly wasn't about to give up her foul mood, and he was just going to have to let her work it through. Erik was leading them somewhere, but wouldn't say where. He said it was somewhere they might be able to stay, *if* it was still secure, but if not, they would have to move on. He wasn't too sure which direction they had come out of Jeffersontown, and what with walking around in the dark, it had taken some time to get on the right track. Jonas didn't care where they were going. Out in the open, away from the town, it strangely felt safer. If they were attacked, at least they would see the dead coming.

As Jonas walked, he realised he should feel relieved. Tyler was the only link to what had happened in the garage, and he had taken Jonas's secret to the grave, yet Jonas didn't feel relieved in the slightest. Tyler should be here now, no matter what he knew, and it pained Jonas for him to be absent. Excusing Dakota, in some ways he felt closer to Tyler than anyone else. It was as if their shared experience in the garage had linked them, their futures inexplicably becoming intertwined the moment Jonas had picked up that axe. Perhaps they still were. Perhaps Jonas would get bitten, or scratched, and end up in a shallow grave by the roadside like Tyler too. Would the others care enough to stop him from coming back? Jonas watched Peter holding Freya's hand as they walked, and knew they would. These people cared about each other, Jonas included. When things got serious, all the arguments were forgotten. No, he couldn't afford to let himself get bitter, or bitten. He was being shunned right now, but he only had one person to blame for that, and there was only one person who could save him from himself. Jonas knew he had to stop over-thinking things, stop being so sensitive, stop thinking about what he had done, and focus on what he could do. He had to find a way to make the others trust him again.

"Hey, Peter, let me take the rucksack. You've got your hands full. Let me help?"

Peter seemed to think over Jonas's offer, and then slipped the rucksack off his shoulders. "Here. Thanks."

Jonas smiled as he took it, but Peter remained calm, his face seemingly incapable of smiling anymore. Jonas wondered how he did it. Freya stuck to Peter like glue, but he was just a kid himself. He was mature beyond his years. Erik had every right to be proud of him.

"You still taking care of that thing I gave you, Freya?" Jonas asked.

Freya looked up at him through sad, blue eyes, a quizzical look on her face.

Jonas leant down to her as they walked. "You know that keychain with the picture of the Fort on it?" he whispered. "Well it's really important. I hope you still have it tucked away somewhere safe?"

Freya slowly drew her hand from her pocket, and showed Jonas the keychain. She held onto it tightly, as if it were an extension of her hand.

"Thanks, Freya," said Jonas, giving her a friendly wink.

He watched her tuck it back into her pocket without saying a word. The poor kid must be out of her mind. She was alert, intelligent, and she knew what was going on, yet she remained in a self-imposed silence. If it helped her deal with things, then Jonas was all for it. He was struggling to understand the new world, so it must be a hell of a lot harder for a nine year old. She had been close with Mary too. There hadn't been much the girls could do together back at Erik's house, cooped up inside without light or electricity. They couldn't run around and make noise like kids should do, so they had to play board games and whisper. It hadn't been much better for the adults either. To pass time they talked, and that was about it. They tried playing a few games, but Erik only had a battered old monopoly set and a pack of cards missing two aces and the seven of hearts. Jonas would give anything to go back to those tedious days, not knowing when they were going to run out of water. Anything was better than living on the run, fending off the dead on an almost hourly basis.

"We're about here," announced Erik suddenly. He paused by a burnt out old Ford truck that had come to rest in a ditch. "It looks promising."

Jonas was weary. He was desperate to believe in Erik, to believe they had found somewhere safe to stay, but looking around, he couldn't see much. There was a tall solid fence, at least ten feet high, with barbed wire along its top. On the other side of the road, just open fields and shambling figures in the distance.

"So what's on the other side of the fence, Erik?" asked Quinn. "You got a plan?"

Something clicked in Jonas's head, a vague memory that there was something important here. He didn't recognise his surroundings, and the fence was unassuming, cold and grey, yet clearly, it was important. Jonas was drawn to the fence, and he studied it closer. Somebody had gone to great lengths to erect it, so whatever lay behind it must be worth protecting. If the fence was intact, then whatever, or whoever was on the other side, was potentially clear of zombies. A thought kept tapping away at his brain, like a knock at a door. There could be somewhere safe on the other side, somewhere without the dead, without the worry of having to watch your back every step, somewhere to rest and sleep. He ambled over to Erik who was looking very tired now. Jonas saw Erik's boots were scuffed, and the jeans he wore were too big for him now, his bulk having slimmed down over the last few months as rations worsened. The back heels of his jeans were frayed and torn, and his shirt was drenched in sweat. He was, as usual, chewing on a licorice roll. Erik offered some around, but no one could stomach it, despite their hunger.

"Erik, what is this place? You know it? You know where we are?" Like a riddle, Jonas felt the answer coming to him, but it was like his brain was numb, and the answer stayed hidden.

"Saint Paul's."

Jonas recognised the name, but he couldn't place it. Why did he know that name? It sounded foreign, but familiar too. Erik could see the obvious confusion on Jonas's face and explained.

"Saint Paul's golf course. They were building it back when we were growing up, remember? I'm not sure they finished it before you left. We've come out on the eastern side of the city. It's an 18 hole course they use for the Masters. They've gotten more precious in recent years, and they put a fence up around it sometime last year. I'm not much of a golfer myself, but living here you can't help but take an interest. Once a year we get all these golf nuts descending on the city for the Masters."

"I guess they won't be coming this year," said Mrs Danick wryly.

Jonas rubbed his neck. The sun was slowly roasting them alive, and they were going to have to find shelter soon. It was approaching midday, and the heat would just drain them of energy the longer they spent in it. They had no water, and Jonas wasn't keen on being out in the open for too much longer. Those shambling figures in the distance were only getting closer. Finding the physical strength to kill more of the dead was getting harder and harder. They had spent so long being cooped up inside lately that it felt good to be out on the open road. On the other hand, he felt exposed, and he knew the others would be thinking the same, although nobody spoke. He saw Peter holding Freya's hand, looking expectantly at his father. There was a hope in his eyes that Jonas hadn't seen in a long time. Peter was sweating profusely. Like all of them, he was dehydrated, and no doubt had a headache too. Peter had the added pressure of looking after his sister. Occasionally, Freya would run to her mother, but most of the time she stayed with Peter. Terry and Mrs Danick still carried the guns, and with them the weight of expectation. If there was any kind of attack, they were probably going to be the first to shoot. Terry was fragile and Jonas was worried about him. The pressure was showing, and though he didn't like to admit it, Terry had been strongly affected by Randall's death. Terry had slept poorly last night in the back of the truck, and Jonas had heard him crying.

"You know where the front door is?" Jonas asked Erik. "Getting over, or through, this fence looks impossible."

"About a mile away. We're on I58, so if we take the next turn up ahead we'll be there in…"

"Hang on, are you thinking of trying to get in there?" asked Quinn. "Are you sure about this? We don't know what's beyond that fence."

"There's a good chance they have supplies inside. You know, the summer golf tournaments would mean the clubhouse should be well stocked. I know they upgraded everything last year too, so they have solar power, a back-up generator, even their own well. It could be nirvana on the other side of that fence," said Erik.

"Or hell," muttered Dakota.

"Couldn't you do with a bottle of water, or maybe a glass of wine?" Jonas looked at his wife, hoping she would engage in conversation. He would rather she argued than stayed silent.

"I'd take a bottle of anything right now," said Dakota, "but going in there is still a risk. Have you forgotten the garage already?"

Jonas didn't know what or where his hackles were, but they were definitely rising. "What's that got to do with anything?" he asked. "That was different, and you know it."

"Was it?" asked Dakota. It looked like she was about to say something else, only she pushed her lips together and stared down at her feet.

"Look," said Erik, "we're going for it. That's the deal. If you want to tag along, great, if not, you're welcome to make your own way someplace else." Erik wiped his brow, and then took Pippa's hand. "Peter, Freya, come on, we're going."

"I'm coming with you," said Quinn. "It's got to be worth a shot."

Terry followed Quinn, and Mrs Danick followed her, mumbling something about wanting to find a comfy chair and get off her feet.

"Dakota?" Jonas held out his hand to her, but she shoved him away, and began walking after the others. Something was irritating her, yet it was more than the usual, more than just the nagging presence of the dead that surrounded them. He had to sort this out once and for all. Jonas jogged to catch her up, and grabbed her shoulder, pulling her back.

"Let *go* of me," Dakota said trying to shake Jonas off.

"Everything okay, dear?" asked Mrs Danick pausing.

"It's fine," said Jonas as he held onto Dakota. "We'll be right behind you."

"Make sure you are. It's too damn hot to argue," said Mrs Danick quietly, leaving Jonas and Dakota alone.

When Mrs Danick was out of earshot, Dakota looked at Jonas. "I *said* let go of me. What do you think you're doing?"

Jonas refused to let go of Dakota's arm, no matter how much she struggled. "This ends now," he said. "Quit struggling, I'm not going to hurt you. I just need to talk. What's with you?"

Dakota pulled her arm free, rubbing it as she stood there trying to avoid her husband's questioning eyes. "We should get going. We don't want to get left behind."

Jonas positioned himself in front of her, stopping her from walking away to the others. "No way. This has got to stop, Dakota. I don't get it. Are you pissed with me? Something I said, or did? Look, we don't have time to argue, or have a meltdown over something minor. You can't afford to get offended if I say the wrong thing. We have to keep on our toes. Let's leave the arguments behind us, please? Can't we just forget it?"

A faint breeze came through the open field beside them, twisting the air into knots, and it carried with it the scent of death. Jonas saw how the fields were dying, the crops unattended, and weeds sprang forth from every possible place. He could understand anyone losing hope in a world like this, but he couldn't stand to see it in Dakota. He needed to know she was still on his side.

"Dakota, whatever I did to you, I'm sorry. All I've ever done is look out for you. Everything that I do is to protect you, to make sure you still have enough life left in you to get up in the morning. No matter what, even if you lost your faith in me, I will never stop loving you. Tell me what's wrong. Please, honey, I..."

"You don't stop. You never stop." Dakota spoke quietly. She turned to look at the fence, and her eyes followed it until she turned back to Jonas. "We should follow Erik. If the golf course behind this fence is intact, we need to rest. We need to regroup. If you still want to go to Janey then, I won't stop you."

"You mean if *we* still want to go?"

Dakota shrugged. "Maybe. I...I've been thinking. I'm not sure it's the best idea to leave Kentucky. I mean, look at me. Look at yourself, Jonas. You really think you can make it to Canada?"

"Yes, I do." Jonas truly believed in what he was saying. There was something else though. It wasn't the journey that Dakota was worried about. She kept referring to him and her, as if they weren't a couple, as if they were headed on different paths. "Canada is our future. We can find Janey, start afresh, and leave this shit behind us. Kentucky isn't home anymore. It hasn't been my home for a long time, since long before my father died, but I'm not going anywhere without you, Dakota. I'll get us there. *Both* of us."

Dakota sighed, and they both began walking down the road after the others. She walked slowly, so as to remain out of earshot of Mrs Danick. Some things were best kept private.

"Jonas, I love you, but..."

A swelling storm above Jonas's head mushroomed, the white clouds turning grey, looming over him and turning black as they popped and fizzed with electricity. An icy wind ran through his body, chilling his blood, and his head felt like it was on fire. He bit his tongue between clenched teeth, the pressure bringing him back to reality.

Dakota had fallen silent. He had gotten this far with her, and he couldn't stop now. As much as he didn't want to hear the end of that sentence, he had to know.

"But..."

"Yesterday, back at the farm, Mrs Danick and Terry were talking about the coast again. They were wondering if, with our new found arsenal, we might be able to make it south. I don't think they're serious, they just need something to believe in you know, something to keep them going. Anyway, Quinn was walking around the barn outside, with Pippa, making sure we were in the clear while you and Erik searched the house. Peter was trying to coax Freya into talking, and getting nothing out of her as usual, which left me alone with Tyler. He was in a lot of pain, Jonas, and I felt so helpless. I wanted to help him, truly I did, but what could I do? By the end, I think he had numbed himself to the pain, and just accepted what was happening."

Jonas could see Dakota was on the brink of tears. Did she hold him responsible for Tyler's death? "We looked in the house for medicine, but there was nothing. I tried, Dakota, but you can't blame me for…"

"Damn it, Jonas, just shut up and listen for a minute, will you? Stop trying to second guess me. Stop trying to rule my fucking life. At least while I still have one."

"Okay, sorry, go on." Jonas saw up ahead the others had stopped, and were looking at the fence. Whatever was eating away at Dakota, he had to get it out of her now. Once they caught up with Erik, he would lose her again. He had lost track of what he was saying sorry for anymore, but he knew more than to question his wife when she was on a roll.

"Tyler was dying while you and Erik were fighting. What the hell were you doing?"

As Dakota wiped a tear from her eye, Jonas saw the cut on her wrist was healing up. He felt guilty about the fight with Erik, but he couldn't change the past, and he had already apologised for that. He decided that Dakota wasn't really looking for an answer. She was venting, opening up to him, and this time he was going to listen.

"While you were wasting time in the farmhouse, I was caring for Tyler as best I could. Other than holding his hand, there was very little I could do. I kept telling him he was going to be fine, that you were going to find help." Dakota looked accusingly at Jonas, then back at the road. "Before he died, Tyler talked to me. Not much. He was too weak. He told me about his parents, and how they had been killed at the start. He told me he missed them. He told me how sad he was to be leaving us, but pleased he would see them again." Dakota wiped a tear away, but as soon as she had wiped one away, another took its place.

Jonas didn't touch her. He wanted to tell her that it was all right, there was nothing she could've done, life was shitty, and that the dead weren't going to be in control forever, but he knew he had to let her get it out. When it was all over, he would hold her, and he would promise to love her and take care of her as long as he had breath in his body.

"He told me something else too," said Dakota. "He said I should take care of you. He said you had it rough back in the garage; that you all did. He said he felt bad about not being able to help those that had died, and that he hoped God would forgive him."

Jonas looked at Dakota. Her voice wavered as she spoke, and it broke his heart. She was pouring everything out now, holding nothing back. It would be good for her, and good for them. They needed to clear the air, so they could move on, and they would be better for it. Tyler had nothing to feel guilty about. He was so young. He was too young to die.

"I told him that God was looking over us, and he shouldn't worry about it, but then, Tyler told me that He should be looking over you most of all. Before he died, Tyler told me about everything that happened in the garage. He said you tried to save Anna, and Mary, but it was impossible. He said you were amazing, that you fought off so many he thought you must've been killed too."

Remembering the garage brought back nothing but bad memories for Jonas. He didn't feel like a hero. He had tried, but he had lost. The dead had won that day.

"You know what else he said?" asked Dakota.

Jonas shook his head. They were close to the others now. A few more feet and they would be at the turn in the road Erik had mentioned. More of the dead in the fields were approaching. They had to find a way into the golf course soon, or none of them would see the evening. He heard Erik shout something, and then Mrs Danick cried out. Jonas instinctively reached for his axe, but whatever was happening up ahead was not his problem, not yet. He could sense Dakota reaching the end of her story. She was ignoring the others too, looking intently at Jonas with those crystal blue eyes of her, the eyes he had fallen in love with so many years ago.

"Tyler told me you saved us all," said Dakota. "He told me how Cliff led you into that death-trap, and if it wasn't for you, we'd probably all be dead right now. He said Cliff had deserved to die. He told me that you had done the right thing by killing him. I remember Tyler smiled, briefly, and then he died."

A shiver ran the length of Jonas's body as they stopped walking. Dakota had finished crying, and was staring at him. Jonas looked back, looked for the love in his wife's eyes, looking for the woman he loved so much, and yet he saw nothing. A strange woman looked back at him, as if seeing him for the first time.

"You killed him, Jonas. You murdered him. You lied to us, to me. He wasn't bitten. You killed him in cold blood."

"But, he...he was... You weren't there, Dakota, you don't know what it was like." Jonas heard him saying the words, and they sounded pathetic, even to his own ears.

"You had a choice, Jonas, and you chose to kill him. It's as simple as that. I have a lot to think about."

Jonas watched as Dakota walked toward the group. Her face showed no emotion as she left him, and she walked confidently, her head held up high instead of staring at the ground as it had been for the last twenty four hours. Jonas wondered if she was about to go and tell the others about Cliff, and then he realised he didn't care. It was the truth after all, and if it came out, then so be it. He did care about Dakota though, and the way she spoke to him was like nothing he had experienced before. She had been so cold and ruthless, that he didn't know she had it in her. They had been married for years, and he couldn't bear the thought of her being angry with him. This was dangerous territory. This was more than anger. This was a test to her faith, to their marriage, and to everything she believed in. He had to talk to her. He had to make her see reason, and to make her see that he hadn't had a choice. He refused even to contemplate leaving for Janey without Dakota by his side. Christ, he hadn't even thought about Janey. It felt like he was being crushed. There was so much to do. He couldn't do this alone, that much he knew. He didn't *want* to do this alone. Erik was still shouting, while Dakota was walking away, Janey was all on her own, and now he had potentially ruined it. Had he made the right choice? He had to explain to Dakota what had happened, and make her understand.

Before he could say anything, Dakota paused and turned around. She looked at him, her eyes distant. The storm over Jonas's head burst, drenching him with fear as shards of icy electricity burned through his temples.

"You're on your own from now on, Jonas," said Dakota. "I need to think. There's more to this than you and me. From now on, I think you should stay away from me. We need some time apart."

CHAPTER TWELVE

"Rose, stop!"

Ignoring Javier, Rose launched herself at the zombies amassed by the gate. Her first kill was a young black man, dressed in a white shirt and black jeans. His shirt was stained with blood, and he was missing a large part of his shoulder. Rose stabbed him quickly though the temple and he dropped like a stone. Another zombie filled his place and lurched toward Rose, followed swiftly by another.

Javier felt helpless. He had literally nothing but his bare hands with which to take them on. It was pointless letting Rose do all the fighting. There was no way she would be able to take them all down, and it wouldn't be long before she would be overpowered. It looked like she was already surrounded, and he was going to have to do something before they got on top of her. He rushed forward and pulled a zombie back just as it was about to latch its teeth onto Rose's arm. He swung it back into the others, sending them falling like dominoes. With his back to Rose, he hit out at another, smacking it hard with his fists. Rose slashed wildly with her knife, and he heard her cry out in pain.

"You hurt?" he asked as he pushed back another zombie.

"I'm fine," said Rose. "Cut myself."

A dead old man, dressed in blue and brown chequered pyjamas stepped up to Javier, his long grey beard covered in blood, and his teeth chewing on something red and fleshy. The zombie's arms reached out and one hand got hold of Javier's shoulder. He tried to shove the old man away, but at the same time, another man was approaching from the other side, his white eyes staring at Javier's.

"I can't hold them," shouted Rose.

Javier saw arcs of blood spraying around him, and felt Rose's back pressed against his, sweaty and hot. He scoured the ground, looking for something they could use, but all he saw was long grass and dead zombies. He tried pushing the old man back, but there was now another behind him, and there was nowhere to go. Everywhere he looked, he saw the dead. He saw cold fingers reaching for him, lifeless eyes vacantly staring at him, and heard the growing moans of the hungry dead. He knew they were finished, and cursed himself for getting into this situation. He had been weak. He had let them get cornered, and it was going to cost them their lives. Rose would go down fighting, of that, he was sure, but he had no energy left for the fight. It was hard to breathe, and flashing stars kept dancing in front of his eyes, obscuring his vision and making him feel light-headed.

"Rose, I'm, I...I can't..." Javier wanted to tell Rose to fight, to run, to do whatever it took to live, but he couldn't. She didn't need his encouragement. She would keep battling until she was drawing her last breath. Normally, he would do the same, but the crash had wiped him out, and he realised that no matter how much he wanted to live, he simply couldn't do it anymore. His arms were shaking, and his legs were about to go. Keeping them back was getting harder and harder, as more joined the fight.

"Rose? I..."

Three quick pops rang out, abruptly followed by more. At first, Javier didn't recognise what was happening until he saw the head of a zombie explode in front of him. The old man who had hold of him fell back when his skull was blown apart, and the ones behind him began to fall too.

"Get down!" screamed Rose. She pulled Javier down, and he collapsed onto the ground with her as more gunshots rang out, taking down the dead. Javier and Rose lay on the ground holding each other, as one by one the dead fell around them.

"Who's doing the shooting?" asked Javier, but Rose returned him with a blank expression. Her face was covered in blood and he hoped none of it was hers.

As the gunshots slowed, and then finally stopped, Javier poked his head up and looked around. There had to be twenty or more zombies scattered around them, all with their heads blown apart.

"Get up." The command came from a man's voice, but Javier was unable to see from where.

Summoning up his last reserves of energy, Javier stood, and Rose joined him. She grabbed his hand and squeezed it tightly.

"Are you bit?" It was the same man's voice again. Whoever it was, they were close, yet invisible.

Javier looked for the man who was talking, but there was no one there. He had to assume whoever it was had been the shooter, which meant they were probably friendly. They could've left Javier and Rose out there alone, with a guaranteed ticket to Deadsville, and yet they hadn't. They were also armed though, and Javier knew he couldn't assume anything at this point.

"No, we're not bit," called out Javier. He wasn't sure what else to say. Talking to a faceless voice was unnerving, especially knowing there was a gun trained on them. He was going to take this carefully.

"Move over to the gate, *slowly*. Tell the girl to drop the knife."

"Better do it, Rose," said Javier. "You don't want to piss off anyone who's as good a shot as this guy."

Rose reluctantly dropped her knife, and they both began walking over to the gate in the fence. Javier watched the dead on the ground, making sure they were dead, not wanting to get a nasty nip on the ankle, which would surely be followed by a bullet to the head.

The gate swung open, and Javier got his first look at what lay behind the fence. There was no grand entrance, no red carpet or champagne waiting. As he walked through the gate, he saw a small hut and a pile of white, plastic chairs, neatly stacked beneath an old shingle oak tree. Beyond lay the fairway, the pristine grass now a little long, the sand pit littered with fallen leaves, and a lone golf cart, abandoned on its side by the ninth hole where it had been left. The driver was trapped beneath it, and their head was cracked open, brains spread all over the beautifully manicured green.

A man ushered Javier and Rose in, and then locked the gate once they were clear. He slid a bolt across, at both the top and bottom of the gate, and all three stood looking at each other in silence.

Javier remembered the unlocked padlock on the outside of the gate. Locking it from the outside would've been impossible, so this man kept tabs on it from the inside. He looked like a security guard, dressed in a dark blue uniform with a small badge on his left chest in the shape of a star. He wore a cap too, and a belt that housed a radio, a baton, handcuffs, and an empty holster. The man was overweight, and his portly belly hung over his belt.

"You sure you're not bit?" asked the man.

Javier raised his hands as if in surrender. He didn't want to scare the man, or risk any misunderstanding that might end with him and Rose being shoved back out the gate.

"We're not, I promise you," said Javier.

The man took off his cap, wiped his forehead, and then put the cap back on. "You look like shit, my friend."

Javier smiled. He was grateful that the man had helped them, but was starting to feel irritated at the gun still pointed at his head. "You think you could put that away? Happy to stay here and talk as long as you like, *friend*, but it's a little disconcerting with that pointed at me."

The man shrugged. "I ain't taking any chances. We don't get many visitors to Saint Pauls', and the last time I let someone in, they wound up dead. Told me they weren't bit, only turned out they were hiding it. Next thing I know, they'd got Dave, and I had to put them both down."

"I see," said Javier. "Well you're in charge."

"Look," said Rose exasperated, "thanks for saving our asses back there, but we aren't bit. Our ride crashed, we've had a *long* fucking day, and if you ain't gonna shoot us, put the fucking gun down."

"Can I get a please?" asked the man.

Rose looked at Javier, and he shook his head from side to side just an inch, just enough to tell Rose to stay her ground. He could see she was fired up, and armed or not, she would take the man on. She was probably still fired up from earlier, adrenalin still coursing through her body, and she needed to calm down.

The man started chuckling, and then erupted into full on laughter. His belly wobbled as he laughed, and he holstered his gun.

"Jeez, I'm sorry folks, I gotta remember my manners. Look, come on in, I'm sorry about the whole gun thing. It's gone, see, you're good." The man waved his empty hands in the air, and Javier hoped that Rose wouldn't do anything foolish.

"This is Rose, I'm Javier, and you are?"

The man stepped forward holding out a sweaty hand. "Gabe McAllister. Gabriel to my mom, but she's with the boss upstairs, if you know what I mean, so just call me Gabe. I'm chief of staff here. You gotta understand - it's been a while since folk came knocking at our door, and we've got to be careful. Our place is probably the safest place to stay around here for miles. Shit, you do look banged up. Where'd you come from? Not Louisville, surely? We ain't had anyone come from the city in weeks. Last I heard it had been overrun by them dead fuckers. Not a soul left is what I heard."

Javier noticed that Gabe called it 'our place,' which likely meant he wasn't alone. They would do well to find out exactly who was here, before deciding what to do next. Staying the night was not a question. He desperately needed to rest, and once Rose calmed down, she would crash. After the night though, how long would they stay? How long *could* they stay? If Gabe and his friends lived here, there must be a decent supply of food and water. Maybe they could take a few days and rest up before moving on.

"It wasn't pretty. That's why we look like shit," said Javier. It was easier to go along with Gabe's pre-imagined story than explain where they had really been. Telling him about the diner and Jeffersontown was probably not a good idea, and sometimes the truth was just a hindrance. Best to go with the flow, and let Gabe's mind fill in the gaps. "If you don't mind, Gabe, we don't really want to talk about it. We lost a lot of people in Louisville, a lot of close friends, and we barely made it out with our lives. My girl, Rose, she lost her mother only this morning," said Javier putting an arm around Rose. "God rest her soul."

Rose coughed, and buried her head in Javier's shoulder to stifle her laugh. He could feel her shaking against him as she let her laughter be swallowed up by his body.

"She's finding it hard," said Javier to Gabe. "She's still grieving and well, you know how close a mother and daughter are."

"My God, look, let's get you inside. We got some rooms set up you can stay in. Clean water, whatever you need. God bless you both," said Gabe. "Follow me. We'll get back to the clubhouse, and get you two sorted out."

Gabe began to lead Javier and Rose toward the clubhouse. "You're lucky I was here. My shift was about over, and I was just about to head on back in. I saw you from the TV tower. Wasn't too sure at first, but couldn't leave you out there could I?"

"TV tower?" asked Javier.

"Just over there, next to the 18th. Best vantage point over the course, and easier than climbing a tree that's for sure. See?"

Javier saw the structure nestled between two Silver Birches close to the fence. Composed of scaffolding and a thin platform on top, it didn't look too strong, as though it might collapse at any time.

"Almost blew down in that storm we had a couple of weeks back. Pleased it didn't, 'cause there's no way we were getting it back up. Mara can cook a mean roast turkey, but she leaves the heavy stuff to me. Truth is, I like it that way. I'm traditional, you know? I'd rather be out here keeping an eye on things while she's the boss inside. It works for us."

Gabe evidently had no problem opening up to strangers, and Javier wondered if this Mara was his wife or mother. Were there more tucked away inside the clubhouse?

"Will this Mara be as welcoming as you, Gabe?" asked Javier. "I mean, you probably don't get strangers turning up unannounced like we did. I'm afraid we're not in the best condition. After what we've been through today..."

"Oh Lord, Mara will love you, don't you worry about that," said Gabe. "She's not a woman you want to cross, I'll give you that. She's got a temper on her, but you'll find she's fair. Sorry about the interrogation earlier, but you understand we gotta be careful these days. If you're up front with me, then we'll have no problems. You play ball, and you'll find I'm all sweetness and light." Gabe chuckled, as they passed near the upturned golf cart.

Rose looked at the body inquisitively, and Javier looked around the course as the fairway opened up. He couldn't see anything else around, just a few flags fluttering in the evening breeze.

"Trust me, you don't have to worry now. I can't imagine what you poor folk have been through, but you got me and Mara to look after you now. There's just us, and we got plenty to share. I got this place tucked up tight, and I got more where this came from to make sure nothing untoward happens to us." Gabe patted his gun, smiling.

Javier said nothing. He was tired, and wanted to get to the clubhouse where he could sit down. Rose was fading too. He noticed she was dragging her feet, and there was something about Gabe's relaxed nature that put them at ease. Javier felt more assured about the place too, knowing there were only two of them. He wasn't comfortable that Gabe had all the weapons, but that was only a matter of time. He just had to get some strength back.

"Janet Goldbitter," said Gabe noticing how Rose kept looking at the dead woman by the upturned golf-cart. "Or Golddigger as we used to call her," Gabe said chuckling. "We left her there to bake. She was a member, one of the old women who used to play here. Got membership because her current husband was on the board. What was he, her fifth? No, sixth. Anyway, royal pain in the ass she was. Rude as hell, just plain obnoxious. She was always shouting at the staff, demanding this and that. She threw money around just because she could. Liked to rub our noses in it."

"What happened?" asked Rose. The body was largely intact. The woman's head was crushed though, and had been picked at by rats, leaving little of the old woman's face.

"When it all kicked off, I was here alone. We were gearing up for the tournament when things changed. It was pretty clear to me that the authorities couldn't keep law and order, so I told Mara to pack a bag and get over here quick. Unfortunately, Mr Goldbitter had the same idea, and he brought *her* with him. It was just us four to start with. Turns out Mr Goldbitter had been bitten as he was making his way out to his car though; decided to keep it quiet, stupid old fart. Anyway, day two, we got up and found him wandering around the corridors, dead as a deer. I managed to put him down quick. I don't like to sound my own trumpet, but I'm a good shot, I know that. I could take the hair off a rat's ball-sack from fifty yards."

"So you had to take out her too? She was bit?" Javier wondered how Gabe could sound so cheery. The man seemed to retain a smile on his face even when recounting a horrific story.

"Yeah, she was bit. Her husband managed to take a chunk out of the sour old bitch before she got away. She thought she was immune to it though, thought anything could be solved with money. Practically threw a suitcase of the stuff at me if I'd promise to help her. She told me to go fetch a doctor while she played a round of golf. Can you believe it? I told her there was no way I was going out there looking for a doctor, and Mara told her the same, but she wouldn't listen. She refused to do anything about her bite. Thought she could see the infection through, and went out to play some golf. I've been in charge of this place for ten years, never had a day's trouble with any of the members, not really, and I wasn't about to let her ruin it all. So I followed her, took out a ten iron, and smashed her head in. Let the gold digger cook, she got what she deserved. I ain't got no regrets. I did what I did to keep this place safe. That's the way it'll stay too. You play ball with me, and you'll find I'm all..."

"Sweetness, and light, right?" said Javier.

"You got it, pal," said Gabe. "Look, the clubhouse is just over there. I'll take you in the front door. Mara's expecting me, and it's best to stick to the routine around here. Don't want to surprise Mara and get our butts blown off."

As they followed Gabe, Javier looked at Rose, his eyes asking her if she was okay. She gave him a half-hearted smile in return, but said nothing. Her eyes were vacant, and her hands cold. He leant over and kissed her cheek, suddenly feeling not just love for her, but pride too. She had really kicked ass out there, and had jumped into the fight for him to protect both of them from the zombies. Gabe seemed to be on the level too, and the clubhouse looked warm and secure. The day hadn't gone how he'd planned, but Javier was pleased just to be alive.

As they approached the clubhouse, Javier noticed it was on two levels, and looked like an old country mansion, complete with a white picket fence out front, a wooden veranda, and a swing-chair on the front lawn where a woman sat lazily sipping on a glass of water. As they neared, the woman got up and waved at Gabe, who returned the wave. As she saw Javier and Rose, the woman's smile turned into a frown, and confusion spread across her face. Javier saw a gun tucked into her apron, and the woman reached for it, bringing it out just enough for them to see it. Her intentions were clear: mess with me, and you'll regret it.

"Mara, you put that away," said Gabe. "There's no need for that. These two folks have had a difficult day, and we're going to show them some good old southern hospitality."

"That's what I thought I was doing," said Mara, giving Gabe a peck on the cheek as he embraced her. "No trouble out there? I thought I heard gunfire. I take it this is what you were shooting for?"

"Mara, this is Javier and…" Gabe hesitated and his cheeks turned red. "Sorry, darling, I forgot. Robyn, was it?"

Rose looked at Gabe and sighed. "*Rose*. This must be Maureen, right?"

Javier sensed Rose wasn't impressed, but it was hardly anything to get worked up about. He knew she had deliberately said Mara's name wrong, but pulling her up about it now wouldn't be the right time. Mara was still defensive about the two newcomers, rightly so, and Gabe had a gun by his right hand. They couldn't afford to piss either of them off right now, and Javier squeezed Rose's hand hard. Then he let go, and stepped forward.

"Mara, we're sorry to intrude on you like this, but my Rose and I have had a long day. We came across this place by chance, and if it wasn't for your good husband, we would most surely be dead."

Javier could see Mara was beginning to let her guard down. He took a guess they were husband and wife. The way they looked at each other, the way they had embraced earlier, all suggested a familiarity borne of living with someone for years. It was not something Javier knew himself, but he had seen enough of it to recognise it when he saw it.

"My husband's a good man," said Mara. "If he trusts you to let you into our home, then I do too."

Mara was a large woman, and Javier could see she and Gabe made a perfect couple. They had similar features, although thankfully Mara did not have Gabe's pot belly. She had auburn hair, tied up in a bun, and wore a dirty apron, as if she had spent all day baking.

"Anyone else here?" asked Rose bluntly.

"No dear, it's just us," answered Mara.

There was a hesitation before she answered, just enough to let Javier know that she didn't quite trust them fully, not yet.

"Our caretaker, Dave, was the only other one who made it here, apart from the Goldbitters. He taught me how everything works, how the solar panels work, where everything is stored, the whole she-bang. We got enough to see this through, thanks to him."

"All right, Gabe, that's enough," said Mara. "I'm sure these two young folk have had enough of you chewing their ears off. Why don't we go inside? Chicken's about ready. We should eat."

As they walked into the clubhouse, Javier noticed they had kept the place spotless. It looked as if it was ready to host a championship, as if the outside world was still normal, not full of zombies. He could smell the food cooking, and his doubts about Mara would keep. She had looked increasingly worried as Gabe was telling them how they had enough food to last, and how the caretaker had told them how to run the place. She was right to worry. If Gabe gave away all their secrets, then there would be no more need for them. Mara clearly wasn't stupid, and Gabe might be a crack-shot, but Javier suspected his wife was the brains behind the operation.

Inside, Gabe showed them to a room where they could spend the night. It was an office in a previous life, converted into sleeping quarters. Some old blankets lay spread out in the middle of the room, and the desk had been pushed to one side, leaving plenty of room to lie down and stretch out. Tempting as it was to curl up and sleep right then and there, Javier's growling stomach won out, and they went straight back down to the diner to eat. Rose said little as they ate, and Javier had to admit it was delicious. Somehow, Mara had come up with a Moroccan chicken dish, with some peas, carrots, and fluffy rice. The chicken was juicy and they ate it noisily, grateful to fill their bellies. As they ate, Gabe and Mara told them a little about their lives, but it was white noise to Javier. He was more interested in how they had survived for so long, how they managed to keep the food fresh, and produce power to cook.

After eating, Mara reclined to their bedroom, and Gabe showed them where it was, just in case they needed anything in the night. If they were up to it, he promised to show them around properly in the morning, to give them the layout of the grounds, and show them where everything was. If they were keen to stay, they could help with the running of the clubhouse, and Gabe smiled as he left them, content he had done his good deed for the day. After providing them with a bowl of hot water to wash — there wouldn't be enough for a decent shower until winter - he reassured them that they were perfectly safe, and that they could sleep easy. With that done, Gabe retired too.

"I could've eaten a second plate," said Rose as she undressed in the privacy of their room. She kept on her underwear, and then washed the blood and dust from her body.

Javier sat on a leather footstool, watching Rose wash. He had already washed up, and he was down to nothing but his modesty. There were no clean clothes to put on, so they decided they would wash them tomorrow, and spend the night without. As Rose finished, he crept under the blankets. Rose dried off and came over to him, slipping beneath the covers with him. They both lay on their backs, staring up at the ceiling. The night was dark. The office only had thin blinds, so the faint moonlight gave the room a milky-white glow.

"You want to fuck me?" asked Rose. She slid a hand over his leg cautiously.

As much as he wanted to, Javier was exhausted. His body still ached, and knew he was probably going to feel worse before he felt better. The crash had beaten him up badly, and his brain wanted more than his body was capable of.

"Want to, yes. Going to, no. Not tonight. I need to sleep. I need to think about things."

Rose withdrew her hand. "But you'd fuck Cindy if she was here now?"

Javier closed his eyes. Just when he thought Rose was back on side, she threw him a curve-ball. "Rose, just go to sleep."

"What about Mara? You want to fuck her too?"

"Can we not do this, Rose? Can you just, maybe, keep your mouth shut and stop talking shit for one minute?"

"Yes sir, sorry sir, I'll be good. Wake me up when you want to fuck me, and then I'll keep quiet again. Whatever you want sir. I'll be a good little girl. You can fuck me in the mouth, in the ass, do whatever you want with me, then…"

Javier sat up and grabbed Rose. "I told you to be quiet," he hissed. "You want to get us thrown out? You want to go back out there? What the hell's got into you?"

Rose said nothing, and Javier was tempted to demand an apology. She would do what he said, but any apology would be hollow. He didn't want a wet blanket for a girl, but he sure couldn't put up with her in this mood either. "Well? You want to go back outside."

"No. I want you. I want to stop…to stop…"

"To stop what?"

"I want to stop. Period. I'm sick of running all the time. I'm sick of everything. Let's stay here, Javier. We can run this place. We can make it work, keep it safe. You saw it too. I know you did. We can take it from them. Together, we can do anything."

Rose sat up, and Javier looked into her eyes. "I don't know, Rose. It's tempting, but I have to get to my brother. You know that's the plan. Keep heading north."

"I know, I know, keep heading north, but we've got something good here, Javier. Let's stay, just for a couple of days. I know you're banged up, and you can rest here. It'll do us good." Rose ran a hand over Javier's chest tenderly. "At the very least we can have some fun for a while without having to look over our shoulder all the time. There's so much here, we can check it out and stock up before heading to Thunder Bay."

Javier doubted that Rose was in it for the long haul. She said the right things, made the right noises, told him she was with him forever; yet, when he mentioned Canada, she changed the subject, or mentioned staying somewhere along the way, as if she wanted to set up home. When she spoke now, he could tell she was lying. She didn't want to go north. She didn't want to go east, west, south or anywhere else. If she was looking to settle down and raise 2.4 kids, then she had got the wrong man. He thought Rose was a wild card, someone he could finally connect with, but the more that time passed, the more he thought she had other ideas. It might be that he would have to go it alone one day. The time would come when she would have to make a decision whose side she was on. Company was good, but he had been alone before, and he could do it again. His brother mattered more to him than anything, more than Rose did, though he would never admit that to her. He simply *had* to get to him. He had to find him. The idea that he might never see him again was unbearable. His mother had separated them when she'd left, taking only one of them with her, and he was *not* about to let another woman get in their way.

"Fine, we'll stay and see, okay?" Javier lay Rose back down, and curled up around her. He draped one arm over her bare shoulder. "Just a few days, to check it out."

"I love you," whispered Rose.

"You're my eagle," said Javier.

Soon they fell asleep, and the clubhouse fell silent. With nothing to draw them in, with the place quiet and dark, the zombies outside the fence stayed away. It was almost sun up before the house woke, and a lone figure crept stealthily into the kitchen.

Rose couldn't take the lies anymore. She had to make Javier see sense. The crash had made him weak, and she was going to have to take matters into her own hands. It was about time they made things go their way instead of waiting, or drifting. Heading north was a dumb idea, just plain dumb, and when she showed Javier the alternative, he would come round.

With a large butcher's knife in each hand, Rose made her way from the kitchen to Gabe and Mara's bedroom. It was just across the hall from where Javier was sleeping soundly. He would be proud of her when he got up. She was doing this for him, for them. Gabe would be first to go. She remembered the way he looked at her over dinner. She could feel his eyes running over her, undressing her, and it reminded her of the way her father used to look at her. Javier thought Gabe was reliable, but wasn't he the only one with a gun? Gabe wasn't about to share. Gabe and Mara weren't just going to let Javier and Rose take what they wanted.

No, they were going to have to take it by force, and if Javier couldn't see that, Rose was just going to have to make him. The golf course could be theirs, *should* be theirs.

Rose pushed open the door. The room was dark, and just like theirs, it had an old wooden desk pushed up beside a wall. The blinds were drawn open, and Rose could clearly see Gabe and Mara sleeping in the middle of the room. Rose could hear them softly breathing.

"Too easy," she whispered as she crept over to them, and knelt down beside Gabe. His gun was beneath his pillow, the butt just sticking out. Wise man, thought Rose. She could try to slip it out from under him, but he might wake and grab it first. It was too risky.

She raised both knives in the air, keeping one of them just inches from his neck, and the other above his chest.

"Stick, or twist?" Rose said, weighing up her options. She would need to be quick. Once she'd stuck Gabe, she would have to move swiftly over to Mara. She didn't want to get drawn into a fight. It would be best to get it over with quickly.

Gabe rolled over, his ample belly pulling the blankets with him, exposing his pale skin.

Rose smiled. "Stick."

"Stop!" yelled Javier.

He appeared in the doorway and Rose looked up in shock. What was he doing here? She looked down at Gabe, who was staring up at her, his eyes open wide in disbelief, unsure if he was still dreaming.

"My thoughts exactly, you bitch," said Mara. She was brandishing a gun which had been hidden beneath her pillow, and was now pointing it straight at Rose.

"Mara, put that down," said Javier. He stayed in the doorway, unsure whether to approach or not. He couldn't get to Mara without her getting off at least one shot.

"Rose, you put that fucking knife down, *now*," demanded Mara.

Rose looked at Javier. Her shock had quickly gone, and now she was angry; angry that Javier had ruined her plan, angry that Mara had a gun pointed at her, and angry with herself for getting caught. She had forgotten Mara had a gun too. "Javier, help me. Take one of these knives and slit Mara's throat."

Mara pointed the gun at Javier. "Don't you move, mister."

"Rose, stop this. Come on over to me," said Javier, his voice wavering. He knew Rose wouldn't back down and he doubted Mara would either. There was a fierce determination about her, and her hands were steady as she held the gun.

Rose shook her head. "No. We have to do this, honey. This place is *ours*. We're taking it. *I'm* taking it."

Mara whirled her gun back to Rose, cocking the trigger as she did so. From less than four feet away there was no way she would miss. Javier could tell Rose wasn't going to drop it. He felt weak at the knees, and his head was sore, but his senses were sharp, and he knew this was going to end badly. Nobody would back down, and he wasn't about to let Rose take a bullet needlessly.

"Last chance," said Mara.

Rose shook her head again. A tear ran down her face. "Fuck you. Gabe's mine now."

"No!" Javier heard the word ringing in his ears, but he didn't know if he had said it, or Mara. Time was up. He ran into the room as Rose plunged a knife downward, and Mara fired.

Outside the clubhouse, if there had been anyone there, they would've heard plenty of screaming and shouting, and seen the blinds to the room suddenly splattered with fresh blood. There were muffled thuds as a fight broke out, and eventually, silence.

CHAPTER THIRTEEN

"Jeez, that hurts," said Mrs Danick rubbing her ankle.

"Fix it up as best you can," said Erik, "we have to get moving." The fields were filling with the dead. From all directions they came, trudging through the mud, stumbling through ditches, and blindly walking across roads ignoring any obstacles in their path.

"What happened?" asked Jonas as he caught up with them. He ignored Dakota who had gone to stand by Pippa. Mrs Danick was sitting on the road, her ankle being strapped up by Terry.

"I just tripped," said Mrs Danick. "Wasn't looking where I was going. Stupid. I should've just shot it."

"Settle down. You're fine," said Terry. "It could've been a lot worse."

"*He* came off second best," said Erik pointing to a corpse a few feet away. "Jumped out of the undergrowth. Well, I say jumped, more like crawled. See, his legs are gone, probably gnawed off by dogs, or rats, or something. Anyway, caused us a bit of a shock. Mrs Danick tripped, and Peter finished him off."

Jonas looked at Peter. He held Erik's baseball bat in his hands, sticky with blood. Freya stood by his side, scuffing her shoes on the road. Peter didn't look very proud, or even pleased he had helped. He just looked tired.

"All done," said Terry. He helped Mrs Danick up to her feet.

"Can you walk?" asked Erik.

Mrs Danick put some weight on her ankle and winced. "I'm not running a marathon anytime soon, but yeah, I can walk."

"Right, let's get going then," said Erik taking the bat from his son. "I'm sure we're almost there."

"I hope so," said Quinn. "They're getting closer."

"You want me to do anything?" asked Jonas.

Erik passed the aluminium bat to Jonas. "Just watch our backs."

As they all trooped off, searching for the entrance to the golf course, Jonas watched Dakota. She was chatting to Pippa, as if nothing had happened. There was no way she could be serious about finishing with him. They had been married so long that it was as if she was part of him, and he was sure she felt the same. She was just confused, and upset about what Tyler had said. He couldn't blame her for that, but it wasn't fair to put it all on him. Jonas knew he was going to have to let her deal with it the only way she could. She would keep running it over in her mind, thinking it through, and then she would see sense, and that he'd had no choice.

A groan from his right brought his attention to the field. A zombie was no more than fifteen feet away, and as it neared Jonas, it seemed to pick up speed, as if it found more energy from being so close to its prey. Jonas waited for it to get closer, until it was close enough to smell, and then he swung the axe at its head. The zombie fell to the ground, and Jonas bashed its head in, smearing its brains all over the road. When he was done, he jogged to catch up with the others, constantly looking out for others that got too close. Killing was getting easier, as if it was just another chore to do that had replaced taking out the garbage, or mowing the lawn. It worried him that it was becoming so easy to smash another person's head in, no matter that they were already dead. If it became too easy he would let his guard down, and then accidents happened. If Dakota wanted to give him the silent treatment, if she wanted to beat him up for a while, he would take it without complaint. He was still going to watch out for her, and she couldn't stop him from loving her.

"This it?" Jonas heard Quinn ask, as the road widened, and a side-road led up to a larger section of the fence.

"Guess so," said Erik.

There was a large billboard on the side of the road with a picture of a woman in a bikini drinking a new brand of soda. Somebody had painted over the soda's name, and in thick, black paint, it read 'Turn back - dead inside.'

Quinn rubbed her face, and then ran her hands through her short, black hair. "Not the friendliest welcome sign I've seen," she said.

"Think they sell those at Walmart?" asked Mrs Danick.

"I think it's a ruse," said Erik. "I think someone painted that to keep people away. People like us."

"Or it could be true," said Dakota. "What if there's nothing in there but more zombies?"

"Only one way to find out," said Erik. "Problem now is figuring out how to get in."

Jonas noticed the solid grey fence they had been walking around had ended by the main entrance, and been replaced by an ornate steel grill. It was even higher than the fencing, at least fifteen feet high, and surveillance cameras were perched atop the structure. Erik was pushing and pulling on the gate, but it was securely locked, and brute force was not going to be enough to open them.

"You think those work?" asked Jonas pointing at the cameras. "Maybe if they see us, see that we're alive, they'll open up."

Erik chewed on a piece of licorice whilst he looked up at the cameras. "No. There's no power on them. I think they're dead. If they do still have power inside, they're probably saving it for the necessities: hot water and cooking, that kind of thing."

"This is great," said Terry. "All this way, and we can't get in?" Terry began pacing up and down in front of the gates. "What about our guns? Can't we just shoot our way in? Blast a hole in the fence?"

"We could probably punch a hole in the metal big enough to get through yes, but that would ultimately defeat the point of getting in. Not only would we use up all our ammo getting in, but the noise would draw every dead fucker for miles around, and we'd leave a nice big hole for them to follow us through. No, shooting our way in is not an option," said Erik.

"Well what then?" Terry shouted. "We lost Randall today, Tyler too, and now it seems like you're saying we're fucked.

Look, we're getting inside no matter what, whether we go over or through, we *are* getting in there."

"I just don't see how," muttered Quinn. "If we rule out blasting our way in, there's no way of climbing over it, even if we could navigate over the barbed wire. Damn it."

"You're right," said Jonas. "We can't blast a hole in the fence, and we can't climb over it."

"So tell me something I don't already know," said Quinn. She looked at Jonas expectantly, waiting for him to follow up his statement with an explanation.

"So we go under it," said Jonas.

"Are you crazy? Do you know how long it would take us to dig under that fence?" asked Terry. "Need I remind you that we have a hundred zombies behind us, and no way of digging a tunnel in the next five minutes, except with our bare hands?"

"No, I think I know what he means," said Mrs Danick. "I should've said, but there was a ditch just back there where I fell. It's some sort of outlet pipe I think."

"Exactly," said Jonas. "Probably carries storm water away from the golf course. It came out right beneath the fence. We can crawl through it. I'd bet anything we'll come up on the other side."

"Probably not smelling of roses though," said Quinn.

"Let's check it out," said Erik. "I don't like the look of those fields. Pretty soon we're gonna have a lot more to worry about than how to get over a fence."

As they hurried back to the outlet pipe, Jonas looked around at the dead roaming the fields. Did they think anything at all? Did those people know who they were, or remember anything of their humanity? Were they just empty shells, parasites, or leeches looking to feed? They certainly didn't worry about anything, or about others. There was a simplicity about their existence, as if they were the same as wild animals, living only to live, and not having the worries of humans.

"Gold," said Erik.

He was crouching down, examining the outlet pipe that ran into the ditch close to where Mrs Danick had fallen. The ditch was dry, and the pipe seemed to run under the fence. It went deep though, and got dark very quickly. As Jonas predicted, it was a storm-drain, used for overflowing water when the rain storms came. The entrance was easily large enough for someone to fit in.

"We'll have to go single file and crawl through," said Erik. "It's going to be dark and smelly in there, so try to relax. Hold onto the person in front of you. With any luck, we'll be up on the other side in no time. I'll go in first, Quinn you follow. I want everyone else in the middle. Hamsikker, you happy to bring up the rear?"

Jonas agreed. He knew it was risky being the last through, in case the dead caught up with them, but if anyone else had volunteered for the job, he would've shot them down anyway. Erik was taking a risk by going first, and he had a family to look out for. Jonas wasn't convinced he had anything to look out for, but he had to trust that Dakota would come round.

"I guess now's not the time to tell you I'm claustrophobic," said Terry.

"You're right," said Erik, "it's not."

Jonas watched as Erik hugged Pippa and Peter, and told Freya that Daddy was going to go into the pipe, and that everyone was right behind him, and that everything would be okay. The girl stayed silent, her body pressed close up against Peter, and one hand clutching the keychain Jonas had given her.

One by one, they got onto their knees, pushed aside the tall grass and weeds, and climbed inside the drain. Jonas watched as Erik disappeared, followed by Quinn, Pippa, Dakota, Peter, Freya, and Mrs Danick. Before he entered the pipe behind Terry, Jonas checked the road and the fields. The zombies were close, worryingly so, but there was enough distance that he wasn't too concerned. They might find the drain, but he doubted they would have the intelligence to figure out how to crawl through. As he got onto his knees, and put his hands inside the concrete tunnel, he pulled the weeds back in front of the entrance, trying to hide it from view.

The tunnel was cold, and the walls were slimy. The sun hadn't penetrated inside more than a few feet, and the further Jonas went, the more he disliked it. His legs soon became wet, and it was clear they were crawling through months of built-up rubbish, leaves and standing water that had turned to sludge. There were broken branches, and more bugs than he cared for.

Small creatures scurried across his hands, flies bit him, and more than once, he had to brush invisible monsters from his face as the darkness swallowed him up. To his credit, Terry never said a word, and Jonas kept knocking into the soles of his boots. There was the occasional shriek from up ahead as someone put a hand on something that moved, but the group stayed quiet. In the blackness, Jonas's mind imagined a host of creatures down there in the drain with him, as he was sure the others did too. At one point, he heard something moving around behind him, and he was worried a zombie had found its way in. He looked around, which was pointless as he couldn't see anything, and he batted an arm around, finding nothing but air. There was a squeaking sound, and then the noise stopped. They had probably disturbed a rat, and he tried to stop his mind from conjuring up images of giant rats with razor sharp teeth nipping at his heels.

After a few minutes, the darkness turned to grey, and he could make out the outline of Terry's body. A minute later, and the grey turned to light. Suddenly, Terry stopped moving, and Jonas hit his legs. When Terry didn't move, Jonas whispered to him.

"What's happening?"

"I can't tell," said Terry. "I think we've reached the end. Hold on, I can hear them talking."

Jonas waited, trying to listen to the faint voices from up ahead, but they echoed around mixing with each other, making it impossible to tell what was being said.

"There's a grill," said Terry. "Erik's trying to open it."

Jonas hadn't thought about the other end. He had assumed it would be open, but of course, it was likely to have a grill over it. If Erik couldn't get it off, they were going to have to back-track. With the time they had spent in the tunnel, if they went back now they would come out onto a road full of zombies. They couldn't stay put though. Jonas wondered if he had led them all down a dead-end. It seemed like everything he did at the moment turned to crap. He wanted to get out of the tunnel so badly. The air was damp, and the smell was foul.

"You okay, Terry?" asked Jonas.

"Sure. Just tell me that's you holding onto my ankle, right, Hamsikker?"

Jonas realised he had been gripping Terry's right ankle, and let go. "Uh, sorry, kind of forgot about that. I'm sure we'll be out of here in…"

There was a huge clattering sound that rung in his ears, and then they suddenly started moving again. It appeared that Erik had gotten the grill off, and Jonas breathed a sigh of relief. His friend had never let him down, and once again, he had pulled through. He felt bad about the fight at the farmhouse, and knew he had to make amends. Erik should lead the group from now on. Being a cop, he had the training and knowledge to deal with most situations, and he could handle himself. Jonas wanted Erik to take over on his own. A small part of him knew he was being selfish, that he was using Erik as an excuse to shy away from having to make the hard decisions, but he had been faced with so many lately that he just couldn't do it anymore. It had cost people their lives, and possibly cost him his marriage.

Terry's legs shot up into the air, and Jonas realised they had reached the end of the tunnel. He climbed up out of the drain, and Erik's thick arms grabbed him, helping him up. Warm sunlight dazzled his eyes, and he rolled onto soft grass, his eyes watering at the sudden light that blurred his vision.

"Give it a second. You'll be fine," said Erik.

The coldness of the damp tunnel was soon forgotten once they were back in the sun, and Jonas looked around.

"Where are we?" he asked rubbing his eyes.

"Right where we want to be, Hamsikker," said Erik.

Jonas let Erik help him to his feet, and he blinked away the tears. They had come up behind what he assumed was the clubhouse, a two-level brick building covered in ivy. There were a couple of large catering trucks parked up, a delivery van, and some more cars, all parked up neatly in the stone driveway. The drain was sandwiched between the drive and a lawn, and further away was what looked like a vegetable patch. Vines grew lazily around a criss-cross mesh of chicken-wire, and cabbages sprouted from the earth. There were small red fruits too, what looked like strawberries, and Jonas dared a smile.

"I know. Seems too good to be true, right?" said Erik.

Jonas looked at Erik. The big man was smiling back as Peter and Freya ran over to the veggie patch.

"You know what, Erik, I'm sorry. Truly."

"Forget it," said Erik, watching Peter scoop up handfuls of fruit and give them to Freya. "We're all under pressure. The main thing is we're here. We made it, Hamsikker."

"You think we can stay here?" asked Jonas. "For good?"

"Why not? We'll have to check the house out, but we're onto a good thing. As long as those fences stay up, we're looking in good shape. We've got food, and I'm sure we can find water. I remember there was a stream running through this area before they built the course. It'll still be here in some format, which means fresh water. There's probably some sort of irrigation system for the course that we can tap into."

A thought snagged in Jonas's mind. Erik was right: it was almost too good to be true. How could a place like this be deserted? Those strawberries that Freya was tucking into hadn't grown by chance. They would've needed water to grow too, which would suggest someone had been tending to them, watering them. Perhaps the house wasn't empty. It might be that someone had been looking after the place, but had recently left, or had an accident.

"I think we need to check out the house, but go carefully, Erik. We don't know for sure it's vacant. Someone could be watching us right now," said Jonas. "Or there could be, well you know, the dead."

"I hear ya," said Erik. "Why don't we let the kids play for a while? I haven't seen them looking so relaxed in weeks. You happy to come with me?"

The way Erik looked at Jonas when he asked him if he would go into the house with him, told Jonas more than the question did. Erik still had doubts. Jonas felt like he had to prove himself all over again. He looked across at Dakota who was sitting on the grass beside Pippa watching the children play. She expected more of him, he knew that, and he was determined to prove himself to her too. He wasn't about to give up on her, no matter what she said.

"Absolutely. Let's just tell the others. I think it's best if we two go in alone. Let the others rest up out here?"

Erik explained they had to go through the house, just to make sure, and he and Jonas walked toward the building. They took just the bat and axe with them deciding to leave the guns with Mrs Danick and Quinn, as they didn't want to leave the group unarmed. If there were any zombies inside, they didn't want to go shooting the place up and bring the dead from the fields to them. The house was quiet, and nothing moved by the windows, but they couldn't assume anything. The farmhouse had taught them that, and Jonas didn't want a repeat of what happened there again.

The vehicles in the yard were all parked up neatly, and as long as they had gas should still be in working order. Jonas was reluctant to tell Erik he planned on leaving, and tucked away for future reference which cars were in the best condition. To get to Canada was no easy task, and he was going to have to take one of the cars, maybe even one of the trucks. Janey needed him, and Jonas had already decided that once Erik, Quinn, and the others were safe, he was gone. He hoped he could convince Dakota to come with him, but if not, he could leave her here temporarily, satisfied she was in safe hands. He would get Janey, and bring her back. Saint Paul's really did seem like nirvana, just as Erik said.

"What's with that stuff?" asked Jonas as Erik chewed on a piece of licorice.

"This? You sure you don't want some?"

Jonas screwed his nose up. "I'm hungry, but I'm not *that* hungry."

"Yeah, it's gross," said Erik as he swallowed and tucked a piece into his pocket. "It's therapeutic. I don't know what I'm going to do when it's all gone. I foolishly took up smoking when I joined the force. I was trying to give up when you came back for your father's funeral. I'd quit the day before. I remember clearly throwing my last pack out. Took one last drag, then I tossed them all in the garbage. Of course, then we were locked up in my place for so long that I had to go cold turkey. This is my substitute. What with the end of the world and all, smokes are pretty hard to find. I don't know, sounds like bullshit, but it gives me something to do with my hands, you know? I'm still adapting to this. God knows how Peter and Freya do it."

"I guess kids don't have the same hang-ups that we do. They just get on with things."

Erik approached the door to the clubhouse. It was clearly a back door, probably leading to a kitchen or store-room, but it was as good a place as any to start.

"Erik, before we do this, just let me apologise again. I know I've acted like an idiot. It just got to me, what happened back there. I think…" Jonas didn't explain any further. He didn't want to, and he hoped Erik wouldn't push it. "Look, anyway, I couldn't have gotten this far without you. Seriously, man, I know I owe you."

Erik patted Jonas on the back. "Forget it, Hamsikker. You just need to concentrate on yourself and Dakota. Talk to her. I can see there's trouble between you. Whatever it is, sort it out. Family's more important than anything."

"I will, but it won't be easy. She can be so stubborn. She says she needs time to think."

"I know," said Erik, "but I also know how forgiving she is, and how much she loves you. I hear her and Pippa talking sometimes, and…well, never mind, just talk to her, okay?"

"What is it?" Jonas could sense Erik was holding something back. "What do you mean you heard her talking? Did she say something to Pippa?"

Erik rested his hand on the door handle and looked down at his feet. "Damn it, Pippa told me not to say anything."

"Erik Lansky, you'd better tell me what you know."

Jonas watched as Erik pulled a fresh piece of licorice from his pocket and the big man began chewing on it noisily. He glanced back at the garden, then back to Jonas. "I didn't tell you this, right?"

Jonas nodded. He feared the worst. Dakota might've told Pippa she was leaving him, or maybe she had told them what he had done with Cliff.

Erik rested a big hand on Jonas's shoulder. "You're going to be a father, buddy."

"Huh? What do you mean?"

Erik grinned. "She hasn't been able to do a test, but from what I hear, she's quite certain. Couple of months or so."

"Wow, I was *not* expecting that." Jonas wondered if that was why she had taken it so badly about what he had done to Cliff. Dakota didn't need a bully right now, or a psycho intent on killing and running headlong into danger. She needed a man, someone to help her. Damn, could she really be pregnant?

"Sorry, I shouldn't have said anything. You all right, Hamsikker?"

Jonas couldn't help but smile. "Yeah, I mean, well, yeah. Shit, I'm just...wow. I've spent my entire life running away, absolving myself for all the shit that's happened, but I'm not running anymore. I'm going to talk to Dakota as soon as we're finished up here. I've got a lot of stuff to make up for." There was a part of him that knew he could never make up for what he'd done, or not done, in the past, but he was sure as hell going to try. That meant Janey too. If Dakota would just come with him to Canada, Janey could help with the baby. Jonas knew absolutely nothing about raising kids, but his sister had three. It was all starting to fit together.

"Look," said Erik, "we don't have to do this now, we can..."

"No," said Jonas. "I'm good. Let's get inside and get this place sorted out. Maybe then we can find some decent food, and you can get rid of those disgusting licorice rolls. I gotta tell you, they do nothing for your breath."

"Thanks. You're pretty ripe yourself, Hamsikker." Erik pulled on the door handle, and it clicked open. "Ready?"

Jonas raised his axe and gave Erik the nod. As the door opened, Jonas half expected a horde of zombies to rush him. Instead, he was greeted by a blast of cool, fresh air. The room inside was dark, and there were no zombies. There was however, a figure stood in the doorway with a gun pointed right at Jonas's head.

"Step back, both of you."

Jonas froze. They had been too blasé about the place being empty. Of course it wasn't. Somewhere as sweet as this was not just going to fall into their lap. It seemed like for every step forward they took, they were forced to go two steps back. With the gun trained on his head, Jonas thought immediately of Dakota. He couldn't go like this. He had unfinished business. As the man kept the gun trained on him, he thought that he was unlikely to see Dakota again. He was used to facing death, but it would be so stupid to die now, right when they had nearly made it. He still had to tell Dakota how he felt. He still had to find Janey. He had to look after his child now; there was so much left to do, that he really didn't want to die today. Jonas contemplated rushing the man. He could probably knock him down, although undoubtedly the man would get a shot off first. Still, it would give Erik time to overpower the stranger. Should he do it, and give Erik a chance to warn the others?

"*Step back*, or I shoot first and ask questions later," said the man calmly.

"Okay, okay," said Erik. He stepped back from the doorway, pulling Jonas back with him.

Jonas knew that Erik had faced armed attackers before, and knew how to deal with them. He would see how it played out. But if things looked like they were turning sour, Jonas had already decided that he was going to take the man on, no matter the consequences. He wasn't about to let someone else harm Dakota, especially not now.

"You play ball with me, and you'll find I'm all sweetness and light. Understand?"

The door swung open fully, and the man on the other side stepped through into the sunlight. As the man stepped forward, Jonas got a clearer view of who they were dealing with. The man was dressed in a security guard's uniform that was slightly too big for him. Jonas could see his eyes sweeping around the grounds, taking in the others who were resting on the lawn.

"Look, we don't want any trouble, we just need some help," said Erik. "Can we come in, just for a few minutes, please, just let us rest and…"

"You got any guns?" asked the man.

"We don't have anything," Erik said quickly. "Just a lot of bruises."

"Is that so?"

"Please," said Jonas sensing the man wasn't buying it, "we have children with us."

"So I see. I also see what looks like a couple of guns out there. An old lady is cleaning them if I'm not mistaken."

"I'm sorry," said Erik quietly. "I just thought…"

The man shook his head. "We don't get along with liars. My wife and I take care of this place, and we don't need a group of murderers and thugs wrecking it."

"No, no, you don't understand," pleaded Jonas. "We've been looking for somewhere safe, that's all. You can take the guns. Take it all. Just please, we need to stay, even if it's just tonight, and then we'll be on our way. You can lock us in a room if it makes you feel better, just please, give us a chance."

The man's brown eyes flitted from Jonas to Erik and back again. "We had some trouble a couple of days ago with some drifters: a couple who claimed to find this place by chance. A man and a woman showed up right out of the blue, claiming this and that. Said they were from Louisville, but that was a pack of horseshit. Turned out they were nothing but common criminals, out for trouble. Tried to kill me, *and* my wife."

"But they're not here now, right?" asked Erik.

"No sir, I dealt with them. Wasn't easy, but they won't be bothering us anymore. Buried 'em both out front, by the old swing. Now it's just Mara and me, and we don't intend to make the same mistake again. I don't want any more trouble, so you folks had better be on the level. Look, I'm sorry, but I think it's best you leave."

"What's going on, honey?"

Jonas saw a woman appear in the doorway. She held a gun too, but it was low by her side. She was apprehensive, but her posture was not threatening, and Jonas sensed that perhaps she was more open to helping strangers than her husband.

"Mara, get on inside, I've got this," said the man, obviously annoyed at being interrupted. "I was just telling these folk that they need to move on."

Hidden in the shadows of the room, Jonas couldn't see the woman, but he heard her tutting. "Oh come on now, they look harmless enough. Isn't that a child out there in the vegetable patch? We can help them out, for tonight at least, can't we, honey? Put your gun down, and stop being such an ass."

The man sighed, and Jonas could sense his annoyance. They were at the tipping point now. Either the man was going to shoot them, or give in to his wife and let them stay.

"Fine, fine," said the man lowering his gun, "but you're to give me all your weapons, and you'll do exactly what I say while you're here, understood?"

Erik and Jonas nodded. "Thank you. You won't regret it," said Erik.

The man tucked his gun into his belt. "Well, you'd better come on in. Try anything though, and I'll kick you out. You play ball with me, and you'll find I'm sweetness and light." He pulled the cap from his head and held out a hand.

Jonas took it and shook the hand firmly. "Thank you for this. I'm Jonas, and this is Erik."

"Gabriel," said Javier smiling. He looked back at Rose in the doorway wearing Mara's apron, standing there proudly as if she knew how to cook anything but burnt toast. "But you can call me Gabe."

THE END

CHECK OUT OTHER GREAT ZOMBIE NOVELS

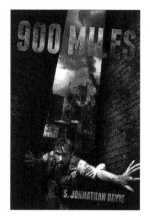

900 MILES
by S. Johnathan Davis

John is a killer, but that wasn't his day job before the Apocalypse.

In a harrowing 900 mile race against time to get to his wife just as the dead begin to rise, John, a business man trapped in New York, soon learns that the zombies are the least of his worries, as he sees first-hand the horror of what man is capable of with no rules, no consequences and death at every turn.

Teaming up with an ex-army pilot named Kyle, they escape New York only to stumble across a man who says that he has the key to a rumored underground stronghold called Avalon..... Will they find safety? Will they make it to Johns wife before it's too late?

Get ready to follow John and Kyle in this fast paced thriller that mixes zombie horror with gladiator style arena action!

WHITE FLAG OF THE DEAD
by Joseph Talluto

Millions died when the Enillo Virus swept the earth. Millions more were lost when the victims of the plague refused to stay dead, instead rising to slaughter and feed on those left alive. For survivors like John Talon and his son Jake, they are faced with a choice: Do they submit to the dead, raising the white flag of surrender? Or do they find the will to fight, to try and hang on to the last shreds or humanity?

CHECK OUT OTHER GREAT ZOMBIE NOVELS

VACCINATION
by Phillip Tomasso

What if the H7N9 vaccination wasn't just a preventative measure against swine flu?

It seemed like the flu came out of nowhere and yet, in no time at all the government manufactured a vaccination. Were lab workers diligent, or could the virus itself have been man-made? Chase McKinney works as a dispatcher at 9-1-1. Taking emergency calls, it becomes immediately obvious that the entire city is infected with the walking dead. His first goal is to reach and save his two children.

Could the walls built by the U.S.A. to keep out illegal aliens, and the fact the Mexican government could not afford to vaccinate their citizens against the flu, make the southern border the only plausible destination for safety?

ZOMBIE, INC
by Chris Dougherty

"WELCOME! To Zombie, Inc. The United Five State Republic's leading manufacturer of zombie defense systems! In business since 2027, Zombie, Inc. puts YOU first. YOUR safety is our MAIN GOAL! Our many home defense options - from Ze Fence® to Ze Popper® to Ze Shed® - fit every need and every budget. Use Scan Code "TELL ME MORE!" for your FREE, in-home*, no obligation consultation! *Schedule your appointment with the confidence that you will NEVER HAVE TO LEAVE YOUR HOME! It isn't safe out there and we know it better than most! Our sales staff is FULLY TRAINED to handle any and all adversarial encounters with the living and the undead". Twenty-five years after the deadly plague, the United Five State Republic's most successful company, Zombie, Inc., is in trouble. Will a simple case of dwindling supply and lessening demand be the end of them or will Zombie, Inc. find a way, however unpalatable, to survive?

CHECK OUT OTHER GREAT ZOMBIE NOVELS

Z BURBIA
by Jake Bible

Whispering Pines is a classic, quiet, private American subdivision on the edge of Asheville, NC, set in the pristine Blue Ridge Mountains. Which is good since the zombie apocalypse has come to Western North Carolina and really put suburban living to the test!

Surrounded by a sea of the undead, the residents of Whispering Pines have adapted their bucolic life of block parties to scavenging parties, common area groundskeeping to immediate area warfare, neighborhood beautification to neighborhood fortification.

But, even in the best of times, suburban living has its ups and downs what with nosy neighbors, a strict Home Owners' Association, and a property management company that believes the words "strict interpretation" are holy words when applied to the HOA covenants. Now with the zombie apocalypse upon them even those innocuous, daily irritations quickly become dramatic struggles for personal identity, family security, and straight up survival.

ZOMBIE RULES
by David Achord

Zach Gunderson's life sucked and then the zombie apocalypse began.

Rick, an aging Vietnam veteran, alcoholic, and prepper, convinces Zach that the apocalypse is on the horizon. The two of them take refuge at a remote farm. As the zombie plague rages, they face a terrifying fight for survival.

They soon learn however that the walking dead are not the only monsters.

Printed in Great Britain
by Amazon.co.uk, Ltd.,
Marston Gate.